*Sheboygan County Chronicle*

D1202551

# SHEBOYGAN COUNTY *Chronicle*

## A Novel by

## James F. D. Martin

*Essence*
PUBLISHING

Belleville, Ontario, Canada

**Library and Archives Canada Cataloguing in Publication**

Martin, James F. D. (James Floyd Dawson), 1953-
     Sheboygan County chronicle / James F.D. Martin.

ISBN 1-55306-816-5.--ISBN 1-55306-818-1 (LSI ed.)

     1. Sheboygan County (Wis.)--History--Fiction. 2. Germans-- Wisconsin--Newspapers. 3. Christian fiction, American. I. Title.

PS3613.A774S53 2004     813'.6     C2004-904131-2

*Essence Publishing* is a Christian Book Publisher dedicated to furthering the work of Christ through the written word. For more information, contact:
20 Hanna Court, Belleville, Ontario, Canada K8P 5J2.
Phone: 1-800-238-6376 • Fax: (613) 962-3055.
E-mail: publishing@essencegroup.com
Internet: www.essencegroup.com

# Acknowledgements

We are a people of stories. Our friend Jesus was a master storyteller who continues to teach His people through the insight of parables. Our memories are stories: collections of events filtered through subjective perceptions and bundled together as individuals, families, and communities of faith. *Sheboygan County Chronicle* is, in part, a story about the good people of Saron Church: our ancestors in faith as well as today's saints. I am grateful to these people for these tales inspired by our life together.

In particular, I am thankful for: Jenny, Ellie, and Andrew and their steadfast support and patient critiques during the many revisions of this material; for Minnette Rautmann, who told me about her search for "elephant eggs" as a child; and for a few good friends whose encouragement and belief in this project helped it to become a reality.

May God bless you in the enjoyment of this story and inspire each of us as we seek the Way, the Truth, and the Life.

# Foreword

Reading James F. D. Martin's historical novel *Sheboygan County Chronicle* brought to mind the words of the ancient philosopher who wrote: "One word frees us from all the weight and pain of life; that word is love." This is a story about love: love that overcomes a multitude of difficulties and challenges, love that is God's promise to the world, love that forms community and sustains a person's life when everything around us appears compromised by contradictions of all kinds. This is a book about life in a small town one hundred years ago. In Mr. Martin's vivid descriptions of that town and its people, one can hear the laughter and experience the tears of those who lived as pioneers before most of us were born. Their humor, their frailties, the wonder and hardship of being alive, the victories and the tragedies we, too, have experienced (or know through the experience of others) are present in this insightful tale of a community of people set in the midst of the fertile (and sometimes stubborn) farmland that once composed Sheboygan County, Wisconsin.

This is a story about faith. It is a story about faith that is tested, faith that is humbled, faith that is accompanied by the reality of doubt, faith that overcomes what the powerful spirituals describe as "the troubles of the world." "What good is it to me," Meister Eckhart asked towards the end of the Middle Ages, "if Mary gave birth to the Son of God fourteen hundred years ago, and I do not also give birth to the Son of God in my time and in my culture… God is always needing to be born." This is a story about God's presence at the center and at the margins of the lives of ordinary people. On many of its pages, one has the sense that one could reach out and touch the characters who appear: Clara, who returns home as a prodigal; Carl, for whom life has turned bitter; Pastor Gustav Vriesen, whose ever patient, wise, and loving pastoral care speaks even louder than his sermons; Calvin Rickmeier, with his fishing pole; and Otto, who breathes the goodness of life. In these pages we meet ordinary people much like ourselves: Jacob with his bowed head and low self-esteem, recalling weaknesses most of us possess and August Schmidt with his self-righteousness and his high self-esteem, bringing to mind our human foibles.

This "chronicle of life" is filled with the delight of humor that often softens some of life's harsher blows, as when a villager seeks to receive a shave and finds himself seated in the chair of a barber named "Nick." There is Edna, constantly feuding with her husband, Emil Dinkmeier. Edna awakens one night to what she is certain is a burglar in the kitchen. "It sounds like he's eating the rest of the torte that we had for dinner!" she exclaims. "Then it's already too late," Emil responds as he rolls over and goes back to sleep. Emil senses no threat since he is aware of the quality of Edna's cooking!

One reads of the "thistles amidst the alfalfa" and is reminded of the realities of our lives: sorrows and joys, disappointments and achievements, deep wounds and gentle healing, the tragedies and wonders of our brief years upon the earth. This book is ultimately about hope. It is, I believe, an Easter story; a tale of resurrection that unfolds, like the lives of all of us, in proximity to the crosses we bear.

"Angels can fly," G. K. Chesterton wrote, "because they take themselves so lightly." In this grand tale of a time now past, you will hear the voices of loyalty and faith and generosity and compassion, as also their opposites. Those voices are believable (and thus a delight) because in the gentle hands of James F. D. Martin, they go about their business (for the most part) lightly, like the angels.

In one of the epistles of the New Testament, we can read these words: "the wisdom from above is pure, first of all; it is also peaceful, gentle, and friendly; it is full of compassion and produces a harvest of good deeds; it is free from prejudice and hypocrisy" (Jas. 3:17, TEV). *Sheboygan County Chronicle* contains all these elements: purity and peace, gentleness and friendship, compassion and good deeds. It does not back away from the presence of prejudice and hypocrisy in our lives. This is why I have so enjoyed the book and commend it to you.

*Frederick R. Trost*
*Easter, 2004*

# Chapter One ⁓

In the fading daylight, the swirling snow outside Martha Schnuelle's kitchen window seemed to draw her thoughts inward. She never imagined she'd be widowed and living alone for so many years. If she had known this ahead of time, she never would have agreed with her husband to leave Germany in search of a better life.

It was Friday, December 15, 1899. *In a couple weeks*, Martha mused, *it will be the year of our Lord 1900, almost twenty-five years since we arrived at Castle Garden in New York City. Imagine. In the first six years of living in Sheboygan County, I gave birth to two children and buried my husband. Wilhelm. Ah, Willie—I miss you. And our children. Conrad, my son. I'm so proud of you—a doctor in Chicago, married three years. But you rarely come to visit. And Clara— oh, my daughter, the pain of my heart! Where are you? When was it you left me? The summer of '96? It's been so long.*

Outside, the gracefully twirling shapes of snow conjured images in her mind from a summer scene years before: little Conrad and Clara swinging in hypnotic rhythm from the outstretched limbs of the bur oak; the day's laundry flapping in the breeze and drying in the sun; Willie coming in from the field, carrying something in his hand—a bouquet of black-eyed Susans. *For me? How thoughtful!* She turned to greet him, but realized she was alone again, peering at a door that wasn't going to open. Her smile faded. A numbing wave of sadness washed over her. She felt listless once more.

On Saturday, Martha awoke in the same blue mood that had become the pattern of her life over the last few years. Again she found herself staring blankly out of the window. Turning her eyes upward, she pleaded with the sky, "How long will I be so lonely?" She wanted to cry, but did not; she wanted to die, but could not.

Yes, her neighbors were kind to her. Otto Steitz, owner of the general store, had been her friend since childhood. August Schmidt from down the road supplied her with firewood. The Rickmeiers sometimes invited her for dinner after church. And dear Anna Klemme often stopped by with some fresh bread or cookies, sometimes two pieces of pie.

When Anna came to visit, Martha usually made coffee and the two women would sit and chat. But Anna's was a busy life; all too soon she'd have to leave, saying something like, "I must be going, but I'll come to see you again next week and we can visit then."

Martha's usual reply was, "Must you leave so soon? Well, thank you for coming. Your bread and pies and cookies always taste so good, like the ones I used to make. I don't enjoy baking or cooking anymore. It's just not the same preparing meals for one person."

On Sunday after worship, Martha was greeted by Otto Steitz, who was the postmaster in addition to the store owner. "Frau Schnuelle," he said, "a letter came for you yesterday. It's from Conrad. I couldn't read all of it—heh, just a little postal humor. It'll be in your post box tomorrow."

*Perhaps it's a Christmas greeting,* she thought. *Oh, it'll be good to hear from him.*

On Monday morning at seven o'clock, she hurried down the

road to the post office inside the general store, found the envelope from Conrad, and opened it excitedly. Instead of a Christmas card, however, she found a note:

*Dear Mother,*

*I hope this letter finds you in good health. We hoped to send you a nice Christmas card again this year, but are coming to visit you instead. Surprise! Charlotte and I plan to arrive in Bierville on Friday, December 22 and will stay with you for a week, if this is agreeable with you. If this is inconvenient, we'll stay at a hotel in Sheboygan. See you soon!*

*With love,*
*Conrad*

"Donnerwetter! Conrad and Charlotte are coming to stay with me? Wunderbar!" She ran over to Otto, threw her arms around him, and kissed him on the cheek.

"Martha!" he said with a smile, his balding head turning a handsome shade of red. "Good news, I take it."

"Yes! Conrad is coming to visit me—for Christmas!" Waving the letter above her head, she scurried out of the store, nearly knocking Anna Klemme over. "Anna! Conrad and Charlotte are coming home for Christmas."

"That's wonderful, Mrs. Schnuelle. How long has it been since you last saw them?"

"Nearly two years. Say, do you have the recipes for your chocolate cake and pumpernickel rolls? I'd like to copy them and do a little baking before my guests arrive."

"It will be my pleasure! Come with me."

The next few days were busy and happy for Martha. She baked cookies, cakes, pies—more than they could eat in a month. The delicious aromas filling her house made her feel alive again. At one point, she appraised the growing assortment and smiled. *We'll simply be making up for lost time. And all the meals we haven't been able to share.*

Martha surveyed her little house with new eyes. *They can stay in the spare bedroom. It was the children's room, after all. But look at the filth!* She began seeing dust she had overlooked for years. With renewed vigor, she started her spring cleaning; she wasn't sure whether it was a few months early or several months late.

On Thursday, her eyes watered much of the day from the ammonia fumes. She washed all of the windows, swept and mopped the floors, and took the rugs outside and beat them till they changed colors. Neighbors on the street asked Martha, "What has come over you? You haven't been this energetic for years."

Her reply was simple: "Conrad is coming." That explained everything.

When the long-anticipated day finally arrived, Martha was exhausted. She was, however, ready. She waited and watched at the front window all day. The clock on the mantle had never moved so slowly and she examined it every so often to make sure it was still working properly.

Shortly after four o'clock, she took the last loaf of bread out of the oven. The sun would be setting soon, but there was no sign of her guests. *Won't they take the train from Chicago and hire a horse and buggy in town?* She scanned the letter again, thinking she had misread it. *No, the twenty-second was correct.* Finally, she heard bells tinkling in the distance, getting louder.

"A sleigh!" she said, stepping outside. "Welcome home, Conrad. Welcome, Charlotte. What a wonderful surprise!" Martha hugged and kissed each of them in turn. "Conrad," she said, "don't they sell razors in Chicago? You look like a wildebeest."

"Thank you, Mother," he said, smiling. "I find that my patients are more inclined to trust me now. The beard makes me look older, more authoritative."

Charlotte said, "I think he looks like a young Alexander Graham Bell. Rather distinguished. I like it."

While Conrad unhitched the horses and got them settled in the barn, Martha and Charlotte brought the luggage inside and finished preparing supper. Martha seated her guests at the kitchen table and brought out a meal that would have fed twice as many: smoked ham, baked potatoes with butter and sour cream, green beans with bacon and onions, pumpernickel dinner rolls, and Bavarian chocolate cake.

"Oh, Mother," Conrad said, swallowing a mouthful of cake, "you've outdone yourself. And you think you're out of practice?"

"Everything's delicious," Charlotte said. "Conrad told me about your wonderful cooking, but it's even more heavenly than he described."

"I'm glad you like it," Martha replied, bowing in gratitude. "Food always tastes better when shared with loved ones."

Conrad leaned back in his chair, folding his hands behind his head. "Ow!" he said.

"Are you all right, dear?" Martha asked.

"Yes," Conrad replied, grinning and rubbing the back of his head. "I was checking the patellar reflexes of one of my patients at my office yesterday, and he kicked me."

"In the head?" Martha said in astonishment. She raised her cup of milk for another sip.

"No. I was startled and lurched backward, banging my head on a shelf."

Martha tried to suppress a laugh with her mouth full, but one finger in the center of her lips was not enough. Two fountains spewed from the corners of her mouth, spraying her guests. Martha was embarrassed, but they all laughed uncontrollably. Charlotte got the hiccups, which only made things worse.

"Don't worry, Mother," Conrad said, chuckling and drying his face with his napkin. "I've gotten worse from baby boys on the examining table." Again they exploded with laughter. Tears trickled down their cheeks.

"Stop, stop!" Charlotte said, giggling hysterically. "I can't breathe."

*Ah,* Martha thought, *it's good to be alive.* "Whew!" she said. "Oh, that was fun! I wish your sister were here for this."

Conrad's smile changed to a scowl. "I don't care if I've seen her for the last time. Mother, look at how she behaves, always carousing and cavorting. The last time she left, how much did she take from you? One hundred dollars? It seems to me you should be glad she's gone."

They finished eating in silence. Later, a dancing fire in the hearth soothed the friction. The three chatted freely into the night.

After breakfast on Saturday, Conrad and Charlotte went out to the woods and cut down a white spruce for trimming. Martha greeted them at the back door. "What a lovely tree you found. We'll decorate it tonight and my home will be festive and alive once more. Thank you."

At about noon, the three of them gathered in the kitchen for a little lunch: ham and cheese sandwiches, milk and coffee, and the remainder of the chocolate cake. There was a knock at the front door. Martha said, "That must be August Schmidt. He's planning to drop off some wood today." She opened the door, but the caller wasn't August.

"Hello, Mama. I'm so sorry for—"

"Clara!" she said, reaching for her daughter. Martha's heart overflowed with a river of joy and a reservoir of grief. She heard the kitchen door close and looked up to see that Conrad had left.

After a moment, Clara spoke again. "Mama, I'm sorry for all

the ways I hurt and disappointed you. I don't have any place to stay. May I spend the night here?"

"Clara, my dear, come in! You must be frozen."

Clara stepped inside, her body in the posture of brokenness, wrapped in a black, full-length, hooded cape. Her movement was stiff and she appeared vulnerable and alone.

"Here," Martha said, "sit next to the fire. Let me take your cape."

"No. I'm fine." Clara huddled in a chair near the fireplace, still wrapped tightly. She appeared to relax somewhat, but wouldn't look up. Charlotte brought a cup of hot tea to her.

Martha said, "Clara, you haven't met Conrad's lovely wife. This is Charlotte. Charlotte, this is my daughter, Clara."

Clara glanced up, managed to smile for a few seconds, and gratefully received the warm gift. Resting the saucer on her knees, she warmed her hands around the cup.

"I'm glad to meet you," Charlotte said, placing a hand on Clara's shoulder.

Martha and Charlotte brought chairs over to the fireplace and sat near Clara. For a few minutes, the three women sat quietly, listening to the snapping and hissing of the burning wood.

Clara started to talk, measuring her words carefully: "After I turned eighteen almost two years ago, I got married to a man named Edward Mackey in Springfield. I thought he loved me and would take care of me, but I was wrong. Seven months ago, when he realized I was carrying our child, he left me. Last Wednesday, he came back and accused me of being unfaithful to him, saying the child I was carrying wasn't his. None of what—"

It was as though the words caught in Clara's throat. She convulsed, as if it were too painful to relive the memory. A heart-rending cry seemed to force its way from the depths of Clara's soul.

Martha groaned, aching for her daughter's misery. Charlotte knelt beside Clara, wrapping her arms around her. Clara hid her face in Charlotte's shoulder and wept. Only the crackling of the fire and the ticking of the clock on the mantle reminded Martha that time had not come to a standstill.

A few minutes later, Clara straightened, took a deep breath, and continued: "It wasn't true. None of what he said was true, but he wouldn't believe me. He said I was no longer his wife, that our divorce became final a few days ago, on the twentieth. Then he hit me with the back of his hand and pushed me into the wall, telling me to get out of his house, to never come back. He grabbed me by the throat and tried to break the chain of my locket and take it from me. I struggled free and ran to a neighbor's house. In the middle of the night, I left. Mama, I have nowhere to go. I'm all alone."

Clara rose slowly and removed her hood and cape. Her matted, dark-brown hair hung over her shoulders. There was a smudge on her forehead and a bruise the size of a silver dollar on her left cheek. Nevertheless, with her dark eyes and fine facial features, hers was the captivating beauty of an angel, albeit a fallen angel. A gold locket hung around her neck and glowed in the warmth of the fire-light. Clara was not, however, completely alone. It was apparent she would give birth any day.

"My dear child!" Martha said. "Did Edward Mackey follow you to Bierville?"

"Oh, I doubt that he'd bother. I never told him where I was from or anything about you. He didn't seem to care."

"I thought I'd never see you again, but now you've come home to me, still in one piece. All is forgiven, Clara. Of course, you can stay with me."

Martha walked outside and found Conrad splitting wood behind the barn. He kept to his task, Martha standing by in silence. Then, in between savage swings of the ax, he vented his anger: "You welcomed her home—didn't you? How could you—after all she—did to you?"

"What concern is it of yours if I forgive her?"

"When she stole that—money from you, I—replaced it out of my—own pocket. One hundred dollars!"

"Is it about money, Conrad? Then I will pay you back and we'll be even."

"Mother, the money's—not important."

"You're right. It's not important. What is important is that your sister who was dead to us is now alive and with us once more. She has had a terrible time of it, Conrad. She was married two years ago, but her husband ran out on her, accused her of infidelity, and beat her. She's expecting a child any day. And you, my son, could have the honor of delivering her baby."

He stared at the ground without saying a word.

She continued: "Conrad, had you not been diligent in making the most of your life and faithful in looking after me, I'm not sure whether I could have survived the grief. It was heartbreaking for me to have my daughter behaving so poorly all those years and gone for so long. I also think it was painfully difficult for you."

He nodded, turning his face skyward. Tears welled in his eyes.

"I remember," she said, "how Clara was always your best friend and playmate. I can still picture the two of you on your swings in the tree there. You two would swing and laugh for hours at a time. She's back, Conrad. She's all right. Welcome her home!"

Conrad looked at his mother and said, "She'll always be my little sister, yet I've never allowed myself to grieve for her pain." He set the ax down and rested his head on Martha's shoulder, letting the years of separation and sadness pour out.

At last, Martha thought, the obedient son has permitted himself to cry for the prodigal.

There were two beds in Martha's house. Conrad and Charlotte snuggled up in one, and Clara lay in the other. Martha curled up in a white goose-down quilt on the floor in front of the fireplace. She didn't fall asleep right away; she was blissfully relieved and wanted to savor the feeling. Her attention was drawn to the reassuring flames of the fire, then to the decorated Christmas tree that stood in the corner. She found it hard to contain her delight until the following midnight. They would light the candles on the tree, causing it to glow with ethereal glory. *We've so much to celebrate,* she thought. *So much.*

Clara didn't fall asleep right away, either. The candle on the nightstand burned brightly and she was grateful for its light. She propped herself up with pillows, making herself more comfortable. She knew she wouldn't sleep soundly. *How can I make sense of all this, these past months? This locket and this child are the only things from my life with Edward that I want to keep.*

Clara was still wearing the locket and realized she'd been fingering it absentmindedly. A gift from her husband, the locket was an exquisite piece of metalwork; the detailed engraving made the flowers and vines on the face seem almost real. She took the locket off and hesitated before opening it.

Inside were two small photographs. On the left side, there was a bust shot of Clara and her husband taken on their wedding day; on the right was a picture of Clara. She picked at the edge of the picture on the left and removed it from the locket. After glancing at the photograph once more, she reached over and held it above the candle flame. In a moment, all that was left of her wedding picture was a curled ash resting in the candleholder and a hazy puff of acrid smoke lingering in the air.

Clara studied the locket again and noticed something she hadn't seen before: a folded piece of paper rested in a cavity that the wedding picture had concealed. She pressed on the other picture, but it felt solid behind. Turning the locket over, she tapped the piece of paper into her open hand and unfolded it. It appeared to be a poem written in red ink:

> *The sweetest sound*
> *my ears have found:*
> *Your love, confessed and brave.*
> *But cross me, dear,*
> *and thine, I fear,*
> *Will be an early grave.*

*What a monster! How could I have married a man I hardly knew, one who grew to have so much contempt for me? Why didn't I realize this before? What else didn't I know about him?*

Clara resolved to put Edward Mackey out of her mind and begin a new life. She blew out the candle and drifted off to sleep.

# Chapter Two ⌒

On a Monday morning in June of 1900, Fritzie, the new stock boy at the general store, handed Clara's basket of groceries to her. She took it with her left hand, holding her baby Liesl with her right. He hurried to the door to open it for her; she smiled and winked at him. He felt himself blush.

"Thank you, Fritzie!" she said. "Good-bye."

He said, "I wish there were something I could do about it."

"So do I," Clara replied.

Otto hurried in from the back room. "Now, Clara," he said, "pardon my eavesdropping, but Fritzie is just learning the ropes here. So if there's a problem you'd like me to take care of, simply ask and it shall be done."

"I had no idea you have such influence. I should be addressing you as 'Your Holiness.'" Clara smiled, winked at Fritzie, and left. His heart melted.

"What?" Otto asked.

Fritzie chuckled. "Rain, Herr Steitz. She wants it to rain."

Otto laughed. "So much for my erroneous assumptions. 'Your Holiness.' Ja! That'll be the day! Pope Otto the Fallible."

Otto couldn't remember such a long dry spell in the spring, being disappointed day after day to be awakened at dawn by bright sunshine and a clear sky. He imagined the little corn plants in the fields crossing their leaves as if they were arms, tapping their tiny feet, waiting impatiently for a good rain so they could shoot up and meet their expected height by the Fourth of July.

Folks weren't frantic yet, but Otto noticed Simon and Anna Klemme from one of the farms down the road doing some unusual things recently: leaving clothes hanging outside all night; having picnics in the middle of the field, far away from any kind of shelter; going swimming in the river. They even washed their buggy and left it outside. Every one of these ideas was a surefire way to cause the skies to open and the showers to fall. However, they received nothing but more blasted, beautiful weather.

At about ten o'clock on Tuesday morning, Otto finished sweeping off the boardwalk in front of the general store and leaned on the broom handle, surveying the sky—another discouragingly cloudless day. His gaze turned earthward and he noticed someone walking up the road toward the village. The man wore a straw porkpie hat and a brown suit and carried an umber leather sampler. "I don't think he's from around here," Otto said to the broom.

When the man was within earshot, he shouted to Otto, "Say, Old Timer. Maybe you can help me."

"I'm not sure anyone can," Otto muttered.

"What say?" the man asked.

Louder this time, Otto said, "I sure will, if I can."

"Say, what are you doing? Studying the weather? I'm too busy for such nonsense myself. I'm looking for the owner of the general store. Do you know who that might be?"

"I have a pretty good idea. Last time I checked, I still am."

"Ya don't say? Well, this is your lucky day, Pappy. I'm in position to do you a favor." He removed his hat and bowed, revealing a strange goat-like toupee. "The name's J. T. Whitley, regional representative for Doctor Whitley's Miracle Elixir. It cures whatever ails you. Gout, distemper, the vapors, rheumatism—especially lumbago—varicosity, biliousness. I'll set up a display for you."

"How much are they?"

"A dollar a quart, twenty-four to the case, plus a ten percent handling fee."

"A dollar? Goodness! Actually, our health around here is pretty good."

"Did I say 'cures' you? I meant it prevents these ailments. You don't want to see your loved ones suffering from biliosity, do you? How many cases can I put you down for? Fifty? A hundred?"

"What we really need is rain."

"Did I forget to mention the best feature of Doctor Whitley's Miracle Elixir? It's scientifically proven to cause rain."

"Is that a fact?"

"Pour about half the bottle into a dish, leave it out overnight, and not only will the neighborhood cats be your friends for life, but in the morning you'll be wanting to build yourself an ark!"

"Hogwash."

"It's good for that, too! Look, Old Timer, why study the weather when you can make it yourself? Rain within twenty-four hours. Completely scientific."

"Mr. Whitley, where do you live?"

"Brooklyn, New York. I have a flat right on Broadway."

"Do you spend much time outside?"

"As little as possible. Only when I'm in places like this—cut off from the outside world."

"Mr. Whitley, look up at the sky for a moment, at the fields and the woods. This is a lot more 'outside' than some human construct where people hide themselves from nature and one another. I bet you're one of those people who think beans grow in cans with labels on 'em and sausages grow all connected."

"Of course not! I've been around the block. All that happens in modern, efficient processing plants. Why, we hardly need the farms anymore."

"Well, most folks here still farm for a living, so we keep a close eye on the weather. Our lives depend on it. Whether or not you realize it, so does yours. Your elixir might make a few cats happy, but it's not going to make it rain."

"So, what's the answer? How many cases can I put you down for?"

"Nein, danke."

"Nine? Well, that's a start. You won't be sorry."

It was too late. Otto already was. "Just what Bierville needs," he said, "a year's supply of feline intoxicant."

"What's that?" Whitley asked.

"Feline intoxicant—to inebriate our cats."

"No. Bierville, did you say? Oh, Pappy! That's the name of this place?"

"Well, unofficially. It's a name that's just sort of stuck."

"Bierville? Well, that's a stupid name! Any idea where it came from? Is there a brewery here or what?"

"No, but I can show you something that should explain it." He led Whitley down the road, in front of the dance hall, and pointed at a large sign hanging over the main entrance. "There," Otto said. "That's where we got the name."

"Pardon me," Whitley said, "but I can't read French."

"Fortunately, I can," Otto said, smiling. "It says, 'Bist du jemand der Bier will?' That means, 'Are you someone who would like a beer?' They don't sell all that much beer there anymore. But the sign's still there."

"Bierville. I get it. But that's still a stupid name!"

"So I've heard," Otto replied. "Now let's go medicate some

cats. I've always heard they can sing pretty well, given the proper disposition."

"Singin' cats! Oh, Pappy! You've given me another idea!"

On Wednesday, Henry Schultz stopped at the post office to get his mail and buy a stamp for a letter. Henry put the letter on the counter. Otto glanced at it and said, "That'll be two cents, Henry," setting a stamp on the counter next to the letter.

"Say," Henry said, "aren't you gonna put that stamp on for me?"

"Ach! My mouth is so dry. Beside that, for two cents the government doesn't supply spit. If you're too dry, then here—use this."

"What is it?" Henry asked, examining the little piece of bent wire.

"I just got a delivery from Germany," replied Otto. "They call it a paper clip. Now, instead of pinning things together, we can clip them together."

"A paper clip. What an interesting innovation. What'll they think of next?"

The farmers were generally reluctant to admit it but they were concerned that if they didn't get rain soon, there would be a complete crop failure. Gustav Vriesen, the forty-two-year-old pastor of the village church, was wondering about it, too. He and his wife Minnie were at the general store, picking up some nails for a project at the church when Herman Rickmeier came in.

"Herr Vriesen," Herman said, "would it be too much trouble for you to dust off some of your rain prayers? We could use some help."

"Herman," Gustav asked, "have you been behaving yourself? Or is it because of you it hasn't rained?"

Herman appeared crestfallen. "Herr Vriesen, do you think it could be something I did that caused this dry spell?"

Minnie poked her husband and said to Herman, "He's joking. What did the Lord Jesus say in the Sermon on the Mount? God 'maketh his sun to rise on the evil and on the good, and sendeth rain on the just and on the unjust.'"

Gustav continued the thought. "God does not withhold rain from sinners, for the righteous would also suffer. Showers from heaven are a blessing for all of God's creatures."

Herman seemed relieved, but another cloud crossed his brow. "We made hay last week and got only about a third of an average cutting. We can't take this much longer."

"You are right," Gustav said, "but remember what the Lord Jesus said. 'Be not therefore anxious for the morrow: for the morrow will be anxious for itself. Sufficient unto the day is the evil thereof.' Try not to worry, my friend."

"Try not to worry? I could lose my farm."

"Oh, I know. Our theologizing and quoting Scripture won't save your farm. Neither will your anxiety. It'll only make you miserable. I know it's hard to be patient, but I am confident that our God in heaven is merciful and just and will not leave us desolate. Creation's rhythms are dependable. The rains will fall again."

On Thursday night, U. S. Senator Harrison Williams addressed the farmers of the area concerning the drought. The meeting was held at the dance hall. Gustav arrived and was amazed at the turnout; people he knew from all over the county came to hear what the senator had to say. He was glad to see that even Bruno, Otto's six-month-old Saint Bernard, was in attendance.

Ida Klietz, the hall owner, walked over to Gustav and greeted him. They stood side by side, chatting together and nodding to the arriving guests. Simon and Anna Klemme entered the hall and went over to stand with Gustav and Ida.

Gustav said, "Ah, the expectant parents! Glad to see you! Say, look over there. Mrs. Klietz took the thermometer down from the wall."

Ida smiled and said, "I didn't want anyone to see how hot it is in here and pass out. Sometimes ignorance is cooler."

Simon said, "Yep, with all these people in here, hotter than blazes, it'd be like handing a mirror to an ugly man and sayin', 'See? It's worse than you think.'"

"What?" Anna said, pretending to stamp on her husband's foot. "Please excuse him. He banged his head in the barn this morning and has been talking gibberish ever since."

Gustav saw Senator Williams approaching the podium on the stage, so he made his way through the crowd to the foot of the stage. Simon and Anna followed. The senator, impressive in stature and girth, prepared to greet the gathering, sweat rolling from every pore, his face like a ripe tomato. A restless hush fell over the assembly.

"Thank you," the senator said, "for welcoming me so—so warmly—to this lovely community of, uh…" He paused and whispered to an aid, "Where are we?"

"Bierville, sir," the aid said.

"Bierville? Really?" The senator spoke for thirty minutes. Every time the audience reacted favorably to what he said, he took a sip of water from the glass at his right hand. When they reacted negatively, he wiped his forehead with the handkerchief in his left hand.

He told them how concerned Washington was over their situation—and he took a sip of water. He said, "You will be able to purchase your seed next year with low-interest loans—" and he wiped his forehead. "Hay will be shipped by rail from Alabama and Georgia, and you will be able to purchase it for fifteen cents per bale—" and up went the handkerchief.

"And, I have just worked out an arrangement with the governor so any farm next to a river or stream can make use of the water for irrigating the fields."

"I beg your pardon, sir," Herman said, rising to his feet. "The rivers are already low and the streams are pert near dry."

Again the senator wiped his forehead.

Simon Klemme stood and asked, "Your Excellency, is it possible for our taxes to be cut for the next two years as a tangible sign of Washington's genuine concern? By then, we should have had a chance to recover."

Senator Williams picked up the glass of water, poured it on the handkerchief, and swabbed his whole face.

After the meeting, the audience milled around. It was time for reactions from the crowd. Gustav looked over at Anna. She nudged her husband. "Where on earth did you get 'Your Excellency'?"

"It's all I could think of. I knew 'Your Royal Highness' wasn't right."

"What about 'Your Mediocrity'?"

"That's a better fit."

Gustav approached the senator, introduced himself, and said, "As a fellow professional orator, you have to score it as a win if they don't start throwing things."

"So my words were helpful?" the senator asked.

"It was everything we'd expected, and so much more. Thank you for coming to Sheboygan County. We're grateful that you made the effort."

Edna Dinkmeier filed past the senator. He shook her hand and asked, "Well, my good woman, how did you find my little speech tonight?"

Edna wrinkled her nose and said, "Ach, it wasn't so little. And dry—about the only thing drier than the weather was your speech! Now if you'd simply done a little dance, it might not have rained, but everyone would have enjoyed it more!"

Gustav wondered all week what he was going to write the sermon about for Sunday. By Saturday night, he had fifteen pages of pointless platitudes. Concern about the dry spell kept creeping into his mind, but what could he say that would help? *Maybe I could use the senator's notes. Now that's a sign of real desperation! Ah, it's past midnight. This is no use. All right, Minnie, here I come.*

He trudged up to bed, thinking about the grim expressions that would cloud the faces of the elders as he stammered his way through the service. *Even German stammering will be an irritation to them.*

On Sunday morning, the spiritual well from which Gustav usually drew his sermons seemed as dry as the parsonage's cistern. He thought of taking a glass of water and a handkerchief up to the pulpit with him but decided a Bible would be better.

Despite the uncomfortably hot weather, there was good attendance for worship. However, his people appeared wilted and spiritless—like sheep without a shepherd. Hymns were sung and prayers were offered, but before the preacher's pump was primed, he was standing in the pulpit, wishing the Bible he was holding would turn into a handkerchief or a glass of water, or that the prophet Elijah would simply come and carry him away. Elijah! That was all the idea he needed.

"My friends," he said, "during the past week I have been pondering our situation in light of the drought we are experiencing, trying to understand what words of comfort God might want to say to us in this difficult time. And the story of the prophet Elijah came to mind."

He opened his Bible to 1 Kings 16 and read about Elijah's confrontation with a nation that didn't trust in the Lord God. He said, "Israel was led by King Ahab, who did more to provoke the anger of God than all the kings of Israel before him. As proof that the God of Israel was supreme over all, Elijah announced there would be no rain for a period of three and one-half years. The drought and the famine were severe."

Gustav paused for a moment and noticed how pensive, even anguished his people appeared. Minnie stared blankly at the ceiling. *Oh, for a handkerchief!* He tried to change course. "However," he said, "I have no doubt that the Lord God is compassionate and good."

He remembered what Jesus said in the Sermon on the Mount, about God sending rain on the just and on the unjust. Gustav started muttering out loud. "That still doesn't explain why it hasn't rained for so long. Even if all of us were scoundrels, God knows we still need the blessing of rain." He wished all the more for a handkerchief.

Gustav noticed the dour expressions on the church elders' faces, and imagined an unusually dry storminess hovering above their heads. One more thought came to mind. He turned to the letter of James 5:7 and read, "'Be patient therefore, brethren, until the coming of the Lord. Behold, the husbandman waiteth for the precious fruit of the earth, being patient over it, until it receive the early and latter rain.'"

He closed the Bible and said, "My friends, I don't know why the early rain of spring is later than usual. But, I do know this. As surely as the Lord God lives and has created the goodness of the earth, we shall survive this drought. Countless people before us have lived through such times, and so shall we. Perhaps as we wait patiently for the coming rains, we shall realize our inability to save ourselves, our dependence upon a strength much greater than our own, and our reliance upon our loving God who knows our names and remembers our needs."

Gustav looked over at the elders—and then at the congregation—and wished for a glass of water.

# Chapter Three ⌒

December twenty-four in the year of our Lord 1900 dawned with all of the promise and goodness that one could hope for. At the Klemme farm, Anna was preparing breakfast, and she had a profound sense of well-being. Bacon and eggs sizzled and snapped in the skillet on the woodstove, coaxing the crisp morning air to cheerfulness. Catherine and Caroline, their four-month-old twins, were sleeping peacefully in the bedroom nearby. Simon came up beside her and draped his arm over her shoulders; it felt to her like a warm shawl. She gazed contentedly out of the kitchen window, past the barn, over the fresh blanket of snow on the fields, and said in a prayerful voice, "God is so good, Simon. God is good."

She reflected on the passing year; it had been a difficult one for their family and neighbors. The spring rains were slow in arriving and miserly in beneficence. The soil was so dry that the seeds germinated only stubbornly. Young plants curled and twisted under the scorching sun. All through June, the bluish-green corn plants remained stunted while the weeds thrived. She remembered Herman Rickmeier saying to her, "If only we could harvest these weeds, why, we'd be a far piece better off."

Through the middle of July, most people in the region who depended on farming for their livelihood were deeply concerned.

However, when the healing rains finally came, the good earth nearly sang with delight. In the end, the crops grew and there was a modest yield, a testimony to the tenacity and re-creative rhythms of life. Now, under a sparkling, soft blanket of snow, it seemed to Anna that all was calm; all was bright.

A quarter mile away, Carl Mueller was in the pantry staring through the window at the pristine expanse of snow outside. His sister Gertrude was in the kitchen preparing breakfast. Carl didn't see anything that gave him a sense of serenity and delight; those were long-forgotten blessings for him.

The day last summer when the rains finally came, he happened to be looking toward the Klemmes' place and saw Simon and Anna run out of the barn and waltz together through the puddles.

"Such foolishness is that!" Carl said out loud, though there was no one nearby. "Don't they know the horses'll gurricken get stuck in the mud now? Sunset strolls, picnics down by the river, an' now this! Them Klemmes spend far too much time havin' fun. Don't they know life's s'posed to be serious? Hard? No! Go ahead, have fun! Ha! Foolishness!"

Carl realized that he spent a great deal of time muttering to himself, but he had convinced himself that he preferred it that way. "I wouldn't be gurricken livin' with a yackety, ol' spinster if my house an' barn hadn'ta been destroyed in that fire. Thirty years now. Hmm. Thirty years since my wife an' son died. That's what tells me life is hard, Simon! An' you'd better not get attached to no one, hey. Love nobody. Something bad'll happen, an' all you'll have is an achin' heart an' broken dreams. No, sir, life is hard enough without gettin' attached to people."

"Carl," Gertrude said, calling him back to the present, "breakfast is ready. Carl? Are you there, or in some other world?"

"I hear ya, ya old maid! Jus' because other people think you're so sweet doesn't mean I have to! Jus' because you go to church every Sunday doesn't mean God loves you, or even that there is a God! An' ya don't have to go on pretending to be nice to me, either. Just because we live together doesn't mean we have to be nice!"

"Carl," she said, her eyes filling with tears, "you're my brother. I love you, whether you like it or not. I should just give up on you, the way you've given up on Bierville. It's not our fault that you're so unhappy. Sometimes I don't know why I bother, other than that I love you."

"All right, Gertrude, don't gurricken go an' get mushy. The food's ready? Fine. Let's jus' sit down, be quiet, an' eat."

Outside the church, Gustav Vriesen was finishing work on an advertising campaign that he hoped would attract people's attention. He and Henry Schultz stood together admiring the new six-by-eight-foot sign they'd just erected facing the road in front of the church.

"Herr Vriesen," Henry said, "das ist eine gute Idee."

"Danke, Herr Schultz," Gustav said. "I received this inspiration from F. W. Woolworth. It might help us to bring some of our lost sheep back to the fold."

The neatly lettered sign read:

*Nur die Engel dürfen sich vom Gottesdienst entschuldigen.*
*Nur böse Geister werden fortgeschickt.*
*Alle anderen werden im Namen Christi begrüßt.*
[Only angels may excuse themselves from attending.
Only demons are invited to go elsewhere.
All others are welcomed in the name of Christ.]

Over at the Rickmeiers, Frieda was getting ready to wrap all the presents she had bought during the past couple of weeks. She arranged them neatly on the kitchen table according to destination.

Herman began circling the table, inspecting the assembled bounty. He grunted and snorted in tones of disapproval. Frieda looked up and asked, "More stomach trouble, my dear?"

"You should stick to making all of our Christmas presents. I am dismayed to see the frivolous trinkets you want to pass off as Christmas gifts. Ornaments, bath oil, fancy bars of soap, wooden figurines, peppermint candies. Such useless, expensive baubles! How can you spend our hard-earned money on these trifles?"

Frieda smiled, patting his hand. "Ach, humor me, Herman, for aren't you the one who bought a year's supply of hair-restoring elixir from that toupee-pated peddler? J. T. Whitley—wasn't that his name?"

"Thank you, Frieda. You've made your point."

"I don't think it's working, Papa," Calvin said.

"Thank you, Calvin," Herman said, the tension in his voice rising. "Perhaps Doctor Whitley hasn't perfected it yet. But some day, modern science will develop a hair-restoring elixir or liniment or some such thing."

"And then what?" Frieda asked. "Men will grow old and hairy? I think the only ones who stand to benefit are the peddlers. You don't need that snake oil. You're as handsome a man as ever there was."

"Well," Herman said, clearing his throat, "I think my rheumatism's pert near better and my eyesight has improved."

That afternoon at the general store, Martha Schnuelle and Clara were showing off the new sweater that Martha had just finished for her granddaughter. She was so proud of it, a fitting gift for the most beautiful grandchild in the world. Martha gazed fondly at Liesl and said, "Can you imagine? She'll be one year old on Christmas day." She watched Otto as he came from behind the counter, approaching the child with obvious delight.

"Donnerwetter!" he said. "Already so big." He looked up at

Fritzie, who was carrying in a hundred-pound sack of flour. Quietly Otto said, "Excuse me, Martha, Clara. I have a little trick to play on Fritzie." Then louder he said, "Hallo, Fritz! What's this I hear about you going to my superior with your concerns?"

Fritzie put the sack down and said in surprise, "Herr Steitz, I haven't done anything of the sort. Forgive me, but aren't you the boss, anyway?"

"Now, Fritz, isn't it true you've been praying about needing more money?" Otto laughed and said, "Here's a Christmas bonus for you, Fritzie. You deserve it—and more. God bless you, son." Otto handed him an envelope.

Fritzie opened it. "Fifty dollars, Herr Steitz! Can this be possible?"

"You don't know how much I appreciate your loyalty and hard work. If I could afford it, I'd give you a thousand-dollar bonus."

"Thank you, Herr Steitz! Thank you!"

Next to the mill, where the road crosses the river on the east side of Bierville, two horses with wagons in tow stood nose-to-nose, right in the middle of the bridge. August Schmidt and his rig had started onto the bridge first, but Carl charged his rig right out to meet him. Carl glared at his neighbor. "I'll never gurricken give way to an idiot!" he shouted, shaking his fist in defiance.

August waved and shouted back, "That's all right. I find it's often the prudent thing to do. Merry Christmas, Carl." He backed his rig out of the way. Flustered and humiliated, Carl had no choice but to proceed.

On his way home, Carl went by the church, read the new sign, and decided to stop and walk around. As he slowly circled the building, his boots made heavy crunching sounds in the snow. He began to relive his Sunday school years, his wedding, the memorial service. A wave of loneliness swept over him, which he covered with anger. "Sure," he muttered, "the season to be jolly. Not for me, hey. Ha, Herr Vriesen, ha! T'ain't any joy to be had in this world! Holidays, holy days, holes in my heart, that's all! Go ahead, Simon, Anna. Have Gertrude over for Christmas again. I still ain't comin'!"

Last week, Simon and Anna had stopped at the Mueller house to invite them to Christmas dinner once again. Carl was in the front room, but could hear the two of them in the kitchen talking with his sister.

He heard Gertrude say, "I'm sorry for my brother's obstinacy, but the one he hurts the most is himself."

And Simon replied, "Maybe one day we'll succeed in overcoming his hard heartedness with kindness."

At sunset on Christmas Eve, Simon had his chance. His attention was drawn to some commotion in front of the house—angry curses and groans coming from Carl. Somehow his rig had gotten mired in the slushy mud in the ditch next to the road; the wagon wheels were buried up to their axles. Carl tugged futilely on the hitch, filling the air with the blue smoke of his frustration. Simon had an idea of what to expect, but he decided to try to help anyway.

Simon drew near, and Carl said, "Stay away, Simon! I don't gurricken need none o' your help!"

"Well, you stubborn, old Schweinkopf!" Simon shouted back. "You're gonna get my help whether you want it or not!"

Before long, Simon had his four big Belgian horses hitched in front of Carl's two. He slapped the lead horse on the flank. The rig jingled and jolted and staggered its way out of the mud onto firm ground. Simon knew better than to expect any gratitude from Carl. So he unhitched his horses and said flatly, "Thank you for letting me help you, Carl. Merry Christmas." And he led his horses home.

It was dark by the time Carl stepped quietly into the kitchen. He saw that the table was already set and Gertrude was putting a few more sticks into the woodstove. She seemed startled by his presence and said, "Oh. Uh, welcome home, Carl. I didn't hear you come in. We'll be ready to eat in a few minutes."

He cleaned up without saying a word and sat in his chair, elbows on the table, his hands covering his face.

"Is something wrong?" Gertrude asked.

Carl was silent for a moment, then said, barely above a whisper, "They gurricken slayed me, Gertrude. Slayed me with their kindness. All o' ya. What've I done all these years? I can't carry this grudge no more."


On Christmas Eve, after tucking the twins into bed, Anna put supper on the table for Simon and herself: black bean soup with ham, oatmeal bread, and cheese. After giving thanks, she said, "Ah! What a lovely end to a good day."

They talked about the events of the day. She glanced outside and noticed a pleasant, warm glow; it took her a few seconds to realize the import. "The barn!" she shouted. She sprang toward the door, nearly tipping the table over.

The night sky shimmered with billowing orange flames, magnificent and horrible against the darkness. Heat, smoke, confusion. Neighbors helping. "Get the animals out!" Standing, watching, weeping. There was little more to do.

Anna stared in stunned silence at the broken, glowing skeleton that remained. Her gaze shifted to Simon standing next to her; he appeared paralyzed, almost lifeless.

August Schmidt walked up between them, draping an arm over each of their shoulders. "You know," August said, "you saved twelve of your cows and all four of your horses. No one was hurt. We're all grateful for that. Think of it this way. You don't have to feed or milk quite as many animals this winter."

By the time worshipers arrived for the Christmas morning service, most people in the area knew about the fire. Gustav welcomed his flock with the compassion of a shepherd tending the needs of the sheep returning from the field. He looked for a moment at the evergreen boughs and red ribbons decorating the main church entrance; their beauty seemed to pale in the presence of heavenly love at work. Carriages, sleighs, and wagons converged on the church property, and people greeted one another with a mixture of joy and concern. When Anna, Simon, and the twins arrived, a greeting line of sympathy and concern formed, the community's assurance that better days were coming.

Gustav glanced up and noticed Gertrude Mueller's rig plowing toward the church. There was someone with her. "It's Carl!" he said in astonishment.

"Carl? Carl?" echoed one voice after another.

Henry Schultz said, "He hasn't been here since, uh—must be thirty years."

Gertrude appeared ten years younger the way she hopped down from the wagon. Carl was not quite as graceful. Without looking up to see the scores of eyes studying him, Carl trudged over to the Klemmes and greeted them with the warmth of an old friend who had been away for a long time.

"Simon," he said, "I'm terrible sorry 'bout the loss of your barn an' your cows. I can maybe help with the barn. When my barn gurricken burned an' my wife an' boy died, I cut and milled all the wood for a new barn. But I ain't never had the heart to rebuild at the old place. That lumber's well seasoned now. It's in one of my sheds. I'd be pleased if you'd take it as a gift, start again next spring."

Tears filled Simon's eyes and a smile brightened his face. The two neighbors embraced in the awkward way that men sometimes do. And Carl began cry, the way people sometimes do.

Simon said, "There's still a place at our table today if you'd like to join us."

Wiping the tears from his eyes, Carl replied, "I'd be most honored. I'd like to get to know these little twins of yours before they're all growed up."

Gustav led his people in the annual celebration of the birth of Christ. To him, it felt even more like Easter.

# Chapter Four 〰

The oil lamp in the parsonage study burned late that Saturday night in May of 1901. Gustav went over the service for the next day and prayed for each family in his congregation, especially the Rickmeiers. It had been a week to remember. Whenever seven-year-old Calvin was present, life was a mixture of unbridled chaos and organized commotion. Only when Calvin was fast asleep could Bierville fully rejoice in the blessing of peace. Still, Gustav thought of him as a true gift.

Last Sunday, Clara had quizzed her students by having them stand in turn and recite Bible passages of their own choosing. "Greta, do you have one?"

Greta Kleinschmidt cleared her throat, stood meekly and said, "The Acts of the Apostles, chapter one, verse eighteen, the second portion. 'And falling headlong, he burst asunder in the midst, and all his bowels gushed out.'"

"Ehhh," Clara said. "An interesting verse, Greta. Calvin, you're next."

Calvin thought for a moment, smiled at Clara, and said, "Here's a good one. The Song of Songs, chapter four, verse five. 'Thy two breasts are like two young roes that are twins, which feed among the lilies.'"

Clara was nonplussed. But she told Herman and Frieda about it, and they didn't let their son out of the corner until suppertime.

On Monday at the general store, Otto moderated an impromptu debate among some of the farmers concerning the weather—which thing they needed first: a warm rain to soak into the fields, then lots of sunshine, then plowing and planting *or* hot, sunny weather so they could plow, then rain, then planting *or* first planting, then rain, then plowing.

Otto noticed Clara heading for the door, groceries in hand. "Heard enough of this nonsense?" he asked.

"Yes," she replied, smiling, "such interesting reasoning! God was mercifully wise not to entrust the control of the weather to a committee such as this."

After the weather debate, Otto said to Fritzie, "You're sure a cheerful soul today. That selection of John Philip Sousa marches you're whistling has put everyone in high spirits. A regular walking gramophone, that's what you are."

Fritzie said, "I'm glad you like it! I'm happy because I'm finally making headway with my girlfriend Bertha. I think she'll agree to marry me soon."

"You're a little young, aren't you, Fritzie?"

"I'll be twenty in six months. And she's eighteen—almost."

"Seventeen? She didn't accept your marriage proposal, did she?"

"Well, not exactly. But yesterday, when I asked her once more to marry me, she said, 'No, and I'm not going to tell you again!' So, I'm almost there."

"Fritzie, I…uh…" Otto paused, looking for the right word. "Take your time."

On Tuesday, Herman saw Carl passing on his cart and called out, "Hallo, Carl! One of my horses has colic. Didn't one of your mares have that last year?"

"Sure did."

"What'd you give her?"

"Gurricken mineral spirits—'bout a quart." Carl continued on his way.

With that advice, Herman set out to remedy the situation.


At the Rickmeiers' place, Frieda caught Calvin coming out of the shed, fishing pole in hand, apparently sneaking down to the river. "Calvin, why didn't you say something about wanting to go fishing?"

"Well, I said I was gonna feed some animals, didn't I?"

"I thought you were talking about squirrels or raccoons, not fish."

He kicked at some pebbles on the ground and said sorrowfully, "Well, if I'd a-said I was goin' down by the river to fish, would you've let me?"

"Of course not. Not without someone along to keep you out of mischief."

"Well, there wasn't much point in my sayin' anything, then, was there?"

"Calvin, you're— uhh!"


Adam Schroeder, the newly-hired farm and home editor at the newspaper in Sheboygan, wasn't having much success being accepted in the area. He'd written a column recently in which he endorsed a new state agricultural proposal that would require all farmers to collect their livestock and have each of them branded. On Tuesday, he received a sarcastic comment from Henry Schultz about the article, saying he'd try to brand all of his animals, but wondered if the "learned farm editor" had any recommendations on how to brand honey bees.

Adam wanted to buy a small piece of land from August on which to build a house. He said to August, "I like this community. You people have been so kind to me. I'd like to make this my home."

August turned him down. "No, I might need that corner for something," he said, clearing his throat. "Even if it is kind of a distant, rolling piece of wooded land. I'm sure you can find something better somewhere else."

Over at the Klemme homestead, Simon and Anna had their hands full caring for the twins, who had just turned eight months old. Anna wrote a letter to Adam at the newspaper for some advice on how to cure diaper rash and foot fungus; the twins were simply miserable. Also in Adam's mail that day was a letter from Carl, asking what he should do this year if his farm were to be overrun by mice, as was the case the year before.

Adam gave thoughtful responses to each problem, but the typesetter mixed up the questions and answers. So, in Tuesday's paper, Carl's mouse question was answered in this way:

The poor dears! The first goal is to keep their feet and bottoms clean and dry. Change their diapers frequently, whenever wet. Mix a teaspoon each of garlic, cinnamon, and cloves in a cup of whiskey; spread this tincture on their bottoms and feet, especially between their toes. Let air dry between treatments. This should fix the situation in no time.

The answer to Anna's toddler question appeared as this:

These nasty pests need to be exterminated before they spread their diseases and eat you out of house and home. Trapping is the only way to go. It is said they especially like apple or nut butter. And don't worry about cruelty. Most experts believe that, unlike you or me, these little critters are oblivious to pain.

The confusion wasn't Adam's fault but he made an easy scapegoat.

On Wednesday, Calvin got dragged along to the Ladies Aid meeting. He wasn't at all happy about it until he heard they were going to make taffy to sell at the church bazaar the next week. Calvin knew he was an angel in the eyes of the Ladies Aid, and he milked it for all it was worth. He'd smile sweetly and they'd say to one another, "Don't you just love him to death?"

To Calvin's delight, several of the women sneaked pieces of taffy to him. With each piece, he smiled and whispered, "Thank you! I've never had taffy before." This was true—before the Ladies Aid meeting. Imagine: all the taffy he could eat. The first pound he devoured was sheer ecstasy. However, after the second pound, everything before his eyes was turning green somersaults, and he was convinced that the ladies had, indeed, succeeded in loving him to death.


On Wednesday night, Gustav met with the elders of the church to deal with Adam's application for church membership. President August Schmidt directed the discussion. "Our church is well established here. We have no need for such newcomers. Schroeder and others like him should look elsewhere for a church."

Gustav could feel is face flush with anger, but he attempted to remain calm. "August, my friend, not too many years ago, none of us lived here. Today you feel well established. You are satisfied with all you have and God has been generous to us all. And what about Adam? Will you not also extend the hospitality of God to your neighbor?"

"He's not going to be my neighbor," August replied, "because I'm not going to sell him any of my land." There was a ripple of laughter from around the table.

Gustav said, "The land you live on was not yours to begin with. It will not be yours in the end. Land is a gift from God to care for, to enjoy, but not to horde."

"But he's the laughingstock of Sheboygan County!"

"He needs a place to call home, August, a church where he will be welcomed as a brother, a land where he belongs. He's a sojourner in the land, the same way you were. If you had been turned away, you might still be wandering. I caution you, 'Forget not to shew love unto strangers: for thereby some have entertained angels unawares.'"

"Schroeder's not an angel. He's just another stranger. His background is quite different from ours. He wasn't even confirmed with the Catechism."

"You are not as different from Adam as you think. The key to discipleship isn't knowledge but love for God and a willingness to follow. After all, this is not our church. It is Christ's. We are the caretakers, not the Owner."

"My father started this church!"

"Jesus Christ started this church. August, the greatness of the Church is not demonstrated by the strength of the walls we build around ourselves, but by the vastness of the bridges we build to spread the gospel and welcome the stranger. There are too many walls in this world already. Let us build more bridges instead."

During the past week, the weather had grown steadily warmer, so by Thursday it was downright hot for April. Riding past August Schmidt's place, Adam stopped to give him some free advice. He surveyed the orchard for a few minutes, scribbled something on a piece of paper, and said confidently, "You're going to have an infestation of scale insects unless you dust those trees right away. The bark's already been scarred and discolored. Here's the formula for an effective mixture that the university just developed. It's great for apples."

"Apples? These are cherry trees."

"Oh, uh," Adam paused, "then that's how they should look. They're fine."

Back at the Rickmeiers' place, Frieda caught her son again. "Calvin, your hair is wet! You've been swimming in the river, haven't you? We told you to stay out of there! Must we punish you again?"

"No, Mama, you mustn't! I didn't go swimming. I was walking over the bridge and I just fell in."

"Ja, sure! And suppose you tell me why you had a towel along."

"Well, I, uh. A fella never knows when he might fall in."

On Thursday evening, Herman met Carl again. "Say, Carl! I gave my horse some mineral spirits yesterday, the way you said. She began bellowin' like a bull, ran about a hundred feet, and dropped over stiff as a board."

"Yep, the same thing happened to mine. That's why I wouldn't gurricken do that anymore. No, sir."

"But I already did!" Herman shouted.

"And I betcha learned your lesson."

"You told me to!"

"I never did. You didn't ask what happened. Nope. Mineral spirits is bad for horses. Even I know that much."

On Friday, Gustav was at the general store when Frieda walked in. He noticed that she seemed preoccupied and was muttering about something. "Hello, Frieda!" he said. "And how are things? Your children?"

Frieda smiled stiffly. "Oh, Emilie's just fine. She does so well in school."

"And your littlest angel Calvin?"

Frieda's fair disposition turned stormy. "I offered to trade Calvin to Herr Steitz for a sack of potatoes, but he wouldn't take him out of fear for the welfare of his store. I don't know what to do with that 'angel,' as you put it."

She told Gustav all the things Calvin had done that week. He listened, chuckled, shook his head a few times, and said, "Frieda, why don't you and Herman find some time to go fishing and swimming with Calvin tomorrow? Give him more of your attention and you won't have to give him as much of your anger."

Early on Saturday, Herman left for Sheboygan to find a suitable replacement for his unfortunate horse. That afternoon, the Rickmeiers followed Gustav's advice; they took their two children on a family outing. Frieda thought it was wonderful. By Saturday night, Calvin was as happy as a clam and about as energetic. He was fast asleep by eight o'clock, and Frieda thought she heard the rest of Bierville breathe a collective sigh of relief. Peace at last.

Frieda knew that her fifteen-year-old daughter Emilie cherished those quiet times when she had her mother to herself. So there they were, rocking and knitting side-by-side. Emilie often sought parental wisdom from her mother on the great issues of life. "Mother, what kind of husband do you think I should look for?"

Frieda clucked and continued rocking. "Child," she said, "you won't be sixteen for a couple more months. But when the time does come to think about such things, don't go looking for any husband to marry. If he's any good, his wife will object. No, find yourself a nice, eligible bachelor. Just wait a few more years. Ten or so."

All Saturday night, Gustav wrestled with God over what his next action should be on Adam's behalf. Before the service on Sunday morning, he stood outside the church and greeted the arriving worshipers. The Rickmeiers approached; Herman was holding his son firmly by the hand. "Calvin," Gustav asked, "do you have a new Scripture verse for today?"

"Yessir," he said. "Colossians, chapter three, verse one says, 'Fathers, provoke not your children to anger, lest they be discouraged.'"

Gustav whisked Calvin up in his arms, kissed him on the forehead, and beamed at him. "You're learning," he said. Setting him down, he turned to Herman and said quietly, "Don't be surprised if God calls your son into the ministry."

Walking inside, Gustav noticed the elders huddled together at the back of the church. August motioned to him and said, "Herr Vriesen, may we speak with you? You gave us a great plenty to think about on Wednesday evening. I've been thinking about how my parents were welcomed to this area. You remember them."

"Of course. They were wonderful people."

"When they arrived here, they settled on land next to the river, near where the Winnebago tribe was living. The Indians were warm and hospitable to my parents. About a year later, my father was caught in a snowstorm, on the verge of freezing to death. Two Indian men recognized him and took him home. He owed them his life."

"I've never heard that story. That's remarkable!"

"At any rate," August said, "we would be honored to receive Adam Schroeder into the membership of this church. I'll be happy to speak with him."

When Adam entered the back door of the church, August walked over to greet him. "Herr Schroeder," he said, "I have some good news, good news for you and the church. We will be pleased to receive you into the membership of this congregation."

"I'm delighted, Herr Schmidt, Herr Vriesen! Thank you for your consideration!"

"Also," August said, "I have a piece of land I'd like to give you for building your house. It's a better piece than the one you looked at before, and it's closer to my orchard. I'm sure you can show me some ways to improve my apples. And my cherries."

"Give me the land? Oh, my! You're too kind. I can't accept such a generous gift as that."

"All right. What if you give me a dollar?"

"You drive a hard bargain, but I can afford that much." The two shook hands vigorously, and Adam went in and found a place to sit, as did the rest of the elders.

Gustav caught August by the arm and said, "My friend, you are a reflection of a generous God. You transformed this morning's sermon from a challenge into an affirmation."

# Chapter Five ⟅

On a crisp Monday morning in late October, 1901, Otto breathed in the goodness of life. He stood on the boardwalk in front of his store, at the leading edge of a flock of ocherous pumpkins. Smiling broadly, his hands on his hips, his long, white apron flapping in the breeze, he was filled with delight. First one wagon, then another passed by on its way to the mill, wagons filled with corn, wheat, and oats. He enjoyed greeting and waving at the passersby: "G'mornin', Henry. Herman—yes, a lovely day. Good day, Simon."

Otto had witnessed this annual cavalcade many times before, but fresh excitement and satisfaction filled the air, blending with the delicious smell of wood smoke drifting by. From time to time, a gust of wind sent a thousand colored leaves swirling and dancing past the wagon wheels and horse hooves, finally racing around the corner of the blacksmith shop on the other side of the road. No one could remember a better harvest.

"This is glorious! Simply glorious!" Otto said, enraptured by the whole scene. He started to hum and sing:

*Come, ye thankful people, come,*
*Raise the song of harvest home;*
*All is safely gathered in,*
*Ere the winter storms begin....* [i]

After supper on Monday at the Rickmeiers was a scene of serenity. Frieda and Emilie sat together, darning socks at the kitchen table. There was a mischievous giggle from the living room where Herman and Calvin were, and Frieda decided to investigate. Herman had dozed off on the davenport, his after-dinner cigar still smoldering in his hand. Calvin sat nearby. "Calvin," she said, "I'm glad to see you sitting so quietly while your father takes a little nap."

"Thank you, Mama. I want to see what Papa does when his cigar burns down to his fingers."

"Calvin!" she hissed. "So compassionate you are! On the other hand, maybe that would teach him a lesson. Just make sure nothing starts on fire—including your father."

On Tuesday afternoon at the parsonage, Gustav sat hunched over his desk, his head buried in his hands, his body shaking with waves of grief that welled up inside. He had just returned from visiting seven-year-old Greta Kleinschmidt, who was being treated for consumption and had been quarantined for nearly six months. Her parents had sent their other children to live with relatives. The only people allowed in Greta's room were Gustav, her parents, and Doctor Hess, and then only if they wore handkerchiefs tied over their faces. Greta told them they looked like bandits.

Gustav was deeply saddened by Greta's plight, but he was also reliving his grief over the deaths of his own children twenty years earlier. During the course of one month, all three of Minnie's and his children died from diphtheria. He and his wife were heartbroken. No more children, Minnie said. No more. Despite the intervening years, Gustav was surprised at the depth of his grief. However, he felt a surprising degree of relief in releasing some of his pain.

When he was at the Kleinschmidt house, sitting next to Greta, Gustav felt the most compelling urge to grab the demonic illness by the throat, drag it out of her, and destroy it in a blazing fire. Of course he couldn't, but he wanted to.

He felt helpless that all he could do was pray for little Greta. Yes, he was praying for her, but he felt as though he had taken the whole burden of her illness upon himself. Now he was exhausted. He wanted to do something more for Greta, but all he had left was prayer. *Merciful God, help me understand! All I can think to do is pray. That's all I can do. All I can do? That really isn't it at all, is it? Prayer isn't a last resort that you give us. It is the very best your children can do. It is like sifting through the gravel to find the nuggets of gold. The treasure you bless us with is the reassurance of your abiding love.*

He remembered what Jesus told his disciples, that they should pray without becoming discouraged. *How foolish I am.* He laughed at himself, wiping away his tears. *Ah, dear God, at least I am one of your chosen fools.*

On Wednesday morning at the post office, Otto was sorting mail. Henry Schultz stuck his head inside and asked, "Anything for me from Northwoods Industries? A couple of weeks ago, I sent for a kerosene lantern on approval."

"On approval? Well, let's see," Otto said. "There's something from Northwoods Industries, but it's just a letter. I don't think there's a lantern in there."

"Hmm," Henry said, frowning. "It's just a letter." He read it out loud:

*Dear Mr. Schultz,*

> *Perhaps you mistook us for "Northwoods Imbeciles." They would gladly have sent the kerosene lantern to you, but they went bankrupt last year. While your proposal is most intriguing, we must regrettably decline. However, we do have*

*a counter proposal: send us your money first. We are certain to approve of it, and we'll be happy to send you the lantern.*

*Sincerely,*
*Northwoods Industries*

"That's discouraging," Henry said. "Whatever happened to trust?"

"I think," Otto replied, "it disappeared with those Northwoods Imbeciles."

Martha came in with a package. "Good morning, good morning!" she said in a melodious tone.

"Morning, Martha," Otto said. "And what have we here?"

"It's something for Conrad and Charlotte—the Schnuelle family Bible. I want them to have it."

"I see you have it nicely packaged and wrapped. I'll have Fritzie finish up with you. Fritzie?" he called. "Could you help Martha here with this package?"

Fritzie came in from the store, smiling. He took the package and asked, "Anything breakable in here, Mrs. Schnuelle?"

She said, "Oh, yes. There are the Ten Commandments, Levitical law, the prophetic dicta, the Great Commandment. Really, they're all quite fragile, but there's no way to insure against such breakage."

Fritzie's eyes glazed over as if in confusion. Martha patted his hand and said, "Don't worry, dear. The world is a perplexing place. The only time to worry is when you think you're beginning to understand it."

Otto looked at Fritzie and said, "That might not be for quite some time."

At the mill on Thursday morning, Jacob Schmalfus and August Schmidt arrived at about the same time to receive payment for the grain they had each brought in. Jacob hid among the shadows in the far corner of the mill while August swaggered around with the confidence of success. Lester Mohr, the miller, stroked his flowing beard as he scribbled calculations to determine the amount he owed each of them. August had his usual prosperous year; Jacob was embarrassed by his comparatively meager harvest.

Lester handed a stack of money to August and said, "You always amaze me with the fine produce you bring in. I truly value the patronage of such an accomplished farmer as you." August nodded in acknowledgement of Lester's compliment, receiving his payment with a smile of satisfaction. Lester turned and said, "But you, poor Jacob, how do you live? It didn't take me nearly as long to figure out your total. Tell me, would you like me to pay you in coins? Your purse would appear fuller that way."

With his head bowed and his heart breaking, Jacob replied, "Dollars'll be just fine."

Jacob left the mill and watched August heading his rig toward home. One admirer after another greeted him: "Guten Tag, Herr Schmidt. Schönes Wetter, nicht wahr?" "Mornin', August. I bet the mill is bustin' at the seams after that load of yours."

There was no one in that part of Sheboygan County who was held in higher esteem than August. He always did everything right, strictly by the book. An elder of the church for more than twenty years, he was known as a model father and husband, caring patiently for his ailing wife, Lena. His was a reputation of success and righteousness. As if in a one-wagon parade heading out of town, August waved to neighbor and friend.

When Jacob drove away in his rig, no one said anything to him. A few people glanced his way, but turned away again, as if they hadn't seen anything important. There was no one in that part of the county who was held in lower esteem than Jacob. Most German bachelor farmers had the reputation of being prosperous and knowledgeable about agriculture. Jacob was the exception; he scraped along year after year. He was painfully aware of his neighbors' opinions of him. To make matters worse, he tended to agree with their assessments.

Sometimes, when Jacob ran short of money, he hired himself out to other farmers. Last summer, he heard that Carl was looking for some extra help at haying time. Jacob asked him, "What'll ya pay me if I work for you this week?"

"Well," Carl said, "I'll gurricken give ya a fair wage for the work ya put in."

"Shucks, 'twouldn't make sense for me to work for that little bit."

Jacob and August had been in the same confirmation class forty years before. Now they barely acknowledged one another's presence when they met in the village. Jacob had stopped going to church a long time ago. He missed it sometimes but, having been away so long, he thought he'd feel out of place inside the church.

On Friday, the weather turned blustery and cold. All day Friday and most of Saturday, Jacob stared blankly into the flames of his fireplace. An unfinished sandwich and eight empty beer bottles lay on the floor around his chair. *Ah, the howlin' winds of autumn. They have such a way of conjurin' up all sorts of ghosts. Bringin' from their hidin' places deep inside. The howlin' winds of autumn, come to spook me again.*

From time to time, he got up to stir the coals and throw a few pieces of wood on the fire. Mostly, Jacob just sat and thought. *Who needs me? Really, no one. I'm no good at farming, but I don't know what else to do. Don't have no friends to talk to. Even Herr Vriesen prob'ly doesn't know who I am. Why should he? They took my name off the church rolls before he ever came.*

Jacob's thoughts carried him back—back to his childhood, his parents, Sunday school, confirmation class, back to better days when he felt that somebody loved him, a time when his life seemed to have purpose. He remembered a project his confirmation class worked on. Down along the river, where it bends through the church property, the students had cleared a lovely place on the flat along the east side. They named it Vesper Point and built an altar out of fieldstones and pews out of split logs. When Jacob was in his teens and early twenties, it was his favorite place on earth; a place where he felt unconditionally loved and accepted, a sanctuary where he felt close to God.

Saturday, as far as August was concerned, started like a bad dream and got worse. The strong winds out of the northwest blew his chicken coop down, and about sixty birds went on the lam. He began to retrieve the chickens and decided he needed some help. "Julius!" he shouted. "Julius?" There was no answer, so he continued chasing birds by himself. After more than an hour, he was only able to capture fifteen.

The gusting winds were also too much for August's windmill; at about noon, with a clatter, a creak, and a crash, it died a violent death. He could see that the pump shaft, under the pile of twisted metal and splintered wood, had bent and snapped. He'd be pumping water in the kitchen and carrying buckets out to the trough for the animals.

"Julius!" he shouted. "Julius? What a fine pickle! I can't ask Lena to lend me a hand—she's of no use to me these days. Ach, it's going to be a long afternoon!"

Finally, after three hours of hauling water, August made the last trip. He thought there'd be enough for his animals to last through the night, and it was time to begin milking his twenty-eight cows. Where was Julius? He couldn't imagine.

He turned and saw his son walking up the road to the house. "Julius! Where have you—" He stopped short. His son approached, head bowed and hat in hand. August knew something was wrong.

"Pa," Julius said, hesitating. "Pa, Rebecca and I have been

courting for nearly two years, and we—well, she's going to have a baby. We're getting married by her priest next Saturday. Pa, I'm sorry. We never meant to embarrass you, so we're going to move away. I'm so sorry, Pa. Good-bye."

August was in utter agony. He could hear the well-ordered structure of his life crumbling and crashing all around him, as if the collapses of the chicken coop and the windmill were portents for what was happening now. Without saying a word, August set the two buckets of water on the ground and walked away. He headed across the hay field, down the road, away.

Jacob got up to stir the fire once more. "What day is it, anyway?" he muttered. "Ja, ja. Still Saturday." He went to a window and looked out. The sun was setting and the winds were settling down. Still deep in thought, he put on his hat and coat, and wandered out of the door. The fading daylight would make it difficult to see, but he was sure he'd still be able to find Vesper Point. It was the kind of place one never forgets.

Jacob walked past the church and found the path into the woods. By the time he reached the twin pines standing sentinel at the path's entrance, he was immersed in a spirit of reverence. Barely daring to breathe, Jacob paused at edge of the clearing, the threshold of holy ground. The surrounding trees and undergrowth had all changed, but the clearing itself, the stone altar, and the split-log pews were just as he remembered.

All at once, something caught his attention. He became aware of a soft, whimpering sound like that of a dog. It came from within the clearing. Slowly, his eyes adjusted to the dimness and he was able to make out the charcoal-gray shape of a dog at the base of the altar. *Will it attack me?* he wondered. *Wounded dogs are unpredictable, sometimes dangerous.*

The wounded shape lifted its head and cried in agony, "My

God, my God, why?"

"August? August Schmidt? Is that you?" Jacob rushed over to him. "Are you all right? What're you doing here?"

Jacob settled on the ground next to him, and the two men sat under a shroud of silence for what seemed an hour. Occasionally, the quiet was broken by waves of grief from August's anguished soul. In the east, the amber gibbous moon peeked over the horizon and climbed into the sky, gradually removing the shroud and bathing the landscape in soft light.

"August," Jacob said, "'member when we cleared them trees, cut the, uh, pews there, made this altar here? It doesn't seem so long ago. I used to feel close to God here. That's why I wanted to come here tonight, though I ain't been here for many years."

August looked over at him, then down again. "Two grown men, sitting in the dirt, next to a pile of rocks. What a picture we make."

"I feel at home in the dirt. It's where I belong."

"No, Jacob. No. That's how people like me have treated you, but it's wrong. I realized tonight that I've been so wrong. You are the one who is justified before God. I am condemned."

"I don't know what you mean."

"I come here to Vesper Point nearly every week, but not like this. I come here to boast, to thank Christ Jesus for making me successful and honorable. Now I see the success I craved all these years is not the victory Christ promises."

"But you're the most successful fella I know."

"Ah, that's what I thought, too. I prayed many self-righteous prayers, but I never took the time to listen to God's response—until tonight."

"An' you heard the voice of God? Truly?"

"Yes, all too clearly. You asked earlier what I'm doing here. I'm not sure. I guess begging God to be merciful to me, a sinner. I've never done that before."

"A sinner, August?"

"Guilty as charged. My chicken coop collapsed. You don't even have a chicken coop. My windmill collapsed. You don't have one of those, either. I resented my wife for not being able to help me, but you've never even been married. And when my own son needed my forgiveness and grace, I remained silent. You have no family at all, and I'm the one who's complaining. Some model Christian I am!"

"C'mon, August. You ain't exactly Attila the Hun. All of this must seem shameful to you, but I been powerful proud of you all these years. A smidgen resentful, too. But powerful proud."

"You were proud of me?"

"I'd look at you an' say, 'He an' I went to school together an', if I could, that's the kind a man I'd be.'"

"Ah, but Jacob. God condemned my arrogance tonight, my hardness of heart, my pride in my own righteousness. I must confess something. I sometimes used to thank God I was not a bumbling buffoon like you. I'm ashamed of myself, of my thoughts toward you, and ask for your forgiveness."

Jacob was astonished. "August, I, uh, I forgive you, I guess. But I gotta say, I've mostly thought the same thing about myself." They chuckled, shook their heads, and sat again in silence.

Finally, August spoke. "You know, for the first time in a long while, I also feel close to God."

The moon was now higher in the sky, shining with a brighter, silvery light. Both men grunted and groaned from their stiffness but managed to make it to their feet. They headed back up the path past the church. Before they parted company, Jacob asked, "August, will there be a place for me at the church tomorrow?"

"Yes, my friend, God will provide room for us both, and I would be pleased if we could sit together. Schlaf im himmlischer Ruhe, Jacob!"

# Chapter Six ∿

*May, May, abundant and glorious,*
*the spring is victorious*
*o'er winter's cold hand.*
*May, May, so verdant and tender,*
*arise in your splendor*
*to bless the good land!*

The first thing Herman Rickmeier did after milking on that Monday in May, 1902 was ride into town and visit the newspaper editor, Daniel O'Brien. He walked into Daniel's office holding a copy of the Sunday paper and said in his best Irish accent, "Top o' the marnin' to ya, Mister O'Brien."

"Herman! What brings you into town so early?"

"Important business, Daniel. I want you to read this column in yesterday's paper here and then study me carefully. Compare the two. Take your time," he said, turning the newspaper to the back of the first section and holding it up next to his own head.

Daniel read the column, looked his friend, referred back to the paper, and again at Herman. "Hmmm, I think I see the problem. You're not dead." They both burst into laughter. "What in the world!" Daniel chortled. "Somehow, that obituary you filed with me 'just in case' must have been pulled out by mistake. From the looks of you, it's rather premature, I'd say."

"To be sure. I was feeling fine yesterday until I realized I was no longer counted among the living."

"Well, I'll be happy to put a correction in the paper, but are you sure you want me to? After all, there are some advantages to having people think you're dead."

"How so?"

"Well, for starters, you're done paying bills. And you find out who your real friends are. If you see people becoming all happy and throwing big parties for the occasion, you'd better keep an eye on 'em."

"Yes," Herman said, "but be that as it may, a correction would still be a good idea. With me off dead, Frieda might get the idea she can go out and find another husband."

"All right, Herman. You're alive again. Talk about the power of the press!"

"Not exactly miraculous, but thanks nonetheless, Daniel. I appreciate it!"


On Tuesday afternoon, Gustav was in his study reading the newspaper. Up the page from the notice about Herman Rickmeier still among the living was another one—about the death of eight-year-old Greta Kleinschmidt. The news of Greta's death continued to spread throughout the area. Gustav looked up from the paper and noticed it was turning stormy outside; the wind was picking up out of the west and the sky was growing dark. *Ah, this is a fitting reminder that even the heavens are grieving for little Greta.*

In the following three hours, they got five inches of rain, more than the fields or streams could hold. By evening, the sky began to clear. Gustav marveled at a magnificent double rainbow projected against the retreating thunderclouds to the east. Children played with wooden boats, wading in the newly-formed lakes. He went outside to admire the sunset; it was breathtaking, life-giving, as if God were saying, "Peace, my children! Greta now rests in my care."

On Wednesday morning, Clara opened her new seamstress shop in the vacant building next to Reiny Hartung's blacksmith shop. Reiny owned the building and was glad to have somebody renting it again. During the building's thirty-year history, it had served as Reiny's home, the village library, and a barbershop run by Reiny's brother Nicholas. Two years ago, Nicholas vacated the building. He had become disgusted with the low number of shaves and haircuts he was doing and moved his barbering business back into Sheboygan.

Just before he moved out, Nicholas went around Bierville complaining, "There are too many shaggy boys and bald ape-men in this village. Why, a barbershop has as much of a chance here as a bridal shop in a convent! A vegetable market in a cannibal village! A...a clothing store in a nudist colony!"

Afterward, Otto joked with Clara about it. He said, "Who wants a shave and a haircut from a man named Nick?"

Nicholas' loss was Clara's gain. Since the barbershop had closed, Clara had her eye on the building. Opening her own business was like beginning a new life. While gratefully accepting her mother's hospitality for the last two years, Clara had been able to find enough sewing and mending work to contribute to the household finances. Her reputation as a seamstress grew and space in Martha's little house shrank. The two of them decided the time was right for Clara to move her operation. The shop would be in the one end of the building; Clara and Liesl would eventually live in the other end.

Clara saved enough money to buy a used Singer sewing machine for the new shop. Altogether, however, the move and setup only took Clara and Martha a few hours to complete. After the curtains were hung, Clara looked around with satisfaction. "Mother, I can't possibly thank you enough. This is wonderful!"

"You made all of the arrangements and earned all the money. I just helped as I could. I'm proud of you."

"Thank you, Mother." Clara burst into tears and hugged Martha. "That's the first time you ever said you were proud of me."

"Oh, Clara. I am. I'm sorry I never told you. It was hard for me to raise two children by myself, and I had an easier time of it with your brother than with you. And, it's true, there were times when I didn't feel proud of you. But I still loved you."

"I know, Mother, and I understand. But it's important to me to hear you say it now—that you love me and are proud of me, instead of wondering if it's true."

"Well, I do love you, and I think you're doing wonderfully well."

"And to think, before Christmas of '99, I had no money and nowhere to live. It's as if I'm starting a new life, and this is the second time you've given me birth."

"It is God who gives us birth, dear. I only try to cooperate as best I can."

On Wednesday evening at seven o'clock, the Rickmeiers welcomed a dinner guest: Adam Schroeder. He was pretty sure that Frieda had a plan for her daughter and him. The mother of the pretty, young woman was playing matchmaker with the eligible bachelor, hoping to get them to fall in love—just not too quickly. He was all for the plan and suspected that Emilie was, too, but that she'd be embarrassed to death to admit it.

Adam arrived on horseback and noticed Calvin on the front porch, a sling on his arm, waiting for him, the guest of honor. The "guest of horror" would be more accurate. Adam was sure that Calvin would be unhampered by a mere sling and wouldn't make things easy for his big sister or her suitor. Before Adam had a chance to dismount, Calvin sprang from his lookout post and initiated his barrage, an all-out *Blitzkrieg.*

"Hey ya, Adam! Are you gonna marry my sister? Ya know what we're having for supper tonight? Roast duck! Last Sunday, after Mama invited you over, she decided right then it was going to be duck for supper. Palaverin' platypuses, it was funny! Ya know that thunderstorm yesterday?"

"I remember," Adam said warily.

"Papa was racing lickety-split up the road in the wagon, trying to get out of the rain. Well, that duck just stood there, and the horses never even saw him and ran him right over. Nothin' was hurt, really, 'cept the head. I guess it was just the duck's way of volunteerin', thereby savin' Mama from making the choice. C'mon, Adam! Let's eat!"

Adam's appetite wasn't much that evening. Had it been the story of the duck's demise? Or love?

On Thursday at the general store, Otto put up a sign announcing that both the store and the post office would be closed during the memorial service for Greta on Friday. He thought that it really wouldn't make much difference; the whole neighborhood would be there, anyway.

Emilie entered the store with a basket tucked under her arm and a shopping list in hand. She knelt down to greet Bruno the Saint Bernard who was at his usual post next to the door.

"Guten Tag, Fraülein!" Otto said, walking over to her. "Say, I hear your brother Calvin fell out of an upstairs window and broke his arm. How'd it happen?"

"You know my brother. He and our cousin Helmut were having a contest. They were trying to see which one could lean out of our tower window the farthest. Calvin won."

Otto laughed. "He's got a few things to learn about winning, I'd say. It's rather a hollow victory if you receive your trophy as you're laid out in a pine box. That little monkey is lucky he wasn't killed."

"Ja, sicherlich! But Calvin seems to think death is something you get over in a few days. He still believes Greta's going to get better."

"Ja, ja. In a way, she is completely healed now, but not in the way we usually think of it."

At the mill, Lester Mohr sauntered over to greet Siegfried Burgener when he arrived for work. Siegfried was a sixteen-year-old hired hand and had been working for Lester for the past few months. "Siegfried, let me ask you," Lester said, his left hand tucked behind his back, his right fiddling with his beard. "Do you believe it is possible to talk to spirits in the great beyond?"

"I, I don't know, Herr Mohr. I suppose it could be possible."

With building excitement, Lester said, "I was skeptical myself until yesterday, but then it happened to me! While you were away at your grandfather's funeral, I saw his apparition here, and he was looking for you. It was so real, the same as I'm talking to you—another dead man! Do that again and you're fired."

On Friday afternoon, warm sunshine poured down upon the mourners gathered at the graveside of Greta Kleinschmidt. There wasn't yet a grave marker for her. Even though Greta had been sick with consumption for nearly a year, she made it through the winter and it had seemed to everyone she was simply too young to die. Bierville had known this sadness many times before.

As part of the committal ceremony, the mourners each threw a handful of soil onto the coffin resting at the bottom of the grave. The handfuls of soil signified three things: that we are but dust and ashes; that the courageous battle was finished, and now—for now—we will say good-bye; that it is only the breath of God, the spirit of life within us, that makes us very different from the elements of the good earth. Everyone cried: Greta's parents and her six surviving brothers and sisters, long-time neighbors and young friends, including Greta's classmate Calvin.

Gustav Vriesen dried his tears, cleared his throat, and said, "Dearly beloved, I assure you God knows exactly how you feel, for God also lost a beloved child. Greta was one of God's children as well. Hear, now, these words of assurance from the Lord Jesus in John 16:22, 'And ye therefore now have sorrow: but I will see you again, and your heart shall rejoice, and your joy no one taketh away from you.'"

When the committal service ended, the entire gathering lingered for a time and took in their surroundings. In spite of the sadness of the day, there was also a sustaining sense of holiness and life that filled the air. The fields and forests nearby were alive with orioles and grosbeaks, meadowlarks and bobolinks, hummingbirds and bluebirds, and dozens of other species trying to raise a new generation of young and keep from going the way of the passenger pigeon.

A warm breeze out of the southwest invited the community to stay awhile longer. It was such a lovely day. All of the people started walking slowly, reverently, through the cemetery in pairs and trios and family groups. They pondered the inscriptions on the headstones of relatives, friends, and neighbors, remembering their loved ones with a mixture of sadness, joy, and affection, especially those whose graves weren't yet covered over with grass. There were eleven more in the last year: from little Elsa Krueger, who lived for only five precious days, to old Walter Heckendorf, who lived ninety-three wonderful, if sometimes difficult, years.

Gustav walked along, his memory spinning back to a day he went to see Greta last fall. During much of their visit, Greta stared out of the window of her room. Finally, after a long silence, she said:

"Everything's dying. I hate it in the autumn when all the beautiful leaves fall from the trees, and they die."

"I know the feeling, Greta. All of the exuberance of spring and the abundance of summer wither and fade, and everything appears to be dying. However, the trees will grow leaves again, and there will be flowers in the spring, just like every year. You'll see!"

"But what if they don't? What if the leaves never come back?"

"Liebchen, God has made the seasons of the year so the earth may be renewed. It is one of the rhythms of life of which we are all a part. Springtime will come again—for the earth, for you, and for me."

Gustav's thoughts came back to the cemetery, and he gazed down at a patch of lilies-of-the-valley planted at the edge of the cemetery. Through her young eyes, Greta had seen everything with a wisdom and appreciation far beyond her years, and she had lived long enough to see the flowers of spring once again. He knelt down, picked one of the stems of flowers, sniffed it, and was impressed once again that flowers so small and delicate could have such a delightful fragrance. "They're like little Greta," he thought.

Gustav walked over to Martha Schnuelle, who was reading the stone at her husband's grave:

WILHELM SCHNUELLE

1845–1882

*Ruhe sanft*

Martha wiped her eyes and said, "Forgive my tears, Herr Vriesen, but even after these twenty years, my heart still aches. Sometimes I weep for him, and sometimes I weep for myself, for our dreams that never came to be."

"Martha, if it never hurt, I would wonder. Your tears testify to your love and that you are still alive and well. The Lord Jesus wept for his loved ones, as we do for ours. We're in good company."

"Yes, I know you're right. Often, when I'm in the middle of grief, I feel so alone. Yet later, when I look back on those times, I realize the arms of God were holding me all the while."

"Martha, remember Paul's words of faith that have sustained a great many people over these nineteen-hundred years? 'For I am persuaded, that neither death, nor life... nor any other creature, shall be able to separate us from the love of God, which is in Christ Jesus our Lord.' Hold onto that faith."

On that Friday in May, through the touch of the breeze, Gustav was aware of the healing hand of God at work again. He watched his people—God's people—leave the cemetery. On foot, on horseback, and in wagons and carts, they returned to their homes. *Dear God, bless them. I know our sadness will linger for a time, and it will also heal. Thank you for a renewed sense of gratitude for the gifts of life and hope and love. Thank you for this reminder of who we are and whose we are.*

# Chapter Seven 〜

Otto stood in the doorway, broom in hand, watching the leaves tumbling to the ground. He reflected on what he saw. *Autumn of 1902 will probably be remembered as arriving a little late. Nevertheless, the annual drama of life's struggle to survive is playing itself out. The pumpkin vines, mortally wounded by a heavy frost, have finally withered. The air is crisp and clean again. The leaves still on the trees have redoubled their efforts to clothe themselves in their brightest costumes, only to perform their farewell, bow to the changing season, and exit the stage of life for another year.*

He looked down at Bruno, the Saint Bernard, who was taking his customary morning snooze on the boardwalk. "Another glorious, mid-October day, eh, my friend? Can't ask for a better start to the week. Of course, where your weeks begin and end, I have no idea."

Otto turned his attention back to the leaves. "See, Bruno? It's as if they're alive. Some are like delicate spots of color floating ever so gently down and down, then swirling up with a passing breeze, and again down, settling together in a company of friends. Others race recklessly toward the ground, with the one landing first proclaimed the winner of that heat." Bruno's eyes remained closed.

Otto marveled at what he saw, smiling with delight. Flight

after flight of geese passed overhead, honking their way toward the marshes in the west. A flock of warblers flitted about in the nearby leaf-littered grass, searching for bugs to fuel their migration south. He remembered with gratitude the wisdom of Ecclesiastes: "To every thing there is a season, and a time to every purpose under the heaven." *Ah, the rhythms of life.*

An interruption to Otto's serenity came in the form of Reiny Hartung, storming across the road from his blacksmith shop, wiping soot and sweat from his forehead, kicking at any leaves that dared get in his way.

"Reiny, Reiny," Otto said, "what could possibly be the matter on such a lovely day as this?"

"Morgen, Otto. I tell you, the young people these days are good-for-nothing loafers! All the boys who have ever worked for me—they don't know what they're doing. They make foolish mistakes. So I yell at them, and they give up and quit."

"Hmm. That's strange, Reiny. I find just the opposite to be true. The young people working in my store over the years have all been very bright and willing to learn. Oh, sure, they make mistakes. They may do some unfortunate things. But no one feels worse about it than they do. If you plant thorny seeds and tell them they're stupid, they'll be thorny and stupid. However, if you plant seeds of encouragement, they'll grow stronger and straighter, and will blossom to be their best."

"Ach! Well, thank you, Mr. Happy Talk! You don't understand. You always get the good ones, while I get the good-for-nothings."

Turning to go inside, Otto said, "You know, it might not have as much to do with the young people as with you."

Otto found Fritzie stacking canned goods. Otto walked over, patted Fritzie on the back, and said, "You're a fine young man, an exemplary employee, and a good friend. I appreciate your good work!"

Fritzie looked up, smiled shyly, and said, "Thank you, Herr Steitz!" As if on cue, the tower of cans Fritzie was stacking came cascading down; with clattering commotion the cans scattered across the floor.

"Eh, Fritzie," Otto said with a smile, "let me help you with those."

On Tuesday, the weather turned cold again. Over at the Dinkmeier house, however, things were just heating up. Emil and Edna were having another one of their donnybrooks; this had become an almost-daily event during their thirty-seven years of marriage.

"You big buffoon!" Edna said. "You told me you were a wealthy man before we were married! I've never seen anything of it!"

"It's true! I had a wealth of happiness until I said 'I do.' But, as soon as I did, I didn't! Why, I was a fool to get married. Ever since our honeymoon, you've been treating me like a lazy hound."

"Well, you act like one! All you do is howl and growl and lie around all day, scratching and snorting!"

Their life together could best be described as two maniacs in a death grip, each afraid of letting go and allowing the other to declare victory. Their favorite category of contention was The Past, anything related to ancient or recent history.

One of the neighbors heard Emil and Edna going at it all morning and grew increasingly concerned as the battle raged on into the afternoon. She asked Gustav Vriesen if he might venture over to their house to try to help them make peace with each other. Reluctantly Gustav accepted the mission, but less than five minutes after he arrived both Dinkmeiers turned on him and had him wondering which way was up, reaching for the doorknob to let himself out.

Gustav rode home pondering the Dinkmeiers. *They've planted so many seeds of discord over the years, how can they hope to harvest anything else? Last Sunday's sermon title was, "As Ye Sow, So Shall Ye Reap," but why should I expect they were listening? Those whom God has joined together, let no one separate. Lord, have mercy!*

At school on Wednesday afternoon, Miss Benson, the teacher, noticed that Calvin Rickmeier, normally quite a handful to manage, was amazingly well behaved all day. She thought she would take the opportunity to encourage him: "Calvin, you've been a good student today. Thank you."

"Yes, ma'am," said Calvin. "I think maybe I'm getting sick."

After school, Calvin had a quick recovery and ran over to Simon and Anna Klemme's farm so he could visit with their children. Catherine and Caroline were well into their Inquisitive Twos. These girls were far from terrible; they loved to learn about everything.

Calvin pulled some coins out of his pocket. "This," he said, "is a dime. You can buy a bag of chocolates with one of these." The twins' eyes opened wide. "And this is a three-cent piece. You can buy five pieces of maple candy with it." The girls smiled appreciatively. "This one," he frowned, holding up a penny, "ya have to save up with a bunch of other ones before it's good for much, 'cept for the offering at church. They'll take anything."

After chores that evening Simon Klemme came into the house and the girls ran to greet him. Anna was resting in the bedroom, and Catherine and Caroline cuddled on their daddy's lap. He thought it might be a good time to prepare them for the arrival of another child in their family in a few months. He said, "You know, little ones, the stork has been flying over our house lately. I think he's planning to make a delivery soon."

Their eyes widened and Catherine said, "I hope he doesn't frighten Mama."

"Yes!" Caroline said. "She's going to have a baby, you know."

On Friday, Martha Schnuelle accompanied Clara and Liesl to the general store. Clara planned to look for yard goods and Martha was charged with looking after her granddaughter. After about fifteen minutes of browsing Martha bought Liesl a lollipop as a reward for her good behavior. Soon, however, Martha realized it had been a mistake. She turned to say something to Clara, and Liesl learned that her lollipop, when prepared properly, could stick perfectly well to an upright bolt of red gingham.

"Oh, Liesl!" Martha said. "This is not good!"

Clara saw the accomplishment and said, "Thank you, Liesl, for being so helpful. Now I know which piece of cloth to buy."

Innocently Liesl popped the sucker back in her mouth and Clara carried the bolt of gingham to Otto at the counter.

Clara said to Otto, "This material reminds me of a table cloth I used to have in Springfield."

"Yes," he replied, "that's very popular for table cloths. You had one like this when you were married to Edward?"

"Yes," she said, looking down at the cloth. "I try so hard to forget, and then something happens that releases another flood of memories."

"Oh," he said, "I'm sorry. I know what you mean."

"It's all right," she said. "I'm getting used to it. Anyway, it was my mistake. I never should've married him. I'm lucky to be alive. Still, I try to forget what I can and move on."

"Clara," Martha said, approaching the counter, "let me give you some money toward that material. I feel partly responsible."

"That's all right, Mother. It'll wash up just fine. I'll be able to use it."

"You're sure?"

"Mother, don't worry."

"Very well. Why don't you take Liesl home with you? I want to buy something for supper tonight."

After cutting and folding the cloth, Otto said, "There's no charge."

"No charge?" Clara said. "Why, of course there is. How much?"

"Those are damaged goods," he said, smiling. "It wouldn't be right to charge you."

"My Liesl did the damage," Clara said.

"But she got the lollipop from me," he replied. "Please, take the cloth with my best wishes."

"Thank you very much," Clara said, leaving with her red gingham in hand and her sticky girl in tow.

"Thank you, Otto," Martha said. "Now how about two pounds of headcheese?"

Otto cut and weighed her order and asked, "Martha, did you hear about Gerhardt Schultz? I know he was a classmate of your son Conrad."

"No," she said with a sigh, "now what?"

"He's in trouble again, this time with the police and that gang of hoodlums from Milwaukee with whom he's been keeping company. After the gang's latest robbery the other night, these so-called friends of his turned on him and beat him up pretty badly."

Martha closed her eyes and shuddered, remembering her own days and nights of anxiety when Clara was running loose.

He continued: "He was placed in his parents' custody. Hilda and Henry are caring for him at home but they don't know if he's going to make it. If he recovers, he'll be going to jail again. I'm sorry to bring you such upsetting news.".

Martha wasn't surprised, however. She began thinking. Throughout most of Gerhardt's life he went from one kind of trouble to another. At first, when he had run-ins with other children, Henry and Hilda always took their son's side. They said, "No, it couldn't have been our Gerhardt's fault. He's such a good boy." Time after time, the other children were blamed for causing the trouble.

The church reluctantly confirmed him, primarily as an act of grace for his parents, but also in the hope it would help him someday.

Gerhardt grew through his teens, into his early twenties, and his troubles worsened. Henry and Hilda Schultz realized they couldn't protect their son anymore. Burglary, vandalism, assault and battery, armed robbery—the charges against him grew more serious and his friends grew meaner. He was in and out of jail with greater frequency. This time, even his so-called friends turned on him.

"Thank you for the news, Otto," she said. "I wish I knew of something we could do, but it seems the seeds for this sadness were sown long ago."

By early afternoon on Saturday, it was sunny and warm again. However, the weather didn't reflect the heaviness of heart that Gustav felt when he heard about Gerhardt Schultz's latest brush with death. He shook his head and walked over to the Schultz farm to see him.

Gustav approached the river and noticed Calvin sitting cross-legged at the side of the bridge with his fishing pole pointing out over the river, resting on the lower rail.

"Had any luck?" Gustav asked.

"No, sir," Calvin replied. "I only started 'bout an hour ago. But I think they'll start biting any time now."

"What are you using for bait? Worms?"

"No, I prefer the dough ball."

"Dough ball? What's in it?"

"Bread—just the soft part, no crust—vanilla extract, and a dab of salt an' pepper."

"And the fish like it?"

"Oh, they love it! I know I do."

"Well, good luck there, little friend!"

When Gustav arrived at the Schultz farm, Henry and Hilda greeted him at the door, but they seemed embarrassed. "Herr Vriesen," Henry said, "you needn't trouble yourself by visiting Gerhardt. You've done so much for him over the years, and how has he repaid your kindness? With drunken carousing, thievery, and fighting. This is our own sorrow to bear. Ours alone."

Gustav took their hands. "Remember, 'And whether one member suffer, all the members suffer with it: and one member be honoured, all the members rejoice with it.'" He went in to see the patient.

The heavy curtains in Gerhardt's bedroom were closed, providing a tomb-like atmosphere. Gerhardt's right arm was in a sling and his chest was wrapped. Most of his head was bandaged in clean, white gauze. There was a slit in the bandaging at his mouth. Only the areas around his eyes were visible, and they were black and blue.

Gustav surmised the patient would be unable to talk, so he opened the one-sided conversation: "Hello, Gerhardt. It's good to see you again, although not necessarily in your present condition."

Gustav noticed Gerhardt was staring blankly at the ceiling and wondered if anything would get through.

"Gerhardt, let me be frank with you. I understand there's a chance you might not survive these latest injuries. Is your misfortune something to blame upon God? Do you think it's the will of the Almighty for you to be lying here suffering? By no means. Think of your parents, of Henry and Hilda. There is your answer. Your parents are heartbroken over you. They are suffering with you."

Gustav looked at Gerhardt's eyes; they were still directed toward the ceiling, but showed he was paying attention. He continued: "So it is with God. Your misfortune, your misdeeds, your willful sinfulness over the years are simply the harvest you are reaping from the foul seeds that you yourself planted. You need to know that. If you die from all of these injuries there will be no one to blame but yourself."

He paused for a moment, walked over to the window, and threw open the curtains. A flood of autumn sunshine and color bathed the room, causing the pall of death to vanish.

"Having said that, I also want you to know there is still hope for you. Remember, years ago, when your father planted those ten acres to the west of the house with what he thought was good alfalfa seed, but it turned out to be contaminated with thistle seed?"

Gerhardt grunted and nodded his head.

Gustav was encouraged by the response. He said, "If your father had allowed all of those little thistle plants to mature and go to seed, it might not have been many years before the whole farm was taken over. Instead, what did he do? When he saw all of that thistle coming up, he decided to plow it under and start again. Before he lost the farm, he decided to start over. And did you see that field this year? He grew some of the best oats in the county."

Still staring upward, Gerhardt muttered, "It was the only thing he could do."

"Yes," Gustav said. "What you need to do is plow under the past, plant some new seed, and start again. God will give you the strength to persevere."

Gustav noticed Gerhardt's eyes flooding with tears, and he nodded. *Perhaps Gerhardt is seeing things clearly for the first time in his adult life.*

Gustav headed for home again and came across Calvin still sitting on the bridge where he'd been an hour earlier. "Hello, little friend! How many have you caught now?"

"Well, sir," he replied, "if I can catch the one that's been nibbling on my hook, that'll make one."

Gustav chuckled and said, "That is a slow afternoon! I could use one of those. God bless you!"

On Saturday night, Frieda Rickmeier tucked Calvin into bed. "Calvin," she said, "you're as wonderful a child as God ever made. We're very proud of you!"

Quite unexpectedly, the normally irrepressible Calvin began sobbing and buried his face in his pillow. "Oh, Mama, I try to be good, only sometimes I'm not. I don't mean to make Papa and you angry. I don't want to be like Gerhardt."

Frieda lay down next to him, cradling and comforting her son in her arms. She said, "Calvin, my Calvin. Your father and I love you just as you are. You are a joy and delight to us. You're growing in such wonderful ways. You just keep being the best Calvin Rickmeier you can and trust in God to help you grow."

Gradually, Calvin's sobbing eased. He seemed to relax. "G'night, Mama."

Frieda kissed him on the forehead. "Schlaf gut, my little one."

# Chapter Eight ∽

Early on the day after Easter in the year of our Lord 1903, Otto unlocked the front door of the general store, stepped outside for a breath of fresh air, and choked on a snowflake. He turned right around and hurried back inside. *Huh. The calendar says April, but the wind says March, the snow says February, and the mud says November. With April showers like these, we won't see any May flowers until July.* He glanced outside again and shivered. Bending over to scratch Bruno's head, he said, "Well, my furry friend, there aren't any signs of Easter out there today." He shuffled over to the woodstove to fire it up for the day.

By mid-morning, Otto had decided that things looked a little better. The general store was buzzing with activity: folks checking their mail, picking up supplies for the week, stopping for a few games of checkers, and disseminating the neighborhood news. Good stories, factual or otherwise, kept things lively.

Otto noticed Calvin Rickmeier coming through the door. "Good morning, Master Calvin! And how goes your Easter vacation? Enjoying yourself?"

"Yessir, thank you," Calvin replied. "But I'd be enjoying it more if my parents didn't give me all sorts of chores 'n errands to do."

"Well, I'm afraid that's what parents think vacations are for."

"Herr Steitz, could you please give me a quart of your cod-liver oil?"

"Let's see. I have two kinds now. This is the regular one, and this is the new variety. It has a milder, more pleasant taste. Which would you like?"

"Oh, the regular's fine. Makes me no never mind if it's more pleasant. It's for Papa."

"But don't you think he'd prefer the other?"

"No, he likes the regular. It's what he always gives me and he says, 'Stop your fussing! It tastes good!'"

"Well, all right," Otto said, smiling. "Let's go with the regular. What's good for the goose will get even with the gander."

On Tuesday morning, things were bustling again at the general store. Clara Schnuelle was buying yard goods. Three games of checkers were the main attraction. Gerhardt Schultz walked in. The whole place went silent. Reiny Hartung looked up from his checkers and said, "Look who's out of jail! Hold onto your wallets!" The checkers players snickered. Gerhardt turned around and left.

Otto walked out from behind the counter wiping his hands on his apron. "Reinhardt Hartung," he said, "you are a bubble-headed baboon, I must say! Even if you are my cousin! Where are your manners?"

"Otto, he's nothing but a jailbird."

"He's out of jail now, and I believe this time he'll stay out."

"Once a thief, always a thief. That's what I always say."

"Reiny, sometimes you say too much. Have you talked with him since he got out of jail? He's not the irresponsible, self-centered lad who committed those burglaries. I think, since Henry died, he's come to his senses, and he feels an obligation to care for his mother, especially after all he's put her through."

"As well he should! After all, his shenanigans worried his father sick! Henry died of a broken heart to see his son carry on that way."

"Reiny, Gerhardt realizes all that now—that he betrayed his parents and that his own wickedness probably contributed to his father's death. He told me he prays every day, 'God, be merciful to me, a sinner!'"

"Well, it's too late now!"

"Too late to bring his father back to life, certainly. But it's not too late to make something good out of his life."

On Wednesday morning, Emil Dinkmeier brought his wagon down to the mill for some sacks of feed. He and Lester Mohr finished loading the sacks into the wagon and Lester said, "Say, it's slow at the mill right now. Why don't we go on over to Otto's place for some coffee and checkers?"

"Thank you, Lester, but I've already been gone too long. I've got to go home and do some explaining to Edna."

"Why? Are you in trouble?"

"Well, I'm sure I am. But I won't know why till I get home."

Emil returned to the farm and started unloading the sacks of feed. Edna poked her head out of the kitchen door. "So, you're finally home. While you were out lollygagging about all morning, I decided to pamper myself, too. So I walked over to Ida's place for a haircut and beauty treatment. The shop was busy. She made me wait for over an hour."

"Too bad," he said, without looking up. "I see she still didn't have time for you." Emil continued unloading the feed, and Edna slammed the door behind her.

They ate a little lunch together, but barely acknowledged each other's presence through most of the meal. Edna broke the silence. "Emil, we don't talk the way we used to. I don't think you love me as much as when we were first married. Do you?"

"I don't know how I could make it any more obvious, Edna!

Now, stop your yappin' and let me eat in peace!"

"Emil, you're not at all nice!"

"And I suppose you are?"

On and on went the torture.

On Thursday afternoon, the Altar Guild gathered at the church for their monthly meeting; their three members were Gertrude Mueller, Hilda Schultz, and Edna Dinkmeier. The purpose of the Guild was to take care of the sanctuary and make sure things were ready for worship the next Sunday by putting out fresh candles when they needed changing, organizing the hymnals in the back of the church, putting the new hymn numbers on the hymn boards in the front, sweeping, and generally tidying things up. There was, of course, time for coffee and conversation.

They each got a cup of coffee and sat down. Edna took it upon herself to get the conversation going: "So, Hilda, I understand your good-for-nothing son is working at the general store."

Hilda swallowed hard and said, "Yes, Herr Steitz was gracious enough to give Gerhardt a job there. He's shown a lot of trust in my son."

"Well," Edna continued, "I say Otto had better lock up all his valuables and watch that jailbird like a hawk!"

At that, Hilda burst into tears and hurried out of the church.

"How do you like that?" Edna said. "The way she insulted me by running out that way! I wasn't finished with what I was saying! The very idea!"

"Edna," Gertrude said, rising to leave, "have you given any thought to the reason why the Altar Guild has dwindled over the years to a membership of three? Keep that up and it'll be down to one!"

On Friday afternoon, Reiny Hartung walked across the road from his blacksmith shop to the general store. When he opened the door he was startled to see not Otto or Fritzie as he expected but Gerhardt Schultz standing behind the counter. Reiny crossed the room and grabbed him by the shirt collar. "You jailbird!" he said. "Where's Otto? Where's Fritzie? What have you done to them?"

Gerhardt stood motionless. Otto and Fritzie walked out from behind the mailboxes.

"Reiny! Leave him alone! He hasn't done anything to us. He's helping out. Gerhardt needed honest work. I needed an honest worker. It's a perfect match."

"Honest? This jailbird?" Reiny said, releasing his captive.

Otto took Reiny firmly by the arm and said, "Mind the store, will you two? Reiny and I have some talking to do in the back room." He ushered Reiny out.

When they reached the back room, Otto closed the door and said, "You weren't at Gottesdienst on Easter, were you? You missed again the Easter story, what Herr Vriesen said about the new way of life that Easter presents to us, of healing and reconciliation and new beginnings?"

Reiny was quiet for a moment, then said, "Actually, Otto, I really don't believe in Easter, only in the crucifixion, that Jesus died for my sins."

Otto was flabbergasted. "More than 'for' your sins. Because of your sins—and mine—because of how we fallible creatures continue to reject the love of God, betraying and crucifying one another. After all these years, the children of earth still don't seem to understand. We are often called to share the suffering of others, but never to cause it."

"My faith has served me well all these years. It's a private matter between God and me. Whether I choose to believe in the resurrection is my business."

"Reiny, my poor Doubting Thomas! Your lack of understanding shows in the way you treat people—always looking for the worst in them and chaining them to the sins of the past. If that's how you treat others, how can you expect God to forgive you?"

Reiny appeared to be thinking.

Otto continued: "Do you remember the Scripture from Easter? Oh, that's right. You weren't there. The apostle Paul said, 'If Christ hath not been raised, then is our preaching vain, your faith also is vain... If Christ hath not been raised, your faith is vain; ye are yet in your sins.'

"Why haven't I heard this before?"

"Well, if yours is only a Good Friday faith, what do you expect? The gospel doesn't stop at the cross. Actually, if that were the end, it would have died there. But it continues through Easter and beyond. Unless people commit themselves to the ways of Easter, the crucifixion goes on and on. It's the resurrection that begins the healing and opens the way to new life. Without Easter there would be no Church."

"Otto, you make it sound like it's only me."

"Well, of course not, Reiny. We are all tempted toward these destructive ways, the ways of crucifixion. You know how Emil and Edna are always going at it, how Edna is always finding a way to be offended by something."

"It is unpleasant to be around them when they're going at it hammer and tongs. Where will it end?"

"Exactly. This hardheartedness has got to stop, beginning with you and me. That's the only way we will ever see Easter in this village. And then, maybe someday, even Emil and Edna will realize Easter has come."

On Saturday afternoon, Gustav Vriesen was sitting in the church study, working on the sermon for the next day. There was a knock at the door. When he opened it he found Gerhardt Schultz with his hat in his hand. "Gerhardt! Wie geht's Ihnen? Come in!"

"Thank you," he said. Still with his head down, he walked in and sat in a chair next to the desk.

Gustav sat at the desk and said, "Well, Gerhardt, what brings you here? Is there a problem?"

"Yes, Herr Vriesen. I am my own problem. I don't know if I can live with myself. I did terrible things. For the excitement of it, I guess. I was only thinking of myself. But now I am truly sorry!"

"True penitence is an important beginning to a new life. I've seen such a change in you over the past year!"

"I had no idea what I was doing, how much shame and suffering I brought upon my parents. And I can't help but think I caused my father so much sadness that he died of a broken heart. Now I am heartbroken. I want to take my own life."

"Gerhardt, I understand some of your sadness, your feelings of guilt. Of course, what you did was wrong. That's what caused your parents so much suffering. The Gerhardt they saw wasn't the one they loved. But if you took your own life, it wouldn't solve a thing, would it?"

"No, I suppose not."

"Your father would still be dead, leaving your mother alone to also grieve for you. The ways of darkness would have won again."

"But, Herr Vriesen, I don't know if I can stand the pain of living with this guilt. It's awful."

"Gerhardt, I see strong evidence of the healing hand of God already at work in you. The thing to do is make the best of your life from now on. That's what God would have you do. That's what your father would want."

"My father? I should think, by the time he died, he hated me."

"No, Gerhardt, he loved you dearly. Just before he died, he said some things I wanted to tell you at the proper time. This is the time. Although he was deeply sad because of the things you did and your imprisonment, he didn't blame you for his death."

"He didn't?"

"No. We talked about this very thing. He said, 'I forgive him. He doesn't know what he's doing, and someday he'll come to his senses.' Your father had great confidence in you, trusting you would return to yourself and be the kind of person they hoped you would be. He also talked about Easter and the power of the resurrection of Christ. He believed the truth would come to you someday."

Gerhardt leaned forward in his chair, burying his face in his hands, and sobbed. "Papa, I'm sorry! I'm sorry! I'll do better. I will."

When the weeping subsided, Gustav rose and stood in front of Gerhardt, resting his hands upon Gerhardt's bowed head. "There's one more thing. Your father asked me to say this to you—for him—in the Spirit of the Risen Christ. 'Peace be with you, my son! Peace be with you!'"

Bright and early the next day—Sunday morning—Otto opened his door and stepped outside to watch the sunrise. He filled his lungs with fresh air. He listened to the birds singing, savored the glory of the rising sun, and reflected upon the happenings of the past week. "Now," he said, "I see signs of Easter."

# Chapter Nine ∼

Otto stood on the boardwalk in front of the store, looking west. *Here we are, a fine Monday morning in May, the year of our Lord 1903. What an exhilarating time for the people of the land. Last week, springtime broke free from the icy grip of winter. And now the fields have dried out enough for the plowing and planting to commence. Beginning this morning, the scene is miraculously transformed. Teams of horses dot the countryside, working the fields with the exuberance they stored up during the long winter. So many neighbors helping neighbors! The hillsides, forests, and meadows are erupting with new life. Behold the beauty of our Creator!*

Late Tuesday night, there was some excitement over at the Dinkmeier house. Edna woke up with a start and said, "Emil, wake up! There's someone in the kitchen. I think it's a burglar. It sounds like he's eating the rest of the torte that we had for dinner!"

"Then it's already too late," he said, rolling over. "Go back to sleep, Edna."

"Too late? You can still catch him!"

"Catch him? I mean it's too late to save him. Even Doc Hess couldn't help him with a belly full of that torte."

Whap!

"I'll bring his body over to the undertaker in the morning."

Whap!

"Oh, it's probably just the cat, and he still has a few lives left."

Whap!

On Wednesday morning, it was warm and rainy. So, by midmorning, the general store had many more customers than would normally be expected during planting season. Otto was a little irritated because most of them weren't actually there to buy anything. Blocking the front doorway was a huge, wooden crate filled with cast-iron cookware; however, rather than see what they could do to move it, the "customers" either climbed over the box or went around to the back door.

Three pairs of men were locked in fierce combat as they hunched intently over their checkers. Some lingered around the postal counter after picking up their mail. Bruno the Saint Bernard was keeping a sleepy eye on things from over near the woodstove. Otto tried to coax some of the checkers players to help him, but he couldn't make them budge.

"Sorry, Otto," Reiny Hartung said. "If one of us gets up, there's no telling what a mischief-maker might do to move his checkers into more advantageous positions."

"Well, what if you all got up and helped me?"

"No, we can't trust Bruno either. He eats checkers as if they were candy."

With resigned frustration, Otto leaned against the wooden box, watching the raindrops splash in the puddles outside. Carl Mueller rolled up in his wagon. "Just in time," Otto said. "Hey, Carl! Give me a hand with this, will ya?" Carl was quick to come to the rescue.

They each took a different end of the crate and lifted and pushed and pulled on it until they were completely worn out. Every time they made a little progress, it slipped back the other way.

Finally, gasping for air, Otto straightened himself and said, "It's no use, Carl. We'll have to empty it before we can get it inside."

With his hands on his hips, Carl snorted. "Whaddaya mean? I thought we was takin' it outside."

They succeeded in dragging the box inside. Another wagon came down the road. It was from the hardware company in Sheboygan. The driver was a new man, Eduardo D'Angelo, in his mid-thirties. Otto had met him before, but no one else from Bierville had seen him. When Eduardo stepped inside, the checkers games stopped suddenly; all eyes were upon him. Holding his dripping hat in both hands, he glanced around the room, recognized Otto, and walked over to him.

"Your name is Eduardo, isn't it?" Otto asked. "Eduardo D'Angelo? Do you have my hardware order?" Eduardo looked perplexed for a moment, then fished a folded piece of paper from an inside coat pocket and handed it to Otto. "It says a dozen boxes. Are they all here?" Otto asked, pointing to the paper.

"Sí. Hardware," Eduardo said, and went out to begin unloading the order.

As soon as he was out the door, one of the checkers players said, "Well, look at him! He must be a Spaniard or maybe a Mexican."

"No," Otto said, "I believe he's Italian. The hardware store said he's been here about a month with his wife and four children."

"I-talian," Hugo Putz said. "Not very bright, I understand— them I-talians. Did ya see the way he just stood there when Otto spoke to him? I hear they're a dirty race, too. Dishonest, quick-tempered, regular religious fanatics. And their bodies are completely numb to pain. And—get this—they go and have dozens of children and simply abandon 'em!"

Otto felt his face flushing. "Hugo, how many Italians do you know personally? Or is Eduardo the first one you've ever seen?"

"Of course. One's plenty."

"Don't you bristle when you hear people tell jokes about us 'dirty krauts'? I would suggest, then, that you keep your eyes and ears open, and your mouth shut. Your ignorance is beginning to show, and it's not at all becoming."

"Say," Reiny said, "what if that's Clara's ex-husband, snooping around, trying to find her?"

"What?" Otto said in disbelief.

"Sure," Reiny said, "that mustache looks phony—too big. It's probably a disguise. Think about it. He's a stranger. His name is Eduardo, nearly the same as Edward. It all fits!"

"Well, thank you, Mr. Sherlock Holmes, for those brilliant deductions! Eduardo has a wife and children, for pity's sake!"

"All part of the disguise," Reiny said, wagging his finger warily.

There was a loud crash outside. The checkers players all ran to the windows and roared with laughter. Eduardo was sprawled face down in a great puddle with a keg of nails scattered in the mud around him. Clara Schnuelle and Gerhardt Schultz were on their way into the store and went over to help him.

Otto addressed the checkers players. "Good Christian gentlemen—or am I presumptuous in calling you that? You ridicule this man and his people, then leave the deeds of kindness to a woman and an ex-convict." He shook his head and headed outside to help.

Gently they assisted Eduardo to his feet; Otto noticed several cuts on the unfortunate man's hands and face. There was a muddy, silver cross hanging on a chain that swung down from around Eduardo's neck. Otto said, "Ah, friend. You bleed just like the rest of us, don't you? Come inside. We'll get you cleaned up."

On Friday, Carl and Gertrude Mueller were in the post office picking up their mail. They were expecting a birth announcement from their nephew in Cleveland any day.

"Sure enough," Carl said, reaching into the box, "here's that ol' letter."

With excitement in her voice, Gertrude said, "Open the letter, Carl. What does John have to say? Oh, I can't wait. Is it a boy or a girl? Is everybody all right?"

"Hold your horses, sister dear! My fingers ain't that nimble no more. Lemme see. It says, uh—oh, this can't be good news, hey." Silently, with his lips forming the words, he reread the brief message. "Oh dear, oh dear."

"Is there a problem?" Gertrude asked.

"Well, for one thing, they gurricken went an' called the baby 'Genesis.' That's a pitiful name!"

"Genesis?"

"Says so right here. For another thing, he's twenty-one pounds, three ounces. That's a powerful huge baby! 'Tain't any way John's wife could survive."

"What?"

"The poor lad must be grievin' somethin' terrible!"

"Carl!" she said after reading the note. "It's a Scripture passage. Something about Abraham, I think."

"Ah," he said with a glimmer of comprehension, "Abraham's a better name, but that's still a whopper of a baby."

"Carl!"

When they returned home, Gertrude looked up the passage. "Here it is," she said, "Genesis twenty-one, verse three. Listen. It says, 'And Abraham called the name of his son that was born unto him, whom Sarah bare to him, Isaac.' Well, that explains everything."

"That explains nothin'. His wife's name 'tweren't never Sarah."

"No, I'm sure John was just trying to be clever, announcing that they have a baby boy and named him Isaac. That's all."

"I bet John's first wife Whatsername went an' died, too. Aw, an' now poor Sarah's dead. An' we ain't never met her."

"Carl, I'm sure everyone's fine."

"Pitiful sad! Pitiful sad!"

When Sunday rolled around, Clara Schnuelle was ready for some Sabbath rest and renewal, but she rarely got it from her class. At Sunday school, she had most of her students spellbound with stories about the work of missionaries in far-away countries. "Just think, children," she said, "in many places around the world, there are millions of people who live where there isn't a single church where they can go to worship and learn about God. Now, what do you think we could do?"

Calvin Rickmeier had an answer. "We could send them our church."

"What an interesting idea! You know, Calvin, the Christian Church is really all of us. So, you think we should all become missionaries and go help them?"

"No. I mean we could send 'em this church. Then we wouldn't have to go anymore."

"Ah. You were trying to get out of something, not into something, weren't you, Calvin?"

"Well, uh. Yes, ma'am."

"Let me tell you—all of you. God has an amazing way of changing our minds, our hearts. Don't be surprised if some of you become missionaries."

At worship, the Scripture text for the sermon was from the Gospel of John, 15:12: 'This is my Commandment, that ye love one another, as I have loved you.' Gustav chose that passage to encourage his congregation in their neighborliness among themselves, as well as to challenge them in reaching out to others.

"Many times," he said, "I see you offering such warmth and affection to one another that Jesus himself would be pleased. And there is such a sense of anticipation among you! Why, just yesterday in an envelope addressed to me we received an early order for our pig roast next month. The note says simply, 'Schweinkopf!' Apparently, someone has reserved the entire head of a pig. The only problem is, there's no signature or return address. However, we'll be sure to set aside a pig's head for whichever of you placed this fine, early order."

Gustav noticed Hugo Putz scrunching down in his pew, trying to hide himself from view. *So, it was you, Hugo.* He went back to his sermon: "I would, however, encourage this congregation to open its heart more to those outside of this church, to the many immigrant families who are settling in the area, to people in far-away lands who are still God's creatures and children. You know what it is to feel joy as well as heartache. You know what you feel when a loved one is injured or becomes ill."

Many people nodded with understanding.

"Why is it, then," he continued, "that we think people of other countries, other races, or other religions feel any less pain than we do under similar conditions of suffering? They also love their homelands, their families. They want to live without the fear of war and famine as much as we do. Yes, the world is changing and we are part of that change, and we dare not neglect the command of the Lord Jesus to love as he has loved even us. Remember, beloved, the scope of God's loving embrace is much broader than we tend to think."

It was a beautiful spring evening on Sunday, and there was a surprise party at the church. Gustav was completing his tenth year as pastor of the congregation, and the church sponsored a banquet to honor his wife Minnie and him. Folks from all over the area came to share in the festivities. The jovial crowd filled the church basement and flowed out into the churchyard. It was an evening of smiles and surprise guests, handshakes and hugs, eating and more eating. After dinner, August Schmidt, who was the president of the church elders, stood up to make a presentation:

"Herr Vriesen, Frau Vriesen, the congregation is most appreciative of your ministry among us during these past ten years. We have decided to send you away on a grand vacation. One month in beautiful Des Moines!"

There was warm applause, and Gustav stood to receive the envelope. He thought for a moment and said, "I am unsure of how to accept this generous gift of yours, because I can think of at least two things that might happen as a consequence of such a long absence. One possibility is you might all pine away, missing your shepherd so. It is also possible that you'll enjoy my absence so much that you'll want to make it a permanent arrangement. At any rate, Minnie and I are deeply grateful. Your generous surprise leaves me speechless."

A ripple of good-natured laughter flowed through the crowd.

Accustomed to listening to sermons lasting an hour or more, August smiled and said, "Well, Herr Vriesen, perhaps we should surprise you more often." Again there was laughter.

Gustav continued: "Now, I have a surprise for you. I must confess that I had some inkling about the festivities this evening. You know how hard it is to keep secrets around here. I've taken the liberty of inviting a world-renowned organist to favor us with a concert on our church's pipe organ. So, if you would be so kind, please adjourn to the sanctuary for a special treat."

Excited speculation rippled through the assembly; they paraded upstairs and settled themselves in the pews. Once again, Gustav stood before them. "Before we begin, I would like to introduce our guest to you. He has been in America only a short time. He and his family escaped from years of political upheaval and repression in their homeland, and now we are blessed by having them in our midst. Otto, will you please stand for a moment?"

Otto stood uncertainly.

Someone remarked, "Otto has trouble playing his concertina, let alone a pipe organ." The assembly rippled with laughter.

"This, I know, is true," Gustav said, smiling. "However, it was Herr Steitz who first mentioned our guest to me, though he did not realize the full giftedness of this man. I recognized his name as that of one of the premiere concert organists in the world. It is my great pleasure to present to you Eduardo D'Angelo, his wife Maria, and their children."

Eduardo entered wearing a concert tuxedo and bowed humbly in response to the enthusiastic applause. He was followed by his lovely wife and their four bright-eyed children. Otto beamed broadly and clapped excitedly. Gustav looked around at the checkers players. They gaped with such stunned surprise that blue birds could have found ready nesting cavities.

Eduardo seated himself at the pipe organ, and Gustav beamed at him. Simon Klemme worked the billows to supply the instrument with plenty of air, and the concert began. Eduardo opened with Bach's Toccata and Fugue in D minor. Music flowed from his fingers and poured through the pipes. Gustav noticed that Eduardo needed no sheet music; it must be written upon his heart.

More than an hour of heavenly sounds followed from Bach and Beethoven, two wonderful German composers, and Alessandro Scarlatti, a fine Italian composer. Never before had the church's pipe organ sung such glorious praises to God. That night, the people of Bierville experienced the saving love of Christ in a new way and an immigrant family found a new place to call home.

# Chapter Ten ∿

Well, Bruno," Otto said, "I don't think life could possibly be any more enjoyable than this." He bent over and scratched his dog behind the ears. Straightening himself, he continued to sweep the boardwalk in front of the general store with methodical meticulousness. He was stalling. By nine o'clock on that Monday in August of 1903, it was so nice outside that he didn't want to go back in.

*Recent weather conditions have been nearly perfect. The days are warm, with just enough of a breeze to keep things comfortable. The nights are cool enough for sleeping. Enough rain has fallen to keep the crops and gardens growing and to provide a few good mud puddles for children to play in. Ah, the blessing of sufficiency!*

Otto noticed four children taking full advantage of some of the puddles down the road near the blacksmith shop. He decided to go over for a closer look.

Calvin saw him coming and shouted, "Hi, Herr Steitz! We been workin' hard all morning. We whipped up a tasty batch of mud pies. Like to try some?"

"Now that's the kind of work I enjoy!" Otto said. "Here I come!" *So, Calvin is teaching Liesl and the Klemme girls the art of mud cookery, molding their impressionable minds in childhood lore. Good for him.* When Otto had nearly reached them, his mouth dropped open. At first, he had thought Calvin was wearing a pair of brown trousers; they were, in fact, blue trousers rolled up to the knees. Calvin's lower half was covered with mud. "Calvin!" Otto gasped.

"What?" Calvin said, looking down at himself. "My shirt's pretty clean."

"And girls! Catherine! Caroline! Liesl!" Otto said in disbelief. "Just look at the three of you!"

"We took our shoes and stockings off," they said in unison, wiggling their little toes in the oozing mud.

Otto chuckled and shook his head. "What will your mothers say? Do they know you're out here?"

"Oh, yes," Catherine said. "They know all about it."

Otto knelt next to the display of mud products. An assortment of earthen confections was neatly displayed on the ground next to the puddle. "What have you children made today—besides a mess?"

"These," Calvin said, "are the chocolate cakes. The blueberry pies are over there. And those prune muffins come plain or special."

"How do you know which ones are special?"

"They have the pig weed on top."

"Yes, that would make them special."

Otto was still kneeling next to the children when the three mothers came out of Martha's house. He heard them shriek and stood to greet them.

"Herr Steitz!" Anna said, smiling and wagging her finger at him. "Was it you who put them up to this?"

"Noooo," Otto said. "They beat me to it. I would have come over here sooner if I'd known I was missing all the fun. I used to play in puddles like this when I was growing up in Germany. The mud there was cleaner, of course."

"My goodness!" Clara said. "We'll have to dunk them in the river in order to tell which child belongs to which mother."

Frieda examined her son. "Calvin, aren't you getting a little old for this?"

"Maybe so," he said wistfully, "but how else are the girls gonna learn how to be a kid unless someone shows 'em?"

"Too old?" Otto said. "Why, if it weren't for my arthritis, I might spend more time making mud pies myself. They say it keeps you young."

The mothers led their little mud balls away to get cleaned up and Reiny Hartung walked out of the blacksmith shop and over to Otto. "Otto," he said, "aren't you the crazy man! I've been watching from my window and I should think you'd have put a stop to this nonsense right away. Life is too serious for there to be time to play in mud puddles, even for children. There are important things they should be doing."

Otto frowned and said, "The twins will be three next week, Liesl's not even four, and Calvin is what, maybe nine? Do you want to send them to work in some coalmine or factory? Weren't you paying attention to Herr Vriesen's sermon yesterday? 'Suffer the little children to come unto me, and forbid them not: for of such is the kingdom of God.' Reiny, you and I could learn something from these children about how to receive God's gift of joy."

"Just the same, they're too old for that kind of nonsense—especially the Rickmeier boy. Now, unlike the rest of the world, I have work to do. I'll leave you here to admire this assortment of foolishness."

On Tuesday evening, Adam Schroeder went over to the Rickmeier house to call on Emilie. It was their first real date—by themselves. Adam was sweating as if he'd just run five miles. When Emilie appeared at the door, he offered her a store-bought bouquet of mixed flowers. "Uh, Emilie? Your beauty is but a shadow of the loveliness of these flowers. No! I meant the other way around. Uh, here!"

Shyly she received the gift. They walked down the road, just past the general store and the mill, to the bridge. When they reached the middle of the bridge, Emilie walked to the north side and leaned over the rail, resting her elbows on top and holding her flowers with both hands. Adam leaned against the rail next to her. Watching the water cascading over the dam, he felt ready to explode. Their elbows were touching.

After several minutes of this ecstasy, Adam tried to pay her another compliment: "Emilie, you sure don't sweat as much as I thought you would. I mean, I do! When I'm nervous! You're not a sweaty girl, no sirree!"

She looked at him quizzically and said, "Thank you, I guess." She started walking back up the road toward home again and he fell in step next to her.

Adam was all too aware that their first date was not going smoothly, so he made another attempt to salvage the conversation in his own debonair way: "Say, I think your makeup is smearing. It's probably from the heat, but it makes you look like you have dark circles under your eyes."

"Oh, you're so mean!" she cried, and threw the bouquet at him. "I'm not wearing any makeup!"

In a moment, Adam was standing alone in the middle of the road, terribly confused and holding the rumpled bouquet.

Calvin walked by and said, "Hey ya, Adam! Are those for my sister?"

"Well, I thought so. But I guess she doesn't like flowers. Or maybe it's just me."

On Wednesday morning, Catherine and Caroline were watching their mother change their baby brother's diapers. Simon Jr. was six months old and the girls loved him dearly. Being veteran observers of the whole diaper-changing operation, they knew just what should happen and they listed the steps to be sure Anna got it right: "Nice and clean, lay out a fresh diaper, fold it in a triangle, put the baby's bottom in the middle...."

Anna completed the routine and the twins jabbered cheerfully. Catherine cautioned, "Don't forget to sprinkle the seasoning on him, Mama!"

"Seasoning?" Anna laughed. "No, dear, it's cornstarch. It keeps him dry. Then his bottom doesn't get chapped."

It was a lovely afternoon on Wednesday, and Reiny took a break from his work on a wheel rim. He brought a chair outside in front of the blacksmith shop and sat for a while in the shade. A black swallowtail butterfly caught his attention, flitting in the sunshine and gliding on the breeze. *Oh, I used to love watching butterflies, go chasing 'em with my net. And, boy, did I get nervous when I'd sneak up on one. I could hardly breathe. I loved catching them, studying their colors and designs, putting 'em in my collection, sometimes letting 'em go. How can a thing so small and delicate fly so well? That was fun.*

Reiny was momentarily lost in thought, but came back to himself as he became aware of voices across the road. Some of the neighbor children were playing with Otto next to the general store. Otto was quite a sight, with a red blindfold over his eyes and his long, white apron flapping. Reiny watched intently. *They're spinning him around. Ah, and he's trying to find them. And, oh! Watch it, Otto. Be careful. You're heading toward the hitching post. Well, look at that. He took off the blindfold, and he's howling with laughter. They're running to embrace him. How they must love Otto.*

Reiny found himself smiling at the sight. He became aware of a wonderfully warm sensation filling his body and brightening his soul. *Why is it there are often children playing next to the general store, but never next to my shop? Sure, he has candy and ice cream and phos-*

101

*phates over there. But maybe it's not so much the store as Otto they like.*

He stood once more and carried the chair inside, frowning and nodding. *Must I become small again? I don't know if I can do that. Perhaps I have already become too brittle.*

On Thursday night, Emilie was waiting impatiently for Adam to stop by again. She had seen him at the general store earlier. After their very awkward first date, Frieda explained to her daughter about nervousness and getting tongue-tied and all, and that Adam was really a nice, young man. There was a knock at the door. It was Adam.

He held out another bouquet of flowers and said simply, "Here, Emilie. I hope you like them."

They enjoyed the evening from the vantage point of Emilie's porch swing. There was more conversation, more perspiration, and more tingling skin. Adam surprised Emilie with a question: "If I ask you for a kiss, will you shrink away?"

"I don't know, but why don't you try and we'll see what happens?" To Emilie's delight, she stayed the same size.

Just before sunset on Wednesday, Reiny decided to take a walk next to the river. It was a beautiful evening. The sky was painted in brilliant fluorescent colors; fiery orange and crimson streaks projected around shimmering clouds of ivory, indigo, and violet. Golden luminosity bathed the fields and forests in a finale of splendor and spotlighted the treetops before receding behind the horizon and giving way to the serenity of twilight.

Reiny continued walking and his ears picked up wisps of a young voice up ahead. After a time, he saw Calvin in his swing under the silver maple near the river's edge and his dog Rex lying next to the tree. Calvin was swinging and singing, facing toward the sunset. Now Reiny was close enough to hear the song:

*Silent night, holy night, all is calm, all is bright*
*Round yon virgin mother and child.*
*Holy infant, so tender and mild,*
*Sleep in heavenly peace, sleep in heavenly peace.*[ii]

Reiny loved that carol, good for all occasions, especially Christmas Eves and summer sunsets—although he liked it better in German. *How I loved to sing like that as a child! When did the song leave my heart? Is it gone for good?*

He thought about the wonderful sunsets he still remembered from his childhood, and the thousands he must have missed because he was too busy working all the time. Before he realized what he was doing, Reiny was standing behind Calvin, pushing him on the swing. Calvin smiled at him and kept on singing. The two of them sang to their hearts' content and watched the twilight colors fade into night.

At seven o'clock on Saturday morning when Otto opened the door of the general store, Fritzie was sitting on the front steps. Otto took one look at him and was immediately concerned. "Fritzie, you look as if you were run over by a stampede of angry elephants! What's the trouble? You're not sick, are you?"

"No, not sick, just stupid. I was playing cards last night with some of the boys and didn't get home until five o'clock this morning. As I was undressing for bed, my aunt woke up and said, 'Why, Fritzie, you early bird, you! You should certainly catch a few worms today!' So, to keep from getting bawled out, I put my clothes back on, made some breakfast, and came in for work."

"By the looks of you, Fritzie, the only worms you're going to catch are the ones who think you're already dead."

By mid-morning, the store was buzzing with activity. Otto enjoyed it thoroughly. The three checkerboards were in constant use and each one had its own cheering section. There were also shoppers, including Gustav and Minnie Vriesen and Reiny Hartung. Clara and Liesl came up the boardwalk, and Gerhardt went over to the door to hold it open for them. *Well I'll be,* Otto mused. *Look at Gerhardt's attentiveness whenever she's around. Hmm. Something to watch.*

Clara and Liesl bent down to pet Bruno, who was resting near the door. "Bruno," Clara said, "I think you're the cuddliest, hand-somest dog I know."

Otto smiled and added, "He's also as good a watchdog as you'd ever hope to see. Why, if I hear a suspicious noise at night, I just wake him up and he begins to bark—if he's not too frightened."

Clara laughed and said, "That's really useful."

"Say, Clara," he said, "I see you're wearing your locket again. I've always meant to tell you how lovely it is. My wife used to have one like it years ago."

"Thank you, Herr Steitz. It was from my former husband." She glanced at Gerhardt, opened the locket, and showed them both the picture of herself inside.

"That's a beautiful picture," Otto said. "Very nice. Your locket is almost identical to Elsa's. I wish I still had it, but I lost it when she died."

"Herr Steitz," Liesl said, "did you hear about the newborn baby that was fed elephant's milk and gained over twenty-five pounds in a month?"

"Ridiculous!" he said, playing along with the joke. "That's impossible! Whose baby is it?"

"The elephant's baby!" she said with delight.

Otto whisked her up off the floor and tickled her tummy. "Liesl," he said, "you're a little ray of sunshine!"

From nine o'clock to noon every Saturday morning during the summer months, Otto offered a free ice cream soda to each of his customers. But over the years, he had noticed something interesting: the vast majority of the grown-ups insisted on paying the regular price for the sodas; the older children mostly said, "No, thank you" and didn't take one. Otto usually replied, "Don't tell me you're too old to accept a gift from a friend."

Only the young children received the free ice cream sodas gratefully and usually only when their parents weren't looking. So, when Otto offered sodas to Clara and Liesl, it didn't surprise him that Clara said, "No, thank you, Herr Steitz. We really don't need any. Oh, very well. One for Liesl, but none for me."

"Thank you very much!" Liesl said.

Smiling, Reiny said, "Otto, you certainly have a way with children."

Gustav was also observing what was happening and didn't miss the opportunity to deliver another of his famous "Saturday Morning Specials." He was aware that these sermons had become something of a joke around Bierville, but the other customers didn't seem to mind too much.

"My friends," Gustav said, "did you see little Liesl receive her ice cream soda from Otto? She didn't try to pay for it or refuse it the way we older folks usually do. She received Otto's gift gratefully, saying simply, 'Thank you very much!' Oh, for the wonder, the joy, the trust, the simple gratitude of children!"

Gustav knelt down, opening his arms to Liesl. She ran to him, her soda leading the way. With Liesl in his arms, enjoying her treat, he stood again and continued. "There are so many wonderful blessings that our God in heaven wants to give us, yet we feel—what? Too old, too sophisticated to receive these simple blessings? No, my friends, there is much more to life than what we earn and accumulate for ourselves. Life passes all too quickly for us to refuse the goodness God has to offer."

Immediately, all twelve of the customers in the store went over and stood in line, waiting for a free soda. Gustav and Minnie were near the front of the line.

"Thank you, dear friend," Otto said, smiling. "That was an effective sales pitch." He handed a glass to the first of his converts. "Now it appears that I might run out of supplies."

Gustav laughed and said, "'Suffer the little children to come unto me, and forbid them not: for of such is the kingdom of God. Verily I say unto you, Whosoever shall not receive the kingdom of God as a little child... shall not enter therein.'"

# Chapter Eleven ❧

For much of the autumn in 1903, it seemed to Gustav that the spirits of most folks around Bierville had been unusually low. This widespread malaise wasn't caused by any catastrophe, but by a confluence of smaller troubles: market prices for farm produce in the region were sagging, commerce was slow for most businesses, some beloved people in the community had died, and many others were affected by nagging colds and influenza that were getting passed around. Area residents mobilized an all-out dispensation of chicken soup, cod-liver oil, and garlic necklaces, but still couldn't keep up with the onslaught of illness.

By world standards, life in Sheboygan County was cozy, even opulent. One could look somewhere else and find others who were much worse off. But for several months, people had been feeling worn down in a depressed kind of way and were beginning to wonder if things were going to stay that way. Thanksgiving Day was one week off. However, with the way most everyone was on edge, even downright cranky, if someone had taken a referendum on the holiday, Gustav expected that people might have voted to forget Thanksgiving that year.

On Thursday morning, a week before Thanksgiving, Otto was inside the store looking out. *Awful weather! No wonder everyone seems so out of sorts! Ah, but is it the weather that influences our mood, or our mood that influences our perception of the weather? Are we such petty creatures that we can't rise above inclement conditions? Or is a spirit of gratitude dependent upon everything being the way we want it to be? That's a sad commentary on the human spirit.*

Edna Dinkmeier came storming inside. "Herr Steitz! I want to complain about that Danish blue cheese you sold me the other day!"

"Why am I not surprised?" Otto muttered.

"Did you say it was imported or deported from Denmark?"

"Verzeihung, Frau Dinkmeier. But you'll remember that I warned you. One has to acquire a taste for Danish blue. It's remarkably piquant, even pungent to some. Here, take two pounds of cheddar with my best wishes."

"Why don't you give me the rest of your blue cheese?"

"But, Edna, it's the same cheese you didn't like before. Here, take the cheddar. It's the only kind I have left."

"No, I want to try some Swiss instead."

Otto was exasperated. "I haven't got any! But here, I'll take the cheddar, drill holes in it, paint it a shade of ivory, and we'll call it Swiss. All right?"

"Herr Steitz, it's amazing that you have any customers at all, with the way you're so crabby all the time."

Things weren't much better over at the checkerboards. Actually, at one of the tables, they were playing poker. Otto warned them when they broke out the cards, "I don't want you gentlemen gambling in here."

"Oh, Otto," Lester Mohr replied. "Your lack of trust wounds us all. Do you see any money on the table? Don't worry. We're just playing for peanuts."

Carl Mueller nodded. "Yep," he said, "just peanuts. Though we dassn't mention that each one o' these puppies is worth a ni—"

"Carl!" Lester snapped.

Otto frowned suspiciously.

After several hands, Jacob Schmalfus had accumulated a large pile of peanuts. He began shuffling the cards again and boasting a little. "Well, boys, looks like I'll be taking home most of the, uh, peanuts again. Just wish I was as lucky at farming as I am at poker."

Lester said, "'Tisn't a matter of luck, Jacob. You can't deal your cows the way you do those cards."

"Oh, ja!" Jacob said. "When you fellas convert these peanuts into—"

Otto walked over to the tables.

"—into peanut butter, then we'll see who's laughing!"

Otto said, "It's a good thing for you Herr Vriesen isn't here. He's not fond of card playing, and he likes gambling even less."

"Well," Jacob laughed, "he isn't here."

In scurried Gustav Vriesen. Peanuts exploded into the air, but somehow the players managed to stuff nearly all of the cards into their pockets. Gustav surveyed the room and the checkers players stifled their laughter. "Otto," Gustav said, "I'm surprised at how you keep this store of yours—peanuts all over the floor. And what's this?" Gustav picked up an ace of hearts and handed it to Otto. "You shouldn't keep poker cards around here. These impressionable cherubs here might get some bad ideas."

"All my work down the sinkhole!" Jacob moaned.

Gustav replied, "Well, it's good they're only peanuts, Jacob. It's not as if they're worth a nickel each or anything." He bent down again, scooped up a handful of peanuts, and went to check his mailbox. As he passed Otto, he smiled.

On Friday afternoon, Carl was outside carrying buckets of water to the troughs for the cows. A stranger walked up to Carl and said in a businesslike tone, "I am a government inspector. Here's my identification card. I'm here to examine your dairy operation."

"Well, I guess that'll be all right, hey," Carl said. "D'ya want me to give ya a tour of the farm?"

"No need for you to accompany me. I've inspected hundreds of farms." He walked past Carl and started looking around.

Carl emptied the buckets he was carrying and walked into the barn. A few minutes later, he heard shrieking coming from the barnyard, so he hurried out to see what the trouble was. The inspector was running laps in the cattle pen, pursued by a burly, black bull. Calmly, Carl opened a gate just enough for the man to slip through, then closed it behind him. The inspector gasped for air.

Carl patted the man on the back. "Why didn't ya gurricken tell me ya wanted to play with Blackie there? He don't have no sense o' humor, but he loves playin' with gover'ment 'nspectors. He 'specially likes the way you fellas bounce."

On Friday night over at the Rickmeiers', the four of them sat around the kitchen table talking. Calvin got up suddenly, hurried into another room, and returned a minute later shuffling a deck of playing cards. Returning to his place at the table, Calvin asked, "Who wants to play poker?"

"Poker?" Frieda said. "Who on earth taught you how to play poker?"

"Well, all the men at the general store. They do it all the time."

"I'm not interested," Emilie said coldly.

Calvin continued shuffling. "Most of the people in this family are not the gamblin' type," he said. "But I am."

"Wait a minute," Herman said. "I have a better idea." Taking the cards from Calvin and smoothing the tablecloth, Herman said, "Let's make card houses. Calvin, run and get three more decks, will you, please?"

For the next hour and a half, the four of them worked together building some real beauties, up to seven stories tall. Nobody lost. Everybody won.

On Saturday night, Adam went over to Emilie's house to pick her up for what had become their customary Saturday night date—already in a rut, and he was just twenty-four years old and she only eighteen. Down the road they headed, all bundled up in the buckboard. Adam said, "Say, Emilie, what d'ya say we do something different tonight? You know, for a change?"

"All right," she said. "What do you suggest?"

He winked and said, "You get fresh with me, and I'll shake my finger at you."

Emilie blushed and popped him one on the shoulder. Adam just smiled.

On Sunday at church, the sermon was about loving one's enemies and was taken from Proverbs, the Gospel of Matthew, and Paul's letter to the Romans: "Vengeance is mine, I will repay, sayeth the Lord. Therefore if thine enemy hunger, feed him: if he thirst, give him drink. For in so doing thou shalt heap coals of fire on his head. Be not overcome of evil, but overcome evil with good."

Gustav ended the sermon on a contemplative note and, as he frequently did, asked one of the elders sitting to his right to lead the congregation in prayer. Speaking just above a whisper, he said to the newest elder, "Elder Schmalfus, will you lead us in prayer?" There was no response. He repeated the request more loudly: "Elder Schmalfus, will you be so kind?" By that time, it was apparent to Gustav that Jacob was no longer in the waking world, so he took two steps to his right, cupped his hand next to his mouth, and said loudly, "Jacob, will you lead?"

Still only half awake, Jacob murmured, "Why don't you lead, Margaret? I'm not a good dancer." *Where is he, and who is this*

111

*Margaret?* In spite of his best efforts, Gustav had difficulty concentrating during the rest of the service.

After worship, Herman and Frieda Rickmeier walked home with Calvin and Emilie. Calvin began telling his family about all the terrible things he was going to get revenge on a little boy at school the next day. Frieda became upset. She said, "Weren't you listening to Pastor Vriesen? About loving your enemies? Have you ever thought about heaping burning coals upon his head instead?"

"Say," Calvin said, "I never tried that! It sounds like a great idea!"

"Son," Herman said, "that's not to be taken, uh, lit'rally. You just be nice to your enemy and it'll feel like burning coals."

"That don't make sense, Papa. Real burnin' coals has to work a lot better."

"Well, that's true, son. Burning coals are pretty effective. Your mother dumps a load on me every so often. How do you think I lost all my hair?"

"Really, Papa?"

Frieda smiled at Herman. "Really, Papa!"

Martha, Clara, and Liesl walked home from church, and they also discussed the service. "Wasn't that a provocative sermon?" Martha said. "'Your purity will be loathsome to them.'"

"Yes," Clara agreed, "challenging and insightful, yet extremely pragmatic!"

Liesl looked up at the two women and said, "My, aren't we using a big vocabulary today!"

"You precocious, little urchin!" Martha said. "Where did you learn such things as these?"

"I listen to Mama and you."

"Then we'd best be careful to say only good things," Martha said.

On Monday morning, Anna Klemme was in the kitchen fixing breakfast: bacon and eggs, with strawberry jam on fresh biscuits. Little Caroline came bouncing down the stairs to breakfast. She said, "Oh, Mama, wasn't that fun?"

"Wasn't what fun, sweetheart?" Anna asked.

"Our dream last night. Wasn't it wonderful?"

"I don't know," Anna said, chuckling. "I haven't any way of knowing what your dream was about."

"Well, you should. You took us on a picnic."

Anna patted her daughter's head and said, "Maybe I just can't remember. Why don't you tell me about it?"

Tuesday morning found Gustav visiting Ida Klietz and Sarah at their home. Three months before, Ida had taken a hard fall and broken her hip. At the time, she had told Gustav that she had given up. Her husband Jonathan had died eleven years earlier, so she lived alone. Business at the dance hall was slow and money was tight. As they were praying together, Ida said, "Lord, I know you want us to give thanks in all circumstances, and all these years I have tried. But this is just too much, just too much."

Ida and Jonathon never had any children of their own but during their life together they had opened their home and their hearts to many orphans from the area. It was like having their own private orphanage, and they were blessed with an instant family. Over a span of eighteen years, they welcomed ten sad and frightened children and raised them as best they could to be ten healthy and happy young adults.

One by one, they left Ida and Jonathon's home and started lives of their own. The last two were still living with them when Jonathon died; after those two moved out six years ago, Ida felt more alone than ever. It was not easy, but she had managed to keep the dance hall going and considered herself fortunate to be in good health for all of those years, until she fell and broke her hip. "I'm sixty years old," she told Gustav. "I should just die. I'm no good to anyone anymore."

For the first few days after the accident, many of Ida's neighbors took turns caring for her. Four days after Ida broke her hip, Gustav was visiting with her and Sarah appeared at the door. Sarah was one of the ten orphans that she and Jonathon had raised.

Sarah said, "I've come home to help you, Mama. To thank you for all the ways you helped me. You were the mother I never had, and now I will be the daughter you never had. Now I'll show you how grateful I've been all these years for your loving care." Sarah knelt down next to the bed and hugged Ida, and the two of them clung to one another.

That had been three months ago. Now, as Gustav sat with Ida and Sarah—mother and daughter together—the world looked so much brighter. "Isn't it amazing," he said, "how a little time and some love and gratitude can warm and brighten the world in ways that few other things can? It's not that we are to give thanks for all circumstances. However, it is essential that, in all circumstances, we find thing for which to be grateful. Sarah, you are like the one that returned to the Lord Jesus to thank him. Your faith has made both of you well."

On Wednesday night, Gustav wasn't expecting to see very many people at the Thanksgiving Eve service. But, one by one and in couples and large families, his people gathered to give thanks. Perhaps they had taken stock of what was truly important and realized their enduring blessings despite the adversities. He was delighted to sense a warm spirit of gratitude in the air. The church was full. Jacob Schmalfus flexed his hands, getting ready to ring the bell. A minute before the service started, in came Ida Klietz with her cane in her right hand and Sarah holding onto her left.

Gustav went to the pulpit and opened the service: "'Rejoice evermore: Pray without ceasing: In everything give thanks: for this is the will of God in Christ Jesus concerning you.'"

# Chapter Twelve ∾

It was a lovely Sunday morning in the summer of 1904 that greeted the people of God gathering for worship. Sunshine lit the stained-glass windows, faded briefly as puffy clouds passed by, then ignited the colors once more.

When the time came for the reading of Scripture, Gustav Vriesen turned to the passage about Mary and Martha. He finished the reading by repeating the words of Jesus with particular tenderness: "'Martha, Martha, thou art careful, and troubled about many things: But one thing is needful, and Mary hath chosen that good part, which shall not be taken away from her.'"

After worship, folks stood outside visiting, then began to make their ways home on foot, on horseback, and by horse-and-buggy. Edna and Emil rode along in their buggy, and Edna said, "So. What did you think of Vriesen's sermon?" Before Emil could say anything, she continued: "I didn't get anything out of it. I just can't understand that passage about Mary and Martha. Emil, why don't you talk to me? I ask you what you think, but you never tell me! All you do is give me the silent treatment. You didn't like the sermon either, did you? Of course not. Emil, why don't you talk to me? I talk to you. I tell you what I think. Why don't you talk to me, Emil?"

Finally Emil said, "Well, I would talk more if I had the chance, if you weren't always telling me what I think."

"I am happy to hear," Edna said, "that you have any thoughts at all in that empty head of yours!"

"Why don't you stop picking on me? I'm trying to do everything possible to make you happy."

"Well, there's one thing you haven't done that my first husband did that pleased me very much."

"And what's that?"

"He went crazy and left town!"

"I can certainly understand why!"


Emil and Edna didn't make it to church very often, but many people, Pastor Vriesen included, were glad whenever they came. On one occasion, Otto said to him, "It's at least a couple of hours out of the week when nobody has to listen to them argue. And who knows? Something good might rub off on them."


The Rickmeiers decided not to go directly home after church, but to take a little ride through the neighborhood. Calvin and Emilie rode in the back seat of the surrey; Frieda rode in front next to Herman who held the reins and guided the horses. She said, "I appreciated Pastor Vriesen's sermon this morning. I like the story about Mary and Martha. I'm not proud to admit it, but I see myself in that story."

"What do you mean, Mama?" Calvin asked.

"Well," she said, "I used to be more like Martha. Always busy, always living two steps in the future, always worried about something. I neglected the more important parts of life, like living in the present and enjoying God's gift of the three of you. Now I think I am more like Mary. Not as worried, more aware of the really precious things. I sometimes still feel a tug-of-war between Mary and Martha inside of myself until I remember what Jesus said."

They rode along through the woods, and Frieda remembered a few years back, when she was more like Martha. When Calvin was about seven years old there was a time when they were having a lot of difficulty with him. In the space of one week alone, Calvin misbehaved in Sunday school, got sick after eating two pounds of taffy, tried to sneak out of the house to go fishing, and went swimming by himself in the river.

Frieda had been tempted to trade him for a sack of potatoes. She confessed all this to Gustav, and he gave her some advice: "Why don't you and Herman find some time to go fishing and swimming with Calvin? Give him more of your attention and you won't have to give him as much of your anger."

Frieda also remembered something that happened with Emilie at around the same time. In addition to doing her regular household chores, sixteen-year-old Emilie was working very hard sewing a new school dress for herself. She reached a difficult part in the project and asked Frieda for help. Frieda said, "I don't have any time to help you! I still have the floor to wash, cookies to bake, and my knickknacks to dust before the party tonight."

Emilie looked at her with tears in her eyes and said, "Mama, you always seem to have more important things to do. You spend more time with your knickknacks than you do with Calvin and me."

Emilie had revealed a painful truth to her mother. Frieda packed her knickknacks away in a box until a time in her life when she'd have more time to fuss with such things. That was her new beginning.

The old Frieda was more like Martha; the new Frieda wanted to be more like Mary. She realized the day would come all too soon when she'd be delighted to have her children ask her to do anything for them. Instead of accumulating and caring for so many things, Frieda began showing more of her love and concern for others at home, at church, in the neighborhood. She still worked hard and most of the work got done, but she saved time and energy for the more important things, the precious things in life that cannot get rusty or dusty, the true blessings of God.

Emil and Edna Dinkmeier arrived home to the neatest, tidiest house in the whole township. The Dinkmeier house set the standard for tidiness in that part of the county. It was, however, an empty home. Years ago, Emil and Edna attempted to entertain guests, but it wasn't very entertaining for Emil. Edna was too busy to visit with them, always fussing with something in the kitchen, washing the pots and pans, cautioning her guests not to make a mess in her house.

In their marriage of thirty-nine years, they raised two children—two boys—but Emil and Edna rarely saw them after they moved out. They had three grandchildren, but had never even met them, all for a simple reason: Edna never allowed her own children to have a childhood. She never made time to play with them, read to them, or help them with schoolwork. She was too busy doing "more important" things, and she insisted that Emil also had more pressing things to do.

Sometimes, when the boys were little, Emil stood at a distance watching them playing together outside and he cried. How he yearned to wrestle with them, to play catch with them, to teach them to play baseball. But Edna always reminded him that he had "better things" to do with his time.

One day he could stand the isolation no more. He started playing with them, reading to them, and helping them with their homework, all in secret. The boys flourished as never before. He rode into town to the glove factory and commissioned them to make three baseball gloves; when the three of them weren't playing catch out behind the barn, they hid the gloves in the hayloft where Edna never ventured. Emil said, "Don't tell your mother! It'll be our secret!" He knew Edna would never approve.

The only rooms in the house the boys were allowed to enter were the kitchen and their bedroom upstairs. When Emil and Edna got into one of their arguments, the boys were pushed farther away; they either went to their room or found something to do outside. Even as toddlers, if they ever wandered into the parlor or some other restricted area, they were severely punished. Why? Edna had too many figurines, carvings, and other valuable acquisitions on display to risk their destruction by careless children.

Beneath her rigid exterior, Edna did have a conscience and a heart; she did have the capacity to love. Over the years, however, she had become preoccupied with many things, and they took control of her life.

Edna made it clear that as soon as the boys turned eighteen, they'd have to set out on their own. So, the day after the oldest one's eighteenth birthday, both boys moved out. Edna rejoiced. Emil felt as though his heart would break.

"Don't be so emotional!" she said. "It's time they grow up and leave us alone. It's for their own good, you know."

On Monday morning down at the post office, Otto was putting the mail into the boxes and folks began arriving to pick it up. Edna came in and scowled at her mail box, noticing that it was, as usual, as empty as their well-ordered house. The post office and general store were crowded, but no one spoke to her. Everyone knew that one wrong word to Edna meant risking the loss of one's head. After watching her for a few minutes, Otto said, "I'm sorry, Frau Dinkmeier. Nothing for you today. Maybe tomorrow."

Martha Schnuelle entered and said, "Good morning, Herr Steitz! Do you have my weekly letter from my boy Conrad?"

"Do you need to ask?" he said. "Doctor Conrad is as regular as clockwork."

Martha opened and read the letter from her son. Edna watched her enjoying the letter, three double-sided pages. Slowly Edna became aware of a burning, empty pain from deep within her soul, a pain that wouldn't leave her at peace; some of it was jealousy, but most of it was sadness.

Thump, thump, BANG! Thump, thump, BANG! BANG! BANG! Otto looked up. Hugo Putz opened the front door and looked down the boardwalk. He shouted, "It's the Rickmeier boy! Everybody hide!"

Calvin came bounding into the store. "Herr Steitz?" he said. "Mama says you have something to show me."

"That's right, Master Calvin!" Otto said, coming out to greet him. "Take a look at this! It's a magazine I like to buy every so often, *Popular Science Monthly.* I've had this one for a while and meant to show it to you. Look at this. A report by Octave Chanute."

Calvin sat at one of the checker tables and began reading the article. "Salivatin' salamanders! They made a flying machine and flew in it—Orville and Wilbur White!"

"I believe that's 'Wright.'"

"Sure it is! It says so right here."

"Nicht richtig, Wright. The Wright brothers."

"They sure are! Totterin' toads! I gotta make one of these! Thanks, Herr Steitz!" Calvin disappeared.

"Ach," Otto said, smiling, "he'll get it eventually."

On Tuesday over at the Dinkmeier place, Edna and Emil were at it again: "Emil, whenever I see you, you seem so sullen and depressed."

"Very good, Edna," he said. "Whenever you're near, that's how I feel."

"But don't you have any feelings for me, Emil?"

"Of course I do," he replied. "Most of them are bad."

One time, Gustav thought that it would be the right thing to do to see if he couldn't help Emil and Edna to get along better. He was right; he couldn't. The Dinkmeiers were miserable together and that's how they seemed to like it. They were like two maniacs in a death grip.

On Wednesday, Carl Mueller limped into Doctor Hess' office with a badly swollen ankle. "Sakes alive, man!" the doctor said, taking a quick look at his patient's ankle. "How long has it been in this condition?"

"Oh, 'bout a week, I reckon. I couldn't take it no more," Carl said.

"It appears this ankle is broken. And you've been walking around on it? Good grief, Carl! Why didn't you come to me right away?"

"Well, I sorta hesitated, hey. Every time I say somethin's wrong with me, why, Gertrude says these things wouldn't gurricken happen if I'd a-stop smokin'."

With a fresh wrapping, a pair of crutches, and instructions to "stay off of that ankle," Carl headed out the door—a cigar clenched between his teeth.

No sooner had Carl left when Wolfgang Johannes strolled in. "Hello, Doc. Got some time to give me an exam? Tillie says it's a good idea to get looked at every ten years or so, so here I am."

Doctor Hess gave him a thorough check-up and concluded, "Wolfgang, for a man of seventy years, I'd say you're in remarkable health. How do you do it?"

"Well, when we were married forty-five years ago, Tillie and I agreed that if I got angry about something, I'd go out and chop wood until I cooled off. And if she got angry about something, she'd send me out for a walk until she calmed down."

"Wait a minute. Why didn't she go for a walk, then?"

"I don't know. She said it was better this way. Anyhow, there are certain advantages to exercise and fresh air in the great outdoors."

On Thursday evening, Clara looked out of her shop window and saw that it was just starting to rain. Liesl was staying overnight with Martha, so Clara decided to turn in early and fall asleep to the sound of the rain on the tin roof of her shop.

By Friday morning, the sky was clear, though it was obvious to Clara by looking at the muddy road outside that at least a few good inches of rain had fallen during the night. With a basket hanging from her arm, she headed over to the general store to buy some needles and thread. When she stepped off of the boardwalk and into the road, her bare feet began sinking into the mud. She continued across and sank in deeper.

By the time Clara reached the center of the road, she was stuck in mud up past her knees. "This is horrible!" she thought. There were people on the boardwalks on either side of the road. She opened her mouth to call for help, but no sound came out. "There's Reiny, Hilda, and Fritzie! Are they ignoring me? Why don't they help me?" she wondered.

Up the road, approaching from the west, she saw a wagon pulled by four black horses racing toward her. She couldn't tell who was at the reins; a dark hood covered the driver's head and face. The horses were fierce and menacing. She tried to move, but her feet were stuck.

Again she cried for help. Still there was no sound. Fritzie walked toward her to the edge of the boardwalk, but stopped and just stared at her. She tried to shout "Help me!" at the top of her lungs, but her mouth wouldn't open. The horses and wagon plowed through the mud straight at her.

"Why can't I see who the driver is?" she wondered. "Why is he doing this?" The wagon came thundering down upon her, each horse wild-eyed and foaming at the mouth. "I'm going to die!" she thought, and—

She bolted upright in bed, her heart pounding, her skin cold and clammy. Frantically she looked around. She was in Martha's house; it was the middle of the night, and Liesl was sleeping soundly next to her. *What a nightmare! What am I so worried about?* She lay down, but was unable to fall asleep the rest of the night.

On Saturday over at the mill, Lester Mohr greeted Emil when he came in. "Guten Tag, Emil. Say, uh, how are things going at home?"

"Funny you should ask. Now Edna says she's not talking to me and, frankly, I get a lot more peace and quiet this way."

When Emil walked in the kitchen door, Edna was standing near the stove. Her eyes were filled with tears and red from crying. Emil remained by the door and braced himself for the inevitable firestorm, but it never came.

She sat at the kitchen table and said flatly, "Emil, I'm a self-centered, foolish woman. I've been an anxious, troubled Martha all my life, too busy taking care of my frivolous flotsam to pay attention to anyone else, even our own children. I feel so empty. Has my heart become so cold and brittle that I'm unable now to live?"

Emil walked up behind her and rested his hands on her shoulders for a moment. He went over to the roll top desk in the corner and got out some stationery and a pen. Placing them on the table in front of Edna, he said, "Write to the boys, Edna. They've been waiting all their lives for this moment. It's a precious opportunity. Don't let it slip away."

Page after page of indigo inscriptions poured from Edna's heart, freely punctuated by her tears.

# Chapter Thirteen ∾

On a Monday morning in late May of 1905 it was raining—again. Down at the general store, Herman Rickmeier and Carl Mueller hunched over a barrel, absorbed in a game of checkers. Herman looked up at Carl. "What's wrong there? You having a hard time concentrating, or what?"

"Yeah, I been gettin' these gurricken headaches lately. What can I do?"

"Ach, Carl," Herman said sympathetically. "I'll tell you what. When I have a headache, I go to Frieda and first she massages the tension out of my shoulders and neck. Then she rests my head in her lap, kisses me on the forehead, and gently caresses my temples until, finally, I feel like a new man."

"Ah," Carl said, "that sounds won'erful, Herman. Let's go find her."

"I was thinking you could have Gertrude help you."

"But she's my sister, hey. I dassn't do that. Don't hardly seem proper."

"Well, Frieda's my wife." After a moment of thought, Herman said, "You could do what the Indians do. Chew on some willow twigs. The Winnebago people say it's a dandy pain reliever, ya know."

"Frieda'd gurricken be a bunch more enjoyable, I imagine."

"Now, let's not go imagining about my wife, Carl. I think, in the long run, a willow twig would be less injurious to your health."

It rained all day Monday and all through the night. At six o'clock on Tuesday morning, Amelia Rickmeier—Grandma Rickmeier—crawled out of bed and went to her favorite place in her new home: the third-story tower at the top of the spiral staircase of her son Herman's house. She was accustomed to waking up with the sun, but it was raining—again—and the sun stayed well above a thick blanket of gray. She finished her devotions and gazed out through the rain-spattered glass at the puddles forming in the fields. She smiled at the scene below: several robins were gladly rescuing earthworms from drowning. *Well, it's gloomy down here, but if my tower stretched above the clouds, there I could see the sun still shining.*

Amelia picked up her Bible once more and turned to the passage she was meditating about: "For God who commanded the light to shine out of darkness, hath shined in our hearts, to give the light of the knowledge of the glory of God in the face of Jesus Christ. But we have this treasure in earthen vessels, that the excellency of the power may be of God, and not of us."

Amelia had seen a lot of darkness in her life but she had always found strength in the light. She looked at the window again. The raindrops trickling down the pane reminded her of the tears from her pain thirty-five years ago when her husband died. One day she was a happily married woman with two young sons, and the next day she was a grieving widow with two sad and frightened little boys to care for.

She remembered people saying at the time, "If you truly believe, you will not grieve," but they were wrong. Jesus wept for his friend Lazarus whom he loved. She wept for her husband whom she loved.

People said to her elder son, Herman, "Now you'll have to be the man of the house." But Amelia assured him, "You just be my son Herman. I will take care of you, and God will take care of us."

"Time will heal the pain," people said, but it didn't. Not completely. The pain was still there after thirty-five years, but she had learned to live with it and many unexpected joys and blessings came her way during those years.

Wednesday was beautiful, and Simon Klemme decided to take the whole family for a drive into town in their new, dark-blue Oldsmobile Touring Car. It was time to leave, but Simon was the only one who was ready. The motor was running, his driving hat and goggles were in place, and he was anxious to get on the road. Every so often he reached over and gave the bulb on the horn a squeeze. HONK! Finally, Anna staggered to the door carrying little Simon Jr. and dragging Catherine and Caroline; the girls had their hands over their ears.

Simon said, "Let's get going!" HONK! "What took you so long?" HONK!

Anna passed the children to Simon and climbed into the seat. "Simon, dear," she said, out of breath, with irritation in her voice, "the next time we go anyplace, you get everybody ready and I'll sit out here and honk like a silly goose."

"Sorry, Anna," Simon said sheepishly. "Next time, you can be the goose."

On Wednesday afternoon, Gustav Vriesen called on Ida Klietz and her daughters in their house adjoining the dance hall. A few days earlier, Ida's daughter Lydia had returned home. Lydia was another of the ten orphans Ida and her husband had taken in. Gustav had been to the dance hall for many celebrations over the years, but this was a visit he didn't relish making.

James Martin

Lydia had been unable to walk for the last six months following a serious accident in New York. She had been run over by a delivery wagon that badly broke her legs. Her doctor did his best for her, but with the passing of time it didn't appear likely that she'd ever be able to walk again. In recent days, Lydia had slipped into a depression so deep it was unclear whether she'd ever recover.

Ida and Sarah greeted Gustav at the door: "Welcome, Herr Vriesen. Thank you for coming. Lydia is in the dance hall. We know it is a most difficult thing to give hope to someone who has none, but we're grateful for whatever you can do."

Gustav entered the empty dance hall where he found Lydia sitting in a strange chair with wheels, staring out of a window at the bright, spring sunshine, her hands sliding back and forth on her legs, her eyes red and swollen from crying.

"Hello, Lydia. It seems so out of place, doesn't it? To see the sun shining so warmly when all you feel is the chill of darkness?"

Lydia nodded, looked down, and said, "After the accident, I thought I might have difficulty learning to dance again. But now, I don't know if I'll even walk again. Herr Vriesen, what is to become of me? From when I was a child, all I ever wanted to do was dance, but no dance troop in New York will want me now. I know my mother thinks I want to die. I don't. But I don't know how to go on living, or even why I should."

Gustav thought for a moment and asked, "What about Kurt? The two of you are planning to be married in three months, aren't you?"

"As far as I know, he's still in New York. I haven't seen him since before Christmas. I don't think he wants to see me again."

"Hmm. I'm sorry." Again he paused to think, and said, "Lydia, I'm curious about your chair with wheels. That's an amazing invention! Where did you get it?"

"In New York," she said. "It's called a 'wheelchair.'"

"This could be of great help to you," Gustav said. "You could be a dance instructor. I know of a woman in Chicago who was a marvelous ballerina—not unlike you—until she was stricken with polio. Now, she teaches ballet, using words and gestures to instruct her students."

"I don't think so. The joy of my life was to dance, not to teach dancing."

Again Gustav thought for a moment. Finally he said, "Lydia, we believe hope for living comes from God, not from ourselves. Therefore, your accident didn't change your real value at all. You're still a child of God whose basic purpose in life is to share the love of Christ as best you are able."

"I find that hard to believe. People are valued for what they do, not because of any intrinsic worth."

"That's a common human understanding, but not God's. I know of many dancers and other stage performers who are exceptional at what they do, yet are pathetic human beings. They have no kindness, no love, no joy. The love of God doesn't shine through their lives, but it still can shine through yours."

"Who would ever think of me as a reflection of God's love, especially now, with this broken body of mine?"

"We are hardly more than earthen vessels—easily shattered, as you know too well. Yet, the love of God within us is eternal."

The two of them sat together in silence for a few minutes. The outside world looked so bright. If only the inside world seemed that way, too.

"Think about it," Gustav said, "and be patient with yourself. You have reason to grieve the loss of the old Lydia, and every reason to embrace the new Lydia. The new Lydia is every bit as lovely as the old one. A young man of true character, one who loves you, will be pleased to embrace you as his wife."

On Thursday morning at Clara's seamstress shop, she and Martha were working on a curtain project for the Schmidts. Clara carefully smoothed out a piece of yellow dotted swiss on the cutting table and said, "This material reminds me of the curtains Edward and I used to have in our kitchen."

Martha smiled at her daughter and said, "You know, Clara, you've never told me much about Edward. All I really know is his name."

"There really isn't much to say. I didn't know too much about him, either."

"Where did you meet?"

"In a tavern. I was flirting with a young lad and things got out of hand. He started grabbing me, kissing me. He tore my dress. Edward was sitting at the bar, but came over and pulled the lad away. With one punch, he laid him out cold."

"Oh, my! Well, that was kind of Edward to help you."

"Yes, it was. That's what attracted me to him. We sat at a table and started talking. He said I reminded him of an old sweetheart of his—Elsie or Elsa, I think he said—and he didn't want some rapscallion taking advantage of me. That was fine by me. He's eighteen years older than I am, but that was all right, too."

"Eighteen years! He was almost old enough to have been your father."

"It's funny you should say that. I've been wondering about that, and I think I must have wanted somebody to take care of me the way my own father never could. But no father in his right mind would have treated me the way Edward did."

"Clara, that's all behind you now. You're doing well here, getting stronger by the day—more beautiful, too. You might want to marry again some day."

"Thank you, Mother. I'll keep that in mind."

On Thursday afternoon, Otto was sorting a delivery of hard-ware when Edna Dinkmeier hurried through the door, slamming it behind her. She cried, "Oh, I'm in a terrible pickle! I broke Emil's favorite walking stick. The hickory one."

"Dear me," Otto said, walking over to her. "Does he know yet?"

"Yes, I think the idea is probably sinking in."

"What did he say?"

"Well, he said, 'Don't swing that thing at me! Somebody could get—'"

"You were having an argument?"

"Yes, about our anniversary party on Saturday. Things got out of hand."

Otto shook his head. "I thought you two were getting along better."

"This is better. But we still argue. Sometimes I think we're improving, and then this happens. I'm so tired of it all. If only we could be at peace."

At the school on Friday, the younger students were working on arithmetic and the teacher Miss Benson presented them with a story problem: "If I gave you fourteen chickens and Miss Purdy gave you twelve more, how many chickens would you have? Anyone? Calvin?"

"Well, let me think. Fourteen, twelve—I'd have thirty-six chickens."

"Don't you mean twenty-six?" she asked.

"No, ma'am. I got ten at home."

"All right, that's correct, Calvin. Fourteen plus twelve is twenty-six, and ten more equals thirty-six."

"But one is probably going to die today," he said.

"I'm sorry, Calvin. Thank you."

"Then I'll have thirty-five."

"Thank you!"

"If they all die, I'll still have the twenty-six new ones."

"Calvin!" said an irritated Miss Benson.

"Yes, ma'am. Most of 'em are pretty healthy, anyway."

At the Rickmeier house on Friday night, things seemed wonderfully quiet to Frieda. Emilie, Grandma Rickmeier, and she were sitting in the parlor, working together on a quilt. Calvin was working on his homework at the kitchen table and Herman sat next to him to answer any questions his son might have.

Emilie said, "I'm glad you live with us now, Grandma. Now we can do things like this together."

"This is good for me, too," Amelia said. "I simply didn't want to stay by myself anymore, and I thank you all for opening your home to me."

"You know, Grandma," Emilie said, "this quilt reminds me of the one you made for me when I was a little girl."

"I'm glad you noticed, Emilie," Amelia said, smiling. "It's the same pattern, all right, and even some of the material is the same kind that we used for yours. The red here, and the yellow check, and this blue plaid. Remember?"

"I remember, Grandma." Without a word, Emilie ran upstairs to her room and returned a moment later with the old quilt. "It was in my cedar chest."

"So that's where it was," Frieda said. "I tried to get rid of that ratty, old thing, but I couldn't find it. Emilie, that was your favorite blanket for years and years, since you were three. And soon, you'll be twenty! Where do the years go?"

Frieda looked over at her daughter and noticed that her smile was gone and she had tears in her eyes. "Emilie?" Frieda walked over to her and guided her over to the davenport, where Emilie snuggled up to her mother the way she had when she was little.

"Oh, Mama," Emilie sighed, "I'm not your little girl anymore, but I don't know who I am. I'm not ready to marry Adam Schroeder and leave home. I want things to stay as they are, but they keep changing."

Frieda stroked her daughter's hair. "My dear girl," she said, "you have always been a dream come true for your father and me. I can't believe how wonderfully you're growing and maturing, yet I will always see the little Emilie within you. Adam hasn't even asked you to marry him yet, has he?"

"Oh, no! You're the first person I would have told."

"Well, I imagine he will. But try not to get ahead of yourself. Every time you and Calvin pass another milestone in life we're proud of you, but also a little sad because we enjoy having you live with us. Remember your first day of school? The red lunch pail?"

"Was it one like Calvin's?"

"That was really yours at first. We gave it to you on your first day of school."

"Oh, that's right! Now I remember!"

"That first time you went off to school, swinging your red lunch pail, I cried all day, till it was time for you to come home. Your father might not admit it, but so did he. When we change and the world changes around us, people often grieve over the loss of how things used to be. That's part of life."

"That's why I wonder if it would be better to live with you the rest of my life."

"No, Emilie. It's impossible for things to remain the same. You'd be miserable if you never grew up, and it would be wrong if we didn't allow you to. Yet, we'll always love you, and we'll always save a place for you and all of your loved ones in our home."

On Saturday at the general store, Frieda was doing a little shopping. In came Miss Benson with a basket tucked under her arm.

"Good morning, Mrs. Rickmeier!" Miss Benson said.

"Why, Miss Benson! How nice to see you! Calvin told us the good news. About the chickens. Tell me, when can he expect to receive them?"

Miss Benson burst out laughing and related the school incident to Frieda. The two women giggled hysterically until they cried.

"To tell the truth," Frieda gasped, "I wasn't sure what we were going to do with more chickens."

On Saturday night, there was an anniversary party at the dance hall for the Dinkmeiers. Emil and Edna had been married for forty years without killing each other and they wanted to take the opportunity to celebrate. Most of the community was invited. The band played waltz after waltz and a blissful spirit was in the air.

Also attending the celebration was Lydia Klietz; she wore a lovely pink and white dress, her favorite gown for dances, and one she hadn't worn for a year. This was her first appearance in public since she returned home. Lydia was all too aware of some people's opinion that handicapped people should stay home, out of public view. Nevertheless, she smiled radiantly, and everyone present seemed to be delighted to see her out and about.

At a moment when Lydia wasn't surrounded by well-wishers, the Vriesens took the opportunity to greet her. Minnie said, "Lydia, you look wonderful, just wonderful!" She leaned forward and kissed Lydia on the cheek.

Gustav took Lydia's hand. "Did something I said make sense to you?"

"Indeed," she replied. "The new Lydia believes she will make a wonderful dance instructor. Dance can still be the joy of my life, in a different way."

Lydia glanced up and saw Kurt stepping out of the crowd and walking toward her. For a moment, he stood motionless in front of her. She studied his face for a sign of what might be coming.

"Lydia," he said, "forgive me, please, for my self-centeredness. When it became clear that you might never walk again, I grieved the loss of the woman I thought I loved. But now, before me, I see the woman I really love. The time to mourn has passed. Now it is time to dance."

Kurt bent forward and gave Lydia a light kiss on the forehead, then a passionate kiss on the lips. With one hand, he held Lydia's hand. With the other, he guided her wheelchair out onto the dance floor and danced with his beloved.

# Chapter Fourteen ∾

What a glorious morning it was when Simon Klemme went out to milk the cows on that Tuesday in August of 1905. No, it wasn't the sunrise that made it so lovely. The sun was hiding behind a dark layer of clouds, and it had rained most of the night. And, no, it wasn't an especially pleasant day. It was hot and sticky and muddy, and the mosquitoes and flies were particularly pesky. Nonetheless, Simon said to his cows, "Good morning, ladies. Isn't it a glorious day?" And he kissed each one on the forehead.

No, he hadn't lost his mind. He had regained it. Just the day before, he had been working feverishly. He could feel in his joints that a storm was approaching and there was too much to do: more hay to bring in, the barn to clean, cows to milk, his wife to visit in the hospital, his children to care for. To top it all off, there was a hole in the barn roof to patch.

Simon climbed the tall ladder toward the roof with his repair tools and supplies in hand, cursing his lot in life: "Why couldn't my grandfather have settled in a different part of the country, where they have better weather? Why did Anna have to get sick now? Why don't my cows give as much milk as August Schmidt's do? Why did Carl have to design such an enormous barn? And why is the roof leaking after not even five years?"

Simon wasn't nearly finished with his list of complaints when he reached the top of the ladder. He put his left foot onto the roof, swung his right leg around, and lost his balance. He grabbed for the ladder to steady himself. It almost worked. However, he stepped back onto the ladder and inadvertently pushed away from the barn. For a moment, the ladder and he paused in mid-air. And then—straight back they fell, a flood of thoughts rushing through Simon's mind. All he was able to say was, "Ohhhhhhh!"

Slowly he opened his eyes. He was in the middle of a dark, damp thicket. Dim light filtered through. He noticed it was uncomfortably warm. He muttered to himself, "I always thought that when I died I'd go to heaven. But this must be—OH!" He gasped and choked and began coughing. Struggling to his feet, he realized he was standing chest-deep in a fortuitously placed haystack. *What a relief!* Simon inventoried the various reporting stations of his body. *Nothing's broken here, there, not even a scratch.* And he started whooping and hollering at the top of his lungs. "WhaHOOwha! WhaHOOEEEE!"

That is why Simon danced through the barnyard puddles and sang to his cows on that rainy Tuesday morning. It was truly a glorious day to be alive. He promised himself—and God—that he'd be more grateful after that.

On Wednesday morning at the general store, things were buzzing. Bruno the Saint Bernard was on guard, snoozing near the door. Gustav Vriesen visited with Otto Steitz. Wolfgang Johannes and Jacob Schmalfus played checkers at one table. Doctor Hess, who came in to mail a letter, settled down at another table to peruse the morning paper.

Gustav said, "Say, Doctor Hess, what's this I hear about Anna Klemme having appendicitis Sunday night? Simon brought her to the hospital in Sheboygan and you met them there?"

"Yes, Herr Vriesen. Her appendix had to come out. Doctor Thomas Jenkins did the operation. He's a fine surgeon. Anna's doing quite well. She's likely strong enough to go home early—by Saturday, I should think."

"That's wonderful," Gustav said. "I'll ride into town and see Anna today. Thank you for caring for her."

"Part of my job. But did you hear about Simon?"

"No. What?"

"He tipped over on a ladder from his barn roof on Monday. It could have killed him, but he's fine. Simon said it's the best thing that happened to him in a long time."

"Simon's a little funny that way," Otto said.

"Now," Doctor Hess said, "he's really got his hands full, caring for their three children while Anna's laid up. But Martha and Clara Schnuelle have been looking after them. They'll be all right."

Doctor Hess turned his attention back to the newspaper. After a minute, he burst out laughing. "Say, gentlemen," he said, "listen to this. The South Carolina Academy of Medicine is conducting a comparative study of the human heart. They're asking doctors and lawyers to donate their hearts for this important medical research. The article concludes by saying, 'All donations, however great or small, will be thankfully received.'"

"One thing's for sure," Otto said, "the lawyers' hearts will be much more valuable than those of the doctors."

Raising his eyebrows, Doctor Hess asked, "And why is that?"

"There'll be so few of them, of course," Otto said, laughing. "Just joking."

Doctor Hess smiled. "I know of people in every walk of life who are modern miracles, existing for years without showing any evidence of having a heart."

"Don't give 'em yours, Doc!" Jacob said.

"Why not?"

"Well, wouldn't it kill ya?"

"I think I'll wait till the proper time. Not a minute sooner."

Doctor Hess read quietly again for a while, then said, "Say, here's another one in the 'Quote For The Day' column. It's by Mark Twain. How true I have found this to be! 'If you pick up a starving dog and make him prosperous, he will not bite you. This is the principal difference between a dog and a man.'"

Otto chuckled and looked toward the door. "Dogs know how to appreciate life. I know my Bruno does."

On Thursday evening, Anna Klemme was napping in her hospital bed when she sensed the presence of someone next to her. "Simon!" she said, smiling and reaching up to hug her husband. He pointed to the table next to her bed where there was a vase with two dozen red roses. "Oh, Simon, they're lovely! Can we afford this?"

"We can," he said, "if you're not hospitalized on our anniversary too often. Happy anniversary, sweetheart. We've missed you so, the children and I. Believe me, things at home aren't the same without you. Clara was over earlier and Martha's watching the children now. Oh, here, the children made cards for you. Pretty flowers from Catherine and Caroline, and this one's from Simon Jr."

After studying little Simon's card for a moment, Anna asked, "Is this a rat?"

"I think so," he said. "He's very fond of them. Of you too, of course."

"What a little charmer," Anna laughed, "to give his mother a get-well rat. I can see how he takes after you."

The two of them delighted in their children's artwork, then Simon handed her another card. "This one's from me." Inside the card it read, "Happy tenth anniversary. Love, Simon." Below this he wrote, "My dear, ten years with you is like ten minutes, but ten minutes without you is like ten years."

They embraced again and he said, "You know, Anna, I've been in a foul mood for the last five months. Complaining too much, appreciating too little, taking too much for granted."

"Oh, you haven't been so bad. Nothing a blow on the head wouldn't cure."

"I could have been a lot better. That fall knocked some sense into me. Life is too precious to let it slip away like that. Promise me, please, if I get into one of those complaining streaks again, you'll tell me to go fix the barn roof."

On Friday, the last day of Vacation Bible School, Clara Schnuelle asked her class to make a list of things for which they were thankful. All the students put in a good effort, and Calvin Rickmeier came up with a nice list; among other things, he said he was thankful for skunk lard and handkerchiefs. Clara was intrigued by that because many boys don't admit to having anything to do with either. However, here was a student who was obviously mature enough to appreciate the usefulness of both.

"Calvin," Clara said, "I see you put skunk lard and handker-chiefs on your list. Is there any special reason?"

"Yes, ma'am. I smear a dab of scented skunk lard on the kerfchief, fold it all up, and stick it in my pocket. Then, if some girl tries to kiss me or some boy wants to pick a fight, I just take out my kerchief and wave it around. It's the idea as much as the smell, but it's a jim-dandy deterrent against such things. That's what Papa says. I've got one of my smelly kerchiefs right here. Would ya like to take a whiff?"

"Thank you, no!" Clara said, wincing. "I'll take your word for it."

The first thing on Saturday morning, Clara and Liesl officially set up housekeeping in their new residence. They now would live in the recently completed addition on the back of Clara's shop. In the five years since Clara had returned to the village, her seamstress business had gone surprisingly well. Last April, she made an offer to Reiny Hartung to buy the building and he accepted it. Construction on their private quarters started in May and now it was time for them to move in. Martha helped Clara and Liesl haul their few belongings down the road in a handcart.

"Mother," Clara said, "once again it's hard to believe. Yet another dream come true for us!"

"Yes, it is," she replied, "and once again, I'm proud of you."

"For what? Buying a place of my own?"

"No, not exactly, but I guess that's part of it. It's more that you were in such bad shape when you arrived on my doorstep in December of '99. To see that you're doing such marvelous things with your life, that Liesl's growing so well—all of this warms my heart. I'm deeply grateful for you."

"I was a mess. If it hadn't been for you and God's care through you, I don't think I would have made it. It certainly would've been harder to turn my life around."

"Ah, but I'll miss the two of you living with me."

"We can still have most of our meals together, can't we? Liesl and I wouldn't want to give that up, too."

"I'd be delighted if we could continue that! Mealtime is so much better when it's shared. And, my dear daughter, I still have more to show you about cooking."

By suppertime on Saturday, things at the Klemme household were getting back to normal. When Simon drove up in the Oldsmobile after picking Anna up at the hospital, the children were overjoyed to see her and climbed onto the running board, swarming around like a litter of puppies. Martha Schnuelle—bless her heart—had prepared a complete turkey dinner, with the guest of honor being one of her own turkeys. Martha was about to leave when they begged her to stay for dinner. "All right," she said, "if you'll allow me to do the dishes." They couldn't refuse her offer.

The food was delicious. After everyone was finished, Martha asked, "Caroline, did you enjoy the dinner?"

"Oh, it was wonderful!" Caroline said. "First the turkey got to eat the stuffing, then we got to eat the stuffing and the turkey!"

Martha started to clear the table and Anna said, "Martha, what a truly lovely woman you are. Clara as well. We can never repay your kindness, only give our deepest thanks to God for both of you."

She blushed and said, "We are the ones who are blessed to know such lovely people as you."

Martha left the room with her hands full of dishes, and Anna whispered, "Did you girls remember to thank Mrs. Schnuelle for all of her wonderful care while I was in the hospital?"

"Well," Catherine whispered, "we were going to before."

"But," Caroline continued, "Papa said, 'Thank you very much' to her and she said, 'Don't mention it.' So we didn't say anything."

On Sunday morning before worship, Clara and Liesl were nearing the church. Gerhardt Schultz was holding the door open for people and welcoming them in the role of an usher. When Clara and Liesl drew near, he opened the door with particular flair, bowed, and said, "Welcome, ladies!" Smiling, he extended his hand to Clara and assisted her up the stairs.

"How gallant!" she replied. "Thank you." She paused at the top of the stairs and glanced at Gerhardt. Their eyes met; their souls met for an instant frozen in time. The touch, the glance— that was the beginning of their romance, a moment Clara knew she would always treasure.

"Liesl," Gerhardt said, "you also look particularly lovely this morning."

"And gallant and thanks to you!" she said, following her mother inside.

Gustav Vriesen greeted the Rickmeiers in the back of the church. He said, "Amelia, how are you adjusting to your new home?"

"Oh, remarkably well, thank you. Cleveland was fine and all, but with neither of my sons living nearby, it was high time that I found one who would let me live with him."

Frieda said, "It's a delight to have you with us, and it's so important that Emilie and Calvin get to know their grandmother."

"Beside that, Herr Vriesen," Herman said, "she keeps me humble and honest. Whenever I say, 'When I was a boy... ' and start reminiscing about the old days, her ears perk up and she makes sure I stick to the truth. The problem is, I can't pretend I was the perfect child anymore. But I'm awfully glad she's here."

The service began and Gustav's sermon was, in part, a reflection on some of his observations around the community. By their various reactions, many in the congregation seemed to think the sermon was written especially for them.

"The expression of gratitude," Gustav said, "is nothing less than the gift of a priceless treasure. Appreciation is the mark of a generous and noble spirit, just as the habit of depreciation is the sign of a desiccated soul. When the Israelites complained against Moses that they preferred the yoke of slavery to the trials of freedom, he said to them quite correctly, 'your complaining, your ingratitude is not so much against us, but against God.'"

Simon Klemme thought about his own complaining during the previous week and prayed, "Forgive me, dear God, for whining so freely and trivially. We are really just fine."

"We turn," Gustav continued, "to the Savior and see how tenderly he appreciated even the simple things and the common people around him. Jesus came, at first, to call the people of Israel to repentance and salvation. But when the Canaanite woman implored him to heal her daughter, he marveled at the depth of her faith and had compassion on her. Oh, how life blossomed in his presence!"

From his place behind the organ, Eduardo D'Angelo looked out at the congregation and prayed, "Thank you, gentle Savior, for helping my family to find refuge and hospitality in this place."

"Many of us," Gustav said, "make the mistake of complaining that we are not happy. In doing so, we only increase our misery. Depreciation is like a boomerang, inevitably turning on itself. Appreciation is the catalyst of satisfaction, the pathway to a sense of joy. Do not focus, beloved, upon the blessings that elude you in the present but upon the blessings already gracing your life."

Emil and Edna Dinkmeier glanced at each other and would have held hands—if they could have reached across the center aisle.

"Beloved," Gustav said, "appreciation is the antithesis of depreciation. They are at opposite ends of a tug-of-war within the human heart. Appreciation invigorates. Depreciation suffocates. Appreciation brings out the best in others. Depreciation tears at the human will. Appreciation puts spring back in the steps of the weary and laughter in the voices of those who have fallen silent. Depreciation projects the road ahead as interminable, and multiplies the burdens of life by a hundredfold."

Reiny Hartung smiled at Otto, Fritzie, and Gerhardt, who were sitting together as father and sons.

"What is the secret to this?" Gustav asked. "It is 'love, which is the bond of perfectness.' As the French author, Gautier said, 'To love is to appreciate with the heart; to appreciate is to love with the mind.' When we see through the eyes of love, we see through the eyes of God. God grant us the vision of these eyes!"

# Chapter Fifteen 〜

It was a busy time in the days leading up to Thanksgiving Day in the year of our Lord 1905. On Sunday morning, Martha Schnuelle was at church worshiping with many other folks from the neighborhood, but her mind wasn't focused on the service. She was still recovering from the events of the previous week.

Eight days earlier, on Saturday, her son Conrad had dropped off his two children for several days while he and Charlotte attended a medical convention in Minneapolis. Martha thought she was up to the challenge. She really did. Five-year-old Norbert and four-year-old Martha: how much trouble could they be? After all, Clara's daughter Liesl was nearly five and a "perfect angel." Martha did not remember the expression from her child-rearing years, "One is like none, two is like ten." Selective amnesia can be a merciful thing, if not also deceptive.

They got ready for church the next morning. Martha instructed her grandchildren to be quiet and to sit still during worship. On their way out the door, they met Clara and Liesl walking down the road. Martha said, "Why don't we five all sit together?"

"Three little wigglers. Do you think that's a good idea?" Clara asked.

"I have confidence in you, dear," Martha said. "I'm sure you can manage the one, and I'll be nearby if you need help." Clara just smiled.

They approached the church and Norbert skipped ahead to open the door. He held the door and in went his four "women folk," followed by Gertrude Mueller, who leaned over and said to Norbert, "And how are you, my little man?"

"I'm fine, thank you," he replied politely.

After a pause, Gertrude said, "Aren't you going to ask how I am?"

"No," he said, "I want to go in."

Norbert squirmed between Gertrude and the door and disappeared inside. She smiled and said, "Well, just in case you were wondering, I'm fine, too."

Martha, Clara, and the children walked to the women's side and sat in one pew, adults on the ends, young ones in the middle. Before the service started, Martha reminded the children, "Remember. Pay attention and be good!" They were—at the beginning. The benevolence offering was collected and Martha put in a quarter, so grateful was she to have her grandchildren and daughter with her.

Gustav Vriesen started the sermon. About a minute later, little Norbert said quietly, "Gramma?"

Martha didn't reply.

A few minutes later: "Gramma? Gramma?"

The sermon continued despite Norbert's periodic calls. But she kept her mind steadfastly trained upon Gustav's voice.

All at once, to her utter embarrassment, Martha realized little Martha was no longer sitting next to her, but was standing at the foot of the pulpit, gazing intently up at Gustav, who didn't even notice her. In a few seconds, though, little Martha disappeared again under the pews. Martha peered down beneath pew level to locate her granddaughter. She was startled to see a whole school of small children scooting around, dusting the floor, and navigating past the legs of the oblivious adults. All the while, Liesl sat perfectly still next to Clara, who was smiling broadly.

In another minute, little Martha surfaced again and climbed

back up to her place between Norbert and Liesl. And, from time to time, Norbert's voice could still be heard: "Gramma?"

Finally, Gustav paused and said, "Better see what the boy's question is, Martha. I have a sermon to finish."

Through clenched teeth, Martha said, "What do you want, Norbert?"

"Gramma, what does 'iniquity' mean?"

At that point, Martha simply wanted to evaporate into thin air.

The service finally ended. Martha was still in a daze and there was very little talking as the five of them walked toward home. They reached Martha's house and Clara and Liesl continued on their way.

Liesl said, "Thank you, Grandma. You were very good today."

Clara said, "Thanks for your help, Mother. I don't think I could have done it without you."

Martha and her little guests returned home and the three of them spent much of the rest of the week in self-imposed exile. One evening, the two children cuddled with Martha on the sofa, one on either side. They sat and watched the flickering flames in the fireplace and Martha told them stories about when she was a little girl growing up in Germany, as well as the adventure and uncertainty of sailing across the ocean and coming to a new country.

After about a half hour, little Martha fell asleep, but Norbert showed no signs of letting go of the day. He gazed up at his grandmother, studying her white hair and the wrinkles in her face that were more prominent in the firelight. Looking at her, he felt his own smooth skin and asked, "Did God make me?"

"Yes indeed, Norbert. And you came out beautifully!"

He nodded thoughtfully and asked, "Did God make you, too?"

"Yes, many years ago!" she replied.

He considered this new information. He said, "Well, I guess God hadn't a-made emery boards way back then."

"That might be true," she laughed, giving him a hug.

After another pause, he asked, "Gramma, did you know Adam and Eve?"

"No," she chuckled, "they were from way before my time. On the other hand, Noah's wife and I were good friends."

On Saturday, the children left and Martha's home returned to quiet normalcy. At church on Sunday, when the benevolence offering was being received, Martha put in another quarter. She was grateful, of course, for the time to spend with her grandchildren, even happier they were not permanent residents. She breathed a prayer for them. *What a sad world this would be without children.*

Over at the Dinkmeiers' on Monday morning, Edna was in a foul mood, thinking about Thanksgiving and about all the blessings she didn't have. She said, "Emil, every year it's the same. Thanksgiving comes and I think, 'Well, what do I have to be thankful for?' You always say we can't afford to buy me a new dress for Thanksgiving, so I end up looking like one of the hired help."

Emil frowned at the breakfast concoction before him and muttered, "One thing's for sure. Nobody's gonna mistake you for the cook."

On Tuesday morning at Clara's seamstress shop, she was hard at work on a Christmas dress for her mother. She was so focused on the dress before her that when the shop door opened she was startled. Gasping and looking up, she saw Gerhardt Schultz holding the door open and smiling at her.

"I didn't mean to surprise you," he said. "I'm sorry."

"No. I'm fine. Please come in. Is there something I can do for you?"

"Not really. It's just that, uh." He paused and glanced at the floor. "I've been thinking." He looked at her again, deep into her eyes this time. "I've just never known anyone like you. I don't understand why, but I feel as if I've known you for more than a lifetime, maybe since the beginning of time. And I'm grateful for you. That's all I wanted to say."

"Oh," she said. She wanted to respond with something more meaningful, but all she could do was blush.

"I, uh… I'm sorry, Clara. Why should I think you'd ever have any interest in an ex-convict like me? I shouldn't have said anything. I won't bother you anymore." He turned and left.

On Tuesday evening over at the Rickmeier place, things were relatively peaceful. It was cold outside, but inside it was cozy and warm. In the parlor, Herman read the newspaper while Emilie was absorbed in *Tom Sawyer* and Amelia finished her work on a red and blue scarf. Frieda sat in the kitchen, darning socks.

From time to time, Herman's gaze was drawn upstairs. *Ah, my son Calvin. Up in his room practicing his violin. His third year of lessons and—ah—how handsome he looks with that beautiful instrument tucked under his chin! But—oh—how the sound betrays the picture, and—oohh—how the sound carries! The violin is such a mystery. How can such a sweet instrument produce such sour notes? Calvin plays the classics as no one else. Familiar pieces such as "Squeaky Hinge in G Minor" and "Ode To A Rusty Nail." And who can forget his immortal rendition of "Sonatina for Fingernails and Blackboard"? All the while, his faithful basset Rex sits beside him, mournfully howwwwling for all he's worth. Oh!*

At one point, Herman looked up from his paper and said out loud, "Ach, I know this one. 'Duet For Witch And Ghoul.'" After almost an hour, he could endure it no longer. "My ears!" he moaned. "Calvin, take Rex along to your next music lesson. Maybe

Eduardo can teach him to howl out of tune along with you."

"Now, Herman," Amelia said, "when you were taking violin lessons, you once shattered a window without even touching it! Calvin is just following in your footsteps. And I think he's doing well."

"Thank you for reminding me, Mother."

Finally, Frieda heard Calvin putting his violin away. *The sand in the hourglass must have run out.* She heard him shuffling toward the kitchen. He plopped into a chair next to the table, and put his head down.

Frieda looked up. "What's wrong, dear? You look discouraged."

"I am," he said. "Nothing's going right. The teacher said today that, with Thanksgiving coming, we should all be giving thanks for our blessings. But what do I have to be grateful for? None of the kids at school like me, I got a bad mark on my arithmetic test today, and I think I should quit taking violin lessons because I play terribly. Even Papa thinks so."

"Calvin, your father didn't mean to hurt your feelings, and I'm sure he doesn't want you to quit. You know how well he plays the violin now, yes?"

"Papa's great. But I could never hope to be like him."

"Ah. Grandma Rickmeier says you play better now than he did when he was your age."

"Really?"

"Yes. And as for your arithmetic test, one bad grade won't ruin your life. Talk to your teacher about where you need help and bring your work home next week so we can look at it together."

"All right. But I don't see what the point is. I'm never going to use arithmetic when I'm all grown up."

"Oh, you'll be surprised. Anyway, it helps you to think. As far as friends at school go, I can't tell you how many times I had that same feeling when I was growing up. I do know many of the children like you very much. Even on the days when you think you don't have any friends, remember that Emilie, Grandma, and your father and I will always love you."

"I know, Mama. I love you, too."

"Now, about Thanksgiving. Sometimes people think they need to be grateful only when things are just the way they want them to be, when everything is perfect. That almost never happens."

"It sure doesn't. Things are hardly ever the way I want."

"Living with gratitude makes every day precious. Sometimes people get in the habit of thinking about everything that's wrong and they're never happy. They always find something to complain about. But there are usually many more things going right."

"Is that what's wrong with me?"

"Well, if you're able to see more of the good things in life, you'll be happier."

Calvin thought for a while and asked, "Really, Mama? It really makes a difference for people to live gratefully?"

"Oh my, yes! Life becomes precious. You know, many people keep what's called a gratitude journal. It's a notebook they write in every day about things they're thankful for. I'd be happy to buy one for you. It wouldn't be cheap, so you must promise to use it. Then, every night before you go to sleep, you can write maybe five things that were good about the day. Would you like to try that?"

"Does anybody really do that?"

"Yes. I believe Herr Steitz keeps a gratitude journal. And I can think of no one who lives more thankfully than Otto. I've never told you this story before, but now I think you're old enough to hear it. Many years ago, before I met your father, Otto was married and lived in Chicago, as I understand, on the northwest side. He, his wife, and their two girls lived on the main floor of their house. They also had a boarder, a young, single man who rented the upstairs rooms and ate meals with them. One day, when Otto was gone, the man got into an argument with Mrs. Steitz about something or other. He strangled Mrs. Steitz and their two children."

"And they died? Oh, Mama!"

"Yes. Neighbors reported that the man ran away, but was shot and wounded in the leg by a sheriff who was passing by and heard the commotion. They never did catch the man. When Otto returned home, unaware of what had happened, some neighbors were there to meet him. They told him the sad news that his wife and children had been killed."

"That's awful!"

"Yes, it is. But, you know, there isn't a trace of bitterness in Otto. He could have become hateful and angry. Instead, he remained loving and kind. He never found another wife, but he's like a daddy and a grandpa to many children."

"That's how I think of him and so do my friends. He's like a grandpa."

"I still remember what he said years ago when he told me the story. He said, 'I am deeply grateful I was blessed with a lovely wife and wonderful children, whom I had the opportunity to love and enjoy for a time. Some people never get that chance, and others receive such opportunities, but end up wasting them. I still have some wonderful memories of our life together. Even if my memory of Elsa and the girls fades someday, it won't matter anymore, for our love will still be alive in the heart of God.'"

Wednesday was a cold, blustery day, the kind of a day late in the autumn when a person would rather stay inside. But, after milking, Herman Rickmeier took his deer rifle out of the front closet and went out. He enjoyed hunting. Beside that, they were counting on the meat for their Thanksgiving dinner.

He was out more than eight hours and made a large circle through all of his favorite spots. During the day, Herman had plenty of time to think. *It's been a good year. Not easy, but good. Lots of blessings to count. The crops are in, yields are up, prices are fair—except for wheat and pork. We have enough for ourselves and plenty to share.*

He headed north through seven different wood lots where he usually saw deer. *There's the new roof we got after the chimney fire in March. That was the week after Frieda's father died. He had a good life. Mother moved back to the village, and I have my precious loved ones to care for.*

By early afternoon, he headed west into the hills and followed the foot of the ridge to the south. *Some lucky deer is running out of time to provide us with Thanksgiving dinner. We'll find something to eat—canned beef. That'll be fine.*

The sun was setting and he began following the river back toward home. During the day, he had seen several deer, but wasn't able to get a clean shot at any of them. *Calvin and his violin—my violin. He's so much like me when I was his age. We'll have to get him an instrument of his own. He really is improving. Emilie and he are growing up so well. And Frieda. How grateful I am for her—all of them. What would life be like without loved ones? I hate to think of it.*

All Herman had to show for his day-long hike were burr-covered clothing, a growling stomach that hadn't been fed, and a throbbing right ankle; he twisted it when he fell out of a tree. When he was about three hundred yards from home, he stopped and studied the silhouette of the farm against the evening sky. Tears of gratitude came to his eyes.

"Dear, dear God," he said, "what have I done to deserve such blessings, such wonder? Such a beautiful world you have made. What a privilege you have given us in this gift of life. Thank you. I am honored that you have entrusted my loved ones into my care. May I always cherish these precious gifts."

# Chapter Sixteen ⌒

By eight o'clock on a Monday morning in August of 1906, it was already one of those sultry summer days. The air was hazy and thick. Bruno the Saint Bernard was snoozing in the shade of the American elm on the west side of the general store, taking advantage of the last cool breezes of the morning.

Inside the store, a theological debate raged and Otto was trying to stay out of it. The discussion had to do with Gustav Vriesen's sermon from the day before. The Scripture text for the sermon was Galatians 3:28: "There is neither Jew nor Greek, there is neither bond nor free, there is neither male nor female: for ye are all one in Christ Jesus."

Gustav had asserted that, because the Lord God is the God of all people and all nations, there is a need to include more English in the congregation's worship and other official business. He said, "We will still, of course, embrace our German heritage. However, by including more English, we will help ourselves—adults as well as children—to acclimate more quickly to our new homeland. This will also encourage our English-speaking neighbors to worship with us."

That's what all the hubbub was about. And Reiny Hartung was dead set against it. "Es ist unser Vorrecht, unsere Sprache mit unseren eigenen Leuten zu sprechen!" ["It is our prerogative to speak our language among our people!"]

August Schmidt tried to approach things more philosophically. "Glaubst du nicht, daß Gott Englisch versteht?" ["Don't you think God understands English?"]

"Ja, natürlich!" Reiny said. "Doch wenn Deutsch für den Heiland gut genug ist, ist es auch gut genug für mich!" ["Yes, naturally! However, if German was good enough for the Savior, then it is good enough for me!"]

Otto continued with his work, muttering to himself: "I didn't realize that. Was Jesus the first German-speaking Jew or were there others before him?"

On Tuesday afternoon, Martha Schnuelle came back to the village after having been in Chicago since early June. For the past two months, she'd been taking care of Conrad's family. In late April, Charlotte and Conrad had become the proud parents of little Wilhelm, named after Martha's late husband. After giving birth, Charlotte developed some nagging health problems; in early June she came down with consumption. Conrad was so busy doctoring his patients that he didn't have time to care for his wife, the baby, and their two other children all by himself. The help of another person was urgently needed.

When Martha decided to leave in June, Otto offered to give her a ride to the train station in Sheboygan. She packed a few things, said good-bye to Clara and Liesl, and off they went, over the bridge and out of the village, riding together in Otto's horse-drawn carriage. These two old friends—older than some, younger than others—were life-long companions. They had grown up together through childhood and school in the same town. They had been witnesses at each other's weddings and had emigrated from Germany at the same time.

At first, Otto and his wife lived in Chicago while Martha and her husband moved to Bierville. Within several years of settling in their new homeland, however, each one was widowed. Otto's children also died. He moved to Bierville and opened the general store.

Otto and Martha were never sweethearts, though many people thought they should have married years ago. Now they were over sixty. They weren't in love, romantically speaking, but they did love each other and had the deepest respect and affection for one another.

The train was ready to leave and Martha stepped up into the coach. Otto said to her, "Gnädige Frau, you are the song in the heart of our community. Do the work of an angel for your loved ones, but then hurry home!"

Martha smiled and replied, "The Lord God is our song, Otto. Isn't it a blessing that God is staying with you and coming with me? This way, we may all keep singing."

For a while, they thought lots of sunshine and fresh air would help Charlotte to a speedy recovery. However, by the end of July it became clear things had gotten a little worse. Any recovery would be a long time in coming. So it was with a heavy heart that Martha returned to the village.

On Wednesday a few minutes before noon, Martha walked into the general store and tearfully made the announcement:

"After talking it over with Clara last night, I've decided to move to Chicago and live with Conrad and his family."

Otto walked from behind the counter and took hold of Martha's hand; but neither he nor anyone else in the store could think of a thing to say. Moving? Martha? Bruno raised his head with as sad an expression as ever there was on a Saint Bernard. With big, bloodshot eyes he looked as if he'd already been crying for a week over the sad news.

It was a painfully difficult decision for Martha. Only her love for her son and his family in this time of need caused her to give up the familiar security of the village for life in a big city. She disliked the idea of leaving Clara and Liesl, but believed Conrad needed her more. She told everyone this was a temporary move, but she had no idea when she might come back to the village, if ever.

Martha planned to return to Chicago on Saturday's noon train, so she spent much of the next few days packing and cleaning. From time to time, people from around the community stopped in, expressing their sorrow and offering words of comfort and encouragement.

On Wednesday afternoon, Anna scowled at the prospect of preparing supper. It had already been a frustrating day. She felt overwhelmed by the endless list of farm chores and the necessity of constant attention to her children. What bothered her most was the news that Martha was moving.

When Anna came inside to make supper, she was exasperated to see such a messy house. The children were having trouble learning to pick up after themselves. This was a particular problem for Simon Jr., who had the uncanny ability of cluttering up a room just by walking through it. Anna thought she'd teach them all a lesson.

"Catherine, Caroline, little Simon," she said, "help me make supper. We're having scrambled eggs, toast, and jam."

Anna started cracking the eggs and emptying the contents into a mixing bowl. However, instead of collecting the shells to put into the compost pile, she tossed them on the floor of the kitchen.

"Mama," Catherine asked, "what are you doing?"

"I'm making supper, dear."

"No," Caroline said, "why are you throwing the eggshells on the floor?"

"Oh, I'm just tired of having to pick up after everyone else. If no one else in this family is concerned about having a tidy house, why should I be?"

"Mama!" the girls shouted in unison. "Mama?"

With calculated coolness, Anna kept cracking eggs and dropping the shells on the floor. The girls began to cry.

Anna said to herself, "You've almost achieved your goal. Stay the course!"

Little Simon absorbed it all with wonder and amazement. To Anna's surprise, he seemed to think this was a real improvement and started finding other things to dump out. Split peas, rice, and dried beans bounced on the floor and scattered to the far corners of the room.

Anna didn't know what else to do, so she kept cracking eggs and tossing the shells down. By this time, the girls were close to hysterics:

"Mama, what are you doing? Mama?"

"All right, Mama!" Simon said, "Let's get some flour!"

"Wait!" Anna said. "This is not working." Anna sank to the floor next to the girls, and the three of them cried together. Simon Jr. was unaffected. He shuffled through the beans and rice, making locomotive sounds. With mighty hops he smashed the shells into smaller and smaller pieces.

At the climax of the confusion, Simon Sr. walked in and calmly surveyed the chaos. "Did I miss something here?" he asked. "A tornado?"

Anna looked up at him, sobbing. "I was teaching them a lesson on the importance of tidiness."

"Well, then," he said, "it appears you succeeded. I'm convinced. Well done."

On Thursday afternoon, Clara and Liesl were preparing to leave for a three-day hat-makers convention in New York. Clara was getting started in the hat business and wanted to learn more about the latest styles and trends. Simon parked his Oldsmobile in front of Clara's shop and helped them get in for the trip to the train station. She'd been planning this for weeks; now she didn't want to go.

"Mother, I'm sorry," Clara said. "I wish I could help you more to get ready."

"Don't give it another thought, dear. The important things will get done. Besides, I don't have to clear out my house, just pack and tidy up."

"Take good care of Conrad's family. And have a nice dinner with Mrs. Schultz this evening. Oh, and make sure you ask her for any news about Gerhardt, how he is, then tell me the next time you write. Good-bye, Mother. I love you."

Off to the train station they went.

That evening, Martha was at Hilda Schultz's house for dinner. During the meal, Martha asked, "And how is your Gerhardt? Do you hear from him often?"

"Oh, yes," Hilda said. "He's working in Detroit at an automobile factory. And he's been keeping company with a young French woman named Yvette."

"A French girl!" Martha replied. "Oh, la, la! Trés bien!"

"However, I think it's more friendly companionship than a romantic relationship. He actually talks about your Clara much more. He asks how she is and if I've seen her lately. He says how much he admires her. And misses her."

"Is that a fact? Why, earlier today Clara told me to make sure to ask you about Gerhardt. Oh, Hilda. The two of them should be writing to each other. Enough of this second-hand information. They don't need us to mediate."

The two ate in silence for a while. Hilda said, "Martha, I can never thank you enough for your kindness to us, especially to Gerhardt when he was in trouble so often and in jail. When so many people of Bierville turned their backs on us or didn't know what to say, Clara and you were among the compassionate few who walked with us through the valley of shadows. I'll always be grateful for that."

"It was our pleasure," Martha said, taking Hilda's hand. "What a lonely life this would be if we had no one to accompany us through those difficult times!"

On Friday morning, Martha started carefully packing a steamer trunk with some of her most precious treasures. At one point she stood before the trunk holding a framed photograph taken on her wedding day. There she was: forty years younger, standing with her husband, whom she hadn't seen for so many years. On either side of them were Otto Steitz and his young bride Elsa.

For a moment, the distance of time separating Martha from the people in the picture seemed to melt away. She imagined herself talking with the other three. *Well, Willie dear, what do you think of our newest grandchild? Now we have Liesl—Clara's daughter—and Conrad's three. Norbert, Martha, and now Wilhelm. I'm doing my best to tell them about their grandfather, but I wish they could know you personally.*

Martha was still gazing into the picture when she heard a knock at the door. She opened it and there stood Anna Klemme and her three children.

"Good morning, Anna, children. Won't you come in?"

Anna tried to smile; tears filled her eyes and she said, "Oh, Martha!"

The two women embraced and cried. For a few minutes, they simply held onto one another. Martha noticed the three children looking up at them in amazement. Then, as if not wanting to be left out, they buried their faces in the two long dresses and began to cry. Martha and Anna laughed.

When things were calmer, Anna said, "Martha, I'll never forget all of your expressions of kindness—when Simon and I were first married, when the barn burned down, when our children were born. Your many gracious deeds shine as jewels in a crown upon your head."

"And what a precious friend you've been to me," Martha replied, "sharing with me your spirit of joy, your family, all the times you and Simon helped me with things I couldn't manage by myself. You made me feel useful. Loved. Alive."

Simon Jr. was sitting on the floor, looking at one of the grandchildren's baby photographs. Martha asked, "Who's that, Simon? A baby?"

Catherine pointed to the photograph that Martha was still holding and asked, "Who are those people?"

Martha leaned over, showing them the picture. "This is from my wedding day. This is Otto Steitz and his wife Elsa. And this is my husband Willie. And here I am."

Caroline's mouth dropped open, and she looked back and forth at Martha—and the picture—and back at Martha. "No," Caroline said.

"Yes," Martha said.

"No," Caroline insisted.

Catherine said, "I like the real one better."

"Which is the real one?" Martha asked.

"You are," Catherine said. "She's a picture, and she's pretty. But you're the real one, the one I love."

Martha's heart melted.

By Friday evening, Martha was painfully tired, emotionally exhausted, and famished. She decided to stop for a while and get something to eat. But the pantry was bare, except for six jars of pickled beets. Everything else had been eaten, given away, or packed.

"Last year was good for beets," Martha said wearily. She opened one of the jars, sat at the kitchen table, and bowed her head to pray. There was a knock at the door. It was Gustav and Minnie Vriesen.

"Are we too late?" they asked. "Have you already eaten? We thought we'd join you for supper."

Each of them brought in a basket of freshly-prepared food: green beans with bacon, potato salad, roasted chicken, dinner rolls, apple pie, "And pickled beets," Minnie said, walking to the table and picking up the jar.

"Angels from heaven," Martha said. "That's what you are."

The three of them sat at the table and gave thanks for the feast. They ate and talked, enjoying one another's company.

Martha smiled and said, "So, I believe this is our last supper." She thought for a moment, then continued, "Saying good-bye to this village, to all of you people has been much harder than I expected. But my son's family needs me desperately, so there really is no decision. I must go."

"You know," Minnie replied, "this is a wonderful opportunity for you to be with Conrad's family. They certainly need your help, but you'll also get reacquainted with Conrad and Charlotte, and you'll be able to help the children to grow up and know them in ways you wouldn't otherwise. Gustav and I will keep an eye on Clara and Liesl, but we'll all miss you! We have never had a friend like you in the church, such a wonderful traveling companion on the journey of life."

"That's what you are," Gustav said, "a wonderful companion on the journey of life. We all need them, and you have been so for a great many people, including us. We help one another along the way and share each other's burdens and joys. We try to stay on the path that Christ asks us to follow. Sometimes we sing and play together along the way. All of these good people make life so rich and rewarding."

He paused and became more serious. "You know," he said, "I can't always tell what people believe, even sometimes if they believe anything. Some travelers decide to leave the trail. They get sidetracked, go off on their own, and leave the way of love behind. But you, by the way you live, testify to the truth of the gospel of

Christ. God bless you, Martha! May all of God's children be blessed with a few kindred spirits, a few companions along the way who are as lovely as you."

# Chapter Seventeen  ∽

The Monday before Easter of 1907 was one of those near-perfect April days when, if only for a fleeting moment, everything seems right with the world. Gustav Vriesen was sitting with Minnie at their kitchen table, taking it all in. What is it about morning sunshine that so eloquently conveys a message of optimism to the human soul? The blending songs of robins, wrens, and goldfinches, all staking their claims for a new season, seemed a fitting accompaniment for the grandeur of this new day, a gift from God, a vision of how life can be.

Setting his cup of coffee on the table, Gustav said, "How is it, then, that otherwise good people can allow bastions of evil to remain barricaded within, impervious to God's song of re-creation that a new day such as this rises to sing? Somewhere in there, our human finitude is mixed in."

Minnie nodded and replied, "That people should remain unaffected by so many powerful displays of God's unmerited grace is, indeed, a mystery to me, too. They're all good people. They just can't seem to get along."

For several months, Gustav and Minnie had been mulling over some painful information they received about two separate disputes with very similar circumstances. Two pairs of brothers in their congregation operated their family farms in partnership, but were constantly at each other's throats. The Vriesens cared a great deal for these people and agonized with them, and recently, the tension in both situations had increased. There seemed to be no easy solution for the families involved, but they all deserved better.

Gustav said, "What do the stories of our faith have to say to this situation?" He was speaking as much to himself as he was to Minnie.

"Let us see what wisdom God has to offer," Minnie replied. "In the meantime, it's a beautiful day!"

On Tuesday afternoon, Anna Klemme thought there'd be no harm in taking a little catnap. Her three children were playing circus together in the backyard. Simon was working nearby in the barn. It seemed to be a good idea for about ten minutes, until she was awakened by muffled cries of anguish from outside. When Anna reached the back porch, she was astonished to see Catherine and Caroline, each wearing a wooden keg that covered them down to their knees. The two "kegs with legs" teetered and wobbled on top of a three-foot-high platform.

Simon Jr. stood on the ground, hitting the kegs with a four-foot stick, yelling, "Jump! Jump!"

"Simon Jr.!" Anna said, "What's the big idea? What are you doing?"

"We're doing tricks. They're being grizzly bears and I'm the circus trainer."

Anna lifted the kegs off of the girls' heads, and Caroline said, "It was his big idea! What a dummy!"

"He wanted us to be human cannonballs," Catherine added, "but he couldn't find Papa's gunpowder. So we're being grizzly bears instead."

Anna shuddered. "We need to go in the house and talk." She glared at Simon Jr. and said, "What are you trying to do, become an only child? And you girls!" she said, turning to them. "You're

smart enough to recognize a bad idea. You don't have to do whatever your brother says. Use your heads! While you still have them!"

On Wednesday afternoon, things were pretty quiet at the general store—a little too quiet for Otto's taste. Gustav walked in to
pick up his mail and asked, "Otto, do you have time to join me for
a little coffee? There are some things related to the Easter sermon
I'd like to mull over with you."

"Gladly," he replied. "I always enjoy a good theological discussion."

They poured some coffee for themselves and sat at one of the
checkers tables. Gustav said, "How many times do you think
people have read or heard the Easter story from one of the gospels?
Ten times, twenty-five times, a hundred times or more?"

"Perhaps. It all depends on who the people are—their ages,
how active they are in church, how much they read."

"That's true, but isn't it possible for someone who has heard
the Easter story even a hundred times to miss the point?"

"Yes, of course. It is often the case that, in order for people to
see things differently, to understand a new way of thinking, something has to have changed in their lives. They have to see it from a
different perspective, a different angle."

"Ah, I've been thinking that very thing, Otto. There's a certain
problem I've been concerned about for a long time. I've been perplexed about how to address it in a way that might finally help
people to understand. Thank you. This has helped me a great deal."

Clara Schnuelle came through and went over to check her
mail. Otto smiled and said, "Clara, there's another letter to you
from Gerhardt in Detroit. It seems that things in the automobile
industry have really been heating up."

"Herr Steitz, you're making me blush. Do you watch
everyone's mailbox as closely as you watch mine?"

"No, just the ones of people I especially care about."

Clara opened the letter and read it. "Otto," she said, "do you have a Bible nearby? Gerhardt says, 'Although we have been friends for a long time, I've never known anyone like you, and I realized that the first part of verse four in Isaiah, chapter forty-three is a reflection of my feelings for you, and I wanted you to know.' What does that verse say?"

Gustav said, "I don't think you need to look it up. That's one of my favorites, about God's love for the people of Israel. But, uh." He paused. "Are you sure you want me to tell you? It's a little personal."

"Please. You already know, anyway. And it's just the three of us here."

"Very well. A paraphrase would be something like, 'Thou art precious in my sight, and honoured, and I love thee.'"

"Oh," Clara said, smiling and blushing.

"Ah," Otto said, winking at Clara. "Things in Detroit are really heating up!"


On Thursday, Gustav was serving Holy Communion to some of the homebound people of the parish. He found it deeply mean-ingful to celebrate the Lord's Supper with people who were long-time veterans of the cross. One woman, Anna Kleinschmidt, was hard of hearing after suffering a stroke several years earlier. When they visited, Gustav wrote notes to her on a slate and she responded verbally. When they celebrated the sacrament, he opened his Bible to different passages and pointed to the beginning verse. She began reading in her squeaky, raspy voice and he stayed in time: the Lord's Prayer, the Twenty-Third Psalm, the story of the Last Supper from the Gospel of Luke. Unshakable faith radiated from Anna's soul.

Gustav had also found that some folks were more interested in "spirits" than in spiritual matters. Recently at Wilhemina Heckendorf's house, he had set out the bread and cups of wine and was proceeding with the communion liturgy. He offered her a piece of bread, but before he was able to take a piece for himself, she said in an irritated voice, "Aren't I supposed to get some wine with this?"

It reminded him of the previous time he brought communion to her. After setting out the elements, he had mentioned to her, "At church, we'll be having communion on the Sunday after Christmas."

"But I get mine today!" she said, grabbing her cup of wine and downing it with great relish.

This time he left shaking his head and muttering to himself, "How meaningful can this be? Next time, it's grape juice for Wilhemina."

On Saturday night at the parsonage, Gustav was telling Minnie about the Easter sermon. "I think it's a good sermon, but it's taking a bit of a risk. It incorporates a Jewish folktale in order to get the point across, but I reinterpreted it to speak an Easter message. It's a story I remember hearing from Rabbi Mendelssohn in Hanover."

"Oh," Minnie said, "I haven't thought of him in years! He was such a kind old gentleman."

"And faithful," Gustav replied, "learned and faithful. After talking with Otto on Wednesday, I decided to tell a story as part of the sermon tomorrow. Jesus taught in parables, little stories. The Bible is mostly made up of stories. So using a different approach to the Easter message might be just the thing for helping it to be heard in a new way."

On Sunday during worship, before Gustav started his sermon, he located the two sets of brothers. Each brother sat in perfect opposition to the other on the men's side of the sanctuary. Gustav breathed a silent prayer that the whole congregation, particularly the four brothers, would be open to receiving his Easter message. After reading the Easter story from John, he said:

"This is one of our most important stories. The resurrection of Jesus Christ is the foundation of our faith. Yet, sometimes, because we are so familiar with certain stories, it is difficult to understand them in new ways. Think for a moment. When did the Easter story become real to you? Or is it yet?"

Gustav looked around the congregation and saw people's gazes turning away from him as though they were searching their souls. He continued:

"There are many things here that are not easy for many people to accept at face value. Don't get lost in the details. Instead, focus on the heart of the story. If Christ has been raised by God, then love is more powerful than hatred, life is more powerful than death, and forgiveness has the power to overcome and transform sin."

Several people nodded their heads in agreement; a few of the men were nodding off to sleep. *Hmm. What to do?*

"HOWEVER," he shouted—*that took care of the sleepers*—"it is easy for me to believe the truth of the Easter story because I have seen the same truth at work again and again in human history and in my own life. What I love about the Easter story is that it takes into full account the destructive power of evil and the suffering and sorrow that evil causes. But then the power of God overcomes the evil, heals the suffering, and transforms death into new life."

Gustav looked around at the four brothers. Their arms, which had all been crossed in a defensive posture, were now relaxed and their hands rested quietly in their laps.

"When the Easter story becomes our story, we really begin to live. That's what happened in the lives of Jesus' disciples, the men and the women who followed him. Before they experienced the truth of Easter, they were timid, waffling, fearful creatures who had miserably failed the test of faith. After Easter they were courageous, confident, loving souls. Through the power of God they were strong enough to overcome the power of evil in this world."

Gustav looked over at Otto and recalled the evil and heart-break that Otto had been forced to overcome.

"We see the same transformation in Saul of Tarsus. His greatest pleasure in life had been persecuting Christians, hounding them like animals, having them arrested, and putting them to death. However, the beginning of his metamorphosis into the apostle Paul was on the road to Damascus. When he heard the voice of the risen Christ cry out, 'Saul, Saul, why persecutest thou me,' the transformation was begun. Saul's complete change of heart would not have happened unless he had experienced the reality of Easter in his own life."

Gustav glanced over at Clara and thought of the many ways her life had been redeemed and transformed.

"When the Easter story becomes our story, that's when we really begin to live. Is the Easter story your story yet? Have you seen that love is more powerful than hatred, that life is more powerful than death, and that forgiveness has the power to overcome and transform sin? Some resurrections take longer than others.

"I have an Easter story to tell you from long ago, about a thousand years ago. It's a tale of evil, redemption, and grace."

"In the foothills of the Alps in what is now western Austria-Hungary there lived a man and woman who were good people, newly married at the village church. They tended their flock of sheep and grew grain and other crops. For much of the year the sheep grazed in the alpine meadows. A sparkling, crystal stream, fed by the snow-covered peaks far above, flowed down the mountainside and past their house. The water was delightful. They called it 'Living Water.' It was the perfect place to live, a glimpse of paradise, they thought. A few years passed, and the woman gave birth to a son. And two years later, they had another son. The man thought, 'These boys will be a real blessing in helping us to farm.'

"On Sundays, they would walk together to worship at the village church and to visit with their neighbors, most of whom they hadn't seen since the previous Sunday. The parents loved their sons dearly and the two boys grew. As they grew, they argued and wrestled with one another as boys often do. But, by the time they were young men, their arguments were more heated and their wrestling matches were more ferocious.

"'My sons,' the father said with a smile, 'you are not Cain and Abel. Make sure you don't kill each other.'

"The father didn't realize their childish rivalry had already grown into a man-sized grudge. They didn't really like each other at all. On Sundays, they'd all still worship together at the village church; the boys sat on either side of their parents. But on Mondays, the truces were cancelled and they went back to battle as usual. Eventually, the mother and father did notice that their sons didn't get along well at all. This broke their hearts, because they loved their sons more than they loved their own lives.

"One Sunday, the village priest quoted Jesus, saying in Latin, 'This is my Commandment, that ye love one another, as I have loved you.' The father took this as an opportunity. 'My sons,' he said, 'your mother and I and the Lord Jesus have loved you. Therefore, the two of you should love one another.'

"The older son glared at his brother and said, 'Father, I'm sure the Lord Jesus never meant that I had to love such a lazy oaf as this!' On and on it went.

"Not many days later, the father and his two sons were up in the foothills watching over the sheep grazing in the meadow, and there was trouble. One of the sheep stepped too close to the edge of a steep drop-off and slid into a deep ravine.

"'It's your fault!' the older son shouted.

"'No, you were supposed to be watching!' Back and forth it went: 'It's your fault!' 'No, it's your fault!'

"They began shoving each other. The father hurried toward

them to break up the fight. One son gave the other a hard shove; he fell back into their father, sending him tumbling down into the ravine, where at last he skidded to a stop near the stranded sheep. The two scrambled down the hill to help, yelling at each other, 'It's your fault!' 'No, it's your fault!' On and on they went.

"They reached the bottom and their father struggled to his feet. There was a gash on his forehead and a stream of blood ran down his face. Tears mixed with blood in his eyes, so he could hardly see.

"He blinked and squinted at his two sons for a moment and said: 'Your mother and I have loved you as best we could all these years. But we can't go on like this. You can't go on like this. I will divide the sheep, divide the land. You may build your own homes. Your mother and I will build one for ourselves. We will help you both all we can, but we can't make the two of you love each other.'

"That's what happened. The land and the sheep were divided. The father helped each of the sons to build homes about a quarter of a mile apart. The sons took turns helping their father and mother to build a home for themselves on the mountainside where they kept their long-suffering watch over their sons. The mountain stream served as a natural dividing line separating the two brothers and their sheep and their land. The father built a bridge over the stream, but it was only used by the father and mother. They were the only connection between their two sons. Although the sons weren't living in peace, at least there was an absence of all-out war.

"Time passed. Some things changed and some stayed the same. The parents grew older and didn't come down to help their sons as often as before. The younger brother married and had children. The older brother stayed single. They all went down to the village church on Sundays. Each brother prospered at farming and each carried a heavy load of animosity toward the other.

"More time passed. Something else began to change. Was it the

Living Water that finally started to melt their hearts of stone? Was it all of the prayers that had been offered to heaven from the mountainside? Was it that, one summer day, the older son looked across the field at his brother's children playing together, and the younger son looked at his own children playing together, and they each thought, 'I wish I could do it all over again'? Whatever the reason, things began to change.

"One day, the older brother said to himself, "It is not fair that I have this beautiful flock of sheep all to myself—far more than I need. My brother and his wife have five children to feed, while I have only myself to care for. But there is one thing I can do. I will take one of best sheep from my flock each Sunday evening, carry it on my shoulders, and put it in with my brother's sheep. He will never know." So each Sunday night he carried one of his sheep across the bridge and placed it in his brother's flock.

The younger brother also said to himself, "It is not fair that my family and I have this beautiful flock of sheep all to ourselves—far more than we need. I have five children to care for me in my old age, and my brother has none. But there is one thing I can do. I will take one of best sheep from my flock each Sunday evening, carry it on my shoulders, and put it in with my brother's sheep. He will never know." So each Sunday night he carried one of his sheep across the bridge and placed it in his brother's flock.

"Each Monday morning, the brothers were amazed to discover that, although they had removed one of their sheep the night before, there were just as many in the flock when they counted them again. Summer and autumn and winter passed, and it was spring once again.

"One Sunday night—an Easter night reminiscent of the one when the risen Christ appeared to his disciples—the two brothers met each other at the bridge, each carrying one of his sheep. The riddle was solved and the wound was healed. They exchanged the

Easter greeting, "Peace be with you!" and set down their sheep next to the stream of cool, Living Water. Then, stepping onto the bridge and embracing as the brothers they were meant to be, each one received his brother's gift and returned to his home.

'Throughout the rest of their lives, as long as they were able, the two brothers continued to meet on the bridge to exchange their gifts of sheep.

"Beginning that Easter night and continuing to this day, the Living Water in the mountain stream began to sing. Some said it was simply the water gurgling over the rocks in a new way. Some said it was the voice of heaven rejoicing. But all of the people recognized the hand of God at work."

At first, Gustav wasn't at all sure whether his message had struck a responsive chord with either of the families for which he was concerned. However, after the service he learned what he wanted to know. Out near the horse barn, both pairs of brothers were joined in an embrace of reconciliation. Each pair was surrounded by their parents, their wives, and their children, all wearing Easter smiles. Gustav could picture the years of tension and enmity melting away.

"As it should be," he said with a nod and a smile. "As it should be."

# Chapter Eighteen ∽

On Monday of the second week of September in the year of our Lord 1907, Gustav Vriesen leaned back at his desk and stretched. *What an exciting time for the village. This will be a week to remember, especially for Adam and Emilie, all of the Schroeders and Rickmeiers. Really, all of Bierville shares their excitement. It's been more than two years since the last wedding here, and folks are always looking for an occasion to celebrate. Even after worship yesterday, people were buzzing with anticipation. Hmm. The big wedding seemed so far off when they became engaged more than a year ago. Now it's less than a week away.*

Gustav had been thinking a lot about Adam and Emilie's wedding. To memory, it would be the first time someone from Bierville married someone from outside of the village. Adam's parents weren't even German; they were Austrian—with some German ancestry. He remembered how Adam had been so poorly received when he started work as the farm and home editor for the newspaper in Sheboygan. "All right," Gustav had conceded, "so he's an Ausländer. So he's not even German. Do we love only those who love us? What did Jesus say? 'Do not even the Publicans the same?' Adam Schroeder is a child of God, a long way from home, and he deserves our hospitality and respect."

*Now,* Gustav thought, *with the passage of time, the love of God at work, and because he's marrying Emilie, they treat Adam as one of their own. However, they still say he has a funny accent. Everybody has a funny accent to someone.*

Adam took the week off before the wedding so he could help with preparations. Especially because none of his family lived in Wisconsin, he thought he should help as much as possible. It was different for Adam, living in an area where almost everybody had dozens of relatives while he had none. However, Simon Klemme had befriended Adam and looked out for him as though he were his younger brother. The Klemmes invited him over for holidays and birthdays and family reunions. Because of that, Adam didn't feel quite as much like an outsider.

On Monday afternoon, Adam worked with Simon to fix a fence an angry bull had knocked down the day before. Adam got to thinking: it was the same fence they had been working on a year earlier when he decided to pop the magic question. At that time, he'd been seeing Emilie for three years. So many times he wanted to ask her to marry him, but it never quite happened; the timing wasn't right or he couldn't get up the courage. Something always got in the way.

So, while they were working on the fence the first time, Adam said to Simon, "I want to marry Emilie in the worst way."

Simon looked up, surprised. "'The worst way?'" he laughed. "What do you mean? Club her on the head, carry her off, and force her to marry you at gunpoint? That would be the worst way!"

"No," Adam said, chuckling. "You know. I love her so much. I want to be with her, to give my life to her. Only—" He gazed out over the field and rested his chin on a fence post. "Only I haven't the slightest idea how to ask her."

Simon walked up behind him, put his brotherly hands upon Adam's shoulders, and said, "If you don't ask her soon, all of

Bierville will ask her for you. The two of you fit very well together, so if you speak from the heart, whatever you say will be right."

Adam asked. She agreed. And all of a sudden, there were five days to go.

On Tuesday evening, the oil lamps were burning over at the church. Thirteen-year-old Calvin Rickmeier and his father Herman were warming up with their violins. Even the process of tuning sounded magnificent to Calvin. As special music for the wedding they were preparing a Bach fugue arranged for organ and two violins. Church organist Eduardo D'Angelo, as musically accomplished as he was, beamed with satisfaction at the ethereal blend of music the three of them made. Toward the back of the church Eduardo's thirteen-year-old daughter Dominique watched and listened attentively.

The musicians began their practice, and the sound carried outside through an open door. It drew Gustav and Minnie over to the church for a closer listen. Calvin noticed them come in, go over to Dominique, and sit with her in the pew. Finally, when the practice was through, the audience of three applauded appreciatively. The musicians bowed, and Herman said, "It's a good thing I don't have to sing at my Emilie's wedding. I don't think I could get any sound out."

Both men reached over and patted Calvin on the back. "Calvin," Eduardo said, "these five years of lessons have certainly borne fruit for you. It is a pleasure to perform with a young musician as gifted as yourself."

Calvin felt himself blush. He nodded and said, "Thank you, sir. I'm honored that you think so. But I have a long way to go."

"You're doing remarkably well," Herman assured him. "Your dog doesn't find your playing nearly as interesting anymore. I never thought I'd say this, but I miss the duets that Rex and you used to perform."

With a smile that would melt a glacier, Dominique approached Calvin and, taking his hand, said, "That was beautiful, Calvin! You're great!"

Calvin thought his insides would burst into flames. He smiled sheepishly and saw Herman and Eduardo give each other a knowing wink and a nod. They all laughed, wished one another a good night, and headed for home.

The Vriesens walked across the lawn and Gustav said to Minnie, "Remember how Eduardo was treated at first when he arrived here?"

"Yes," she replied. "Just because he's Italian, some treated him like dirt."

"Then," he said, "they had the idea he was Clara's ex-husband in disguise and wanted to lynch him."

"What a blessing it has been to discover such a lovely and talented person!" Minnie said.

On Wednesday morning at the general store, Lester Mohr was standing near the front windows, sipping a cup of coffee, when he noticed Jacob Schmalfus walking down the road toward the store. Lester hurried to one of the checkers tables, slouched back in his chair, and pretended to be asleep. Jacob came in and Lester muttered, "I'm not a good dancer, Margaret. Why don't you lead?" and burst out laughing.

"Ja, I still remember," Jacob said, smiling in an irritated sort of way. He poured himself a cup of coffee and sat at the table near Lester.

"Say," Lester said, "do you remember the time we were sitting here and Edna Dinkmeier was modeling some of the yard goods over there, trying to see how it would look as a dress?"

"Yessir," Jacob said, laughing, "and Emil says, 'Edna, I admire the way you've kept your girlish figure after all these years.' And Edna says,

'Thank you, Emil. That's the nicest thing you've ever said to me.'"

"And Emil said, 'Yep, somewhere deep inside, you've kept your girlish figure. You've been hiding her in there all these years.' And she gave him a whap."

They both laughed. Jacob said, "Well, hey, but I miss those days. They sure ain't as entertainin' anymore, since they've been gettin' along better."

Otto walked over and asked, "Are you sure that's what you want, that they'd go back to arguing all the time?"

"Naw, you're right," Jacob said. "As entertainin' as it was, the two o' them must have been mis'rable. Ya can't wish that on people. Even if they deserve it."

On Thursday morning at about ten o'clock, Clara was hard at work in her shop, putting the finishing touches on Emilie's wedding dress. There was a knock at the door. "Come in," she said. "The door's open." There was no response. "Come in," she repeated. Still there was no answer. "Honestly!" she said.

Clara went to the door and opened it. Gerhardt Schultz was standing on the boardwalk, holding a bouquet of flowers. "Hello, Clara," he said. "I'm back."

"Gerhardt!" she said, hugging him. They kissed. "Oh," she said, "I'm so glad to see you! Welcome home."

"Home was never like this," he said. They kissed again. "But I think I can adapt."

Someone whistled. Clara pulled back and looked across the road to the general store. Otto was waving at them.

"Gerhardt! Clara!" Otto said. "I see the two of you have met. Welcome home, young man! Why am I not surprised that you stopped to see her first?"

"I'll be there in a minute!" Gerhardt said, smiling. "Make that five minutes!"

"Tell me," Clara said. "Why did you say a couple years ago that you've never known anyone like me?"

"Because I've known you all these years. We were neighbors—good friends. And I suddenly realized that I love you the way I've never loved anyone. That's why."

They kissed again. Holding him close, Clara said, "You're right. You've never known anyone like me. And you don't know how happy that makes me."

"But we need to take it slowly," he said. "Each of us has been through some tough times, and we're used to being pretty independent. Well—and you have Liesl to think about."

"That's true. I'm just glad you're home. Now I get to see you every day. We can actually talk, instead of having to write letters and wait for an answer in the mail. But I will miss getting letters from you. They were wonderfully sweet."

"Who said I have to stop writing you love letters?"


Right after school on Thursday, Calvin entered the general store with a broad smile and a boisterous greeting, "Herr Steitz, would you be so kind as to make me a strawberry soda? I deserve one after a day like this." Calvin plopped his stack of books on the counter and settled onto a stool.

"Calvin," Otto said, preparing the soda, "you seem positively elated. It was a good day?"

"I'll say! I had two tests today and got perfect scores on both."

"Wonderful! Congratulations! For an achievement like that, young man, this one's on the house. I think I'll join you in this little celebration." Otto made a strawberry soda for himself and sat with him.

"Thank you, Herr Steitz! This is most kind of you." Calvin received the drink and sipped it. "Mmmm," he said. "Delicious!"

"So the new school year is going well?"

"Yes! It's the strangest thing. Everything seems to be making sense."

"I'm proud of you, Calvin. I always knew things would come together for you. There's such a wonderful spark within you, and you're making the best of it."

They sat together in quiet for a while, sipping their sodas. Calvin looked across at Otto and said, "Herr Steitz, a couple of years ago, my mother told me what happened to your wife and children when you lived in Chicago. Well, I just want to tell you how sorry I am, and how much I admire your courage."

Otto took another sip of his soda and said, "Thank you, Calvin. It's not something I talk about very much, but it's always in the back of my mind. Do you have any questions you want to ask me about it?"

Calvin thought for a moment. "Who was this man? Did you know him?"

"His name was Evan McKay, a single man in his late teens, maybe twenty, I'd say. He answered our advertisement for a room upstairs we wanted to rent."

"How long did he live with you?"

"I think about eight months. He used to eat meals with us. I remember he told us about his years of growing up. Not a happy life. His mother died when he was small. My wife Elsa always seemed special to him, like a big sister or a mother. I sometimes feel guilty for not seeing the trouble coming, but I never thought he'd hurt anyone."

"Forgive me, Herr Steitz. I—I didn't mean to bring up bad memories for you. I just wanted you to know I'm sorry, and I think you're a wonderful man. You're like a grandfather to a lot of us."

"That means a great deal to me, Calvin. Now tell me about your classes at school. What are you taking?"

Late in the afternoon on Thursday, Adam headed over to the general store for some last-minute supplies for the wedding reception. He entered the store and saw Gerhardt on a ladder behind the counter. "Gerhardt," he said, "how's my best man? And how was your trip? Uneventful, I take it."

Gerhardt smiled and climbed down to greet Adam. "I'm just fine, thanks. And how 'bout you? Still breathing, I see." The two joked back and forth as Gerhardt filled Adam's order. Then Gerhardt became serious.

"Adam," he said, "I can't tell you how grateful I am that you think of me as your friend. When I got out of jail, you were one of the few people here who would have anything to do with me. When my father died, people blamed me. They said that I broke his heart. I guess maybe I did."

"People tell me that your father loved you very much."

"Yeah. I used to wish that I had died instead of him. Emilie and you, Clara and Martha, Otto, my mother, and the Vriesens— the eight of you saved my life, and I'll never forget it. That's why I wanted to move back to the village."

"Now, come on," Adam said, smiling. "Everybody knows it had more than a little to do with Clara."

"All right, that's true. She does make Bierville a lot more interesting."

"Thank you for that confession. Anyway, I think our friendship started because you were just as much of an outcast as I was when I arrived here. And it was wrong that you should be treated that way. You needed a friend."

"It's a risky business keeping company with outcasts, you know."

"I do! I remember, at the first three wedding receptions I was invited to, no one wanted to sit with me. I've always believed that sharing meals together is really important. It builds relationships, a spirit of community. So, I'd go over to sit at a table full of people, and they'd all get up and sit somewhere else. Or they'd ignore me and pretend I wasn't even there."

"Yep. That's what happened to me. Plenty of times."

"After I met Emilie and we saw you sitting by yourself at another wedding reception, that's why we went right over and sat with you, to break bread with you, so you didn't have to be alone. Now you're my friend, and I'm honored to have you as my best man."

Otto came in from the back, having heard most of the conversation. He walked up beside Gerhardt, put his arm over his shoulders, and said, "Gerhardt, I have perfect trust in you. I'm proud of you both."

On Friday, it was already quite warm by mid-morning, especially for September. Emilie came strolling into the general store with a basket tucked under one arm and a short shopping list in hand. Jacob Schmalfus looked up and said to Otto, "Jus' look at her. So young and pretty, so confident and happy. Why, it's hotter than blazes today and she's not even sweatin'!"

"Perspiring," Otto said with a wink. "Women don't sweat."

"All right," he continued, "she's not perspirin', either. Why is that?"

Otto smiled and said, "It must be love." Then, in a louder voice, he said, "Emilie, a package came for you this morning. The postmark says Toledo, Ohio." Emilie smiled. "Why, it's from Aunt Gertrude!" she said. "Thank you!"

When Emilie returned home after shopping, Frieda suggested she open the package in case it was perishable. "Oh, Mama!" Emilie said. "Look at the lovely crystal serving dishes Aunt Gertrude sent for our wedding!"

After barely a glance, Frieda replied, "I believe they're glass, dear."

"Can you be sure, Mama? You've hardly looked at them."

"If they're from Gertrude, they're glass."

Saturday arrived and the excitement of the village peaked. Spirits and emotions ran high. Adam's parents and a host of other friends and relatives arrived from out of town, and the church was packed.

The processional started. Simon Klemme could see just about everything from where he and Anna stood at the front. The groomsmen entered the sanctuary from the front and the bridesmaids from the back. Clara was the maid of honor. Simon thought that Adam had never looked more nervous, Emilie more beautiful, and Herman more like a blubbering wreck.

Anna whispered, "Here comes Emilie, so starry-eyed."

"And here comes Adam," he replied, "so pie-eyed. It must be love."

"I'm sure that's it. But, Herman—he looks like somebody has died!"

"I think someone has," Simon said. "Herman's little girl."

The wedding service commenced. Adam and Emilie appeared to relax and Herman seemed to regain his composure. Herman had told Simon recently that Frieda and he were, in truth, very happy for their daughter and already loved Adam as one of their own. Yet, saying good-bye to the little Emilie was not an easy thing. Still, as hard as it was, they wouldn't have wanted it any other way.

Frieda leaned over and kissed his tear-streaked cheek. She said softly, "I love you, Herman."

Later in the service, the trio performed the Bach fugue, and it was as if heaven and earth were joined as one, so lovely that the angels must have been humming along. Herman looked up to see Emilie smiling at the three of them. Surely they would treasure this gift for the rest of their lives.

Still later, Pastor Vriesen concluded his remarks and said to them, "Adam and Emilie, it is not remarkable to find love at first sight. When two people are still deeply in love after learning to live together for many years, that's when we see the real strength of love. Each of you, look at your parents and the love they still share. That is the testimony of God's enduring love we hope to see in you!"

After the service, the "Klemmemobile" was used as the getaway car. For the first time, newlyweds drove away from the village church in an automobile. Simon and Anna sat in the front, and Adam, Emilie, Gerhardt, and Clara all squeezed into the back seat. With a honking horn, showering rice, cheering guests, and a cloud of dust, the automobile roared away. Simon wondered if Herman would be able to see them driving away, and not because of the dust.

Later at the dance hall, Otto was standing near the punch bowl with Simon and Anna, sipping some delicious strawberry-apple cider. The other wedding guests were still arriving for the reception. Through the door across the hall came a stunningly beautiful, raven-haired *Fraülein* in a fitted, floor-length apricot dress.

Otto's eyebrows rose to attention. "I don't think she's from around here."

Anna replied, "That's Adam's younger sister Cynthia from St. Louis. Frieda introduced me to her this morning."

Otto glanced at Simon, who seemed to be enthralled by the sight of Cynthia gliding across the floor. Anna watched Simon watching Cynthia. She set her glass of punch down and, smiling at her husband, put her arms around his waist. Gradually, Simon seemed to regain consciousness.

"Well? Are you happy now?" she asked.

"I sure am," he said, a far-away smile still on his face. "Why do you ask?"

"You're drooling all over your suit. You're taken, you know." She poked him in the ribs and began tickling him.

"Now come on," he said, laughing and fending off her attack. "I was just looking for family resemblance."

A delicious meal was served, featuring stuffed pork chops and beef tips, two of Otto's favorites. The blessings of life and love and faith were celebrated, and more than four hundred people broke bread together. The people of Bierville welcomed their guests with open arms and hearts and no one was excluded. The Spirit of Christ was perceptibly present among them, serenading the wedding guests well into the night.

# Chapter Nineteen  ∿

One Tuesday in June of 1908, Otto finished sweeping the boardwalk in front of the store, then allowed his eyes to lead his mind along the road to the east, over the bridge, out of Bierville, into the morning sky. *Who could argue with the notion that hope springs eternal on such a glorious day? Lyrics of praise to the Maker wafted through the air, carried ever higher by the fresh, summer breeze. As if descending from the realms of cherubs and seraphs, grace, mercy, and love settled gently upon the earth. Glorious.*

Tuesday evening marked the beginning of the four-day Sunday school camp-out in the church woods. This was Gustav Vriesen's idea, a reward for the students after such a good year together. Ten tents were pitched around the edge of the Vesper Point clearing. A little farther down the flat next to the river, they constructed a fire circle to accommodate all forty campers.

About a half-hour before sunset, Gustav asked Simon Klemme, Gerhardt Schultz, and some of the children to gather firewood from the surrounding woods and build a large campfire shaped like a teepee in the center of the fire circle. By nightfall, a blazing fire illuminated and enlivened the circle. The aroma of wood smoke permeated the air. Gustav led the gathering in singing and Bible stories.

Just before bedtime, Caroline Klemme asked, "Can we have a story?"

"A bedtime story?" Gustav said. "Well, let's see." In no time, in the manner of macaws, a chorus of children parroted the request. Gustav looked at Simon, who looked at Anna, who looked at Fritzie, who looked at Gerhardt, who looked at Clara. "Does one of you have something in mind?"

"Mama," Liesl said, "why don't you tell the story about Eden-on-Eden?"

Clara rose slowly, paused for a moment, and said, "It's a long story, so I'll have to tell it over our three nights together—if that's all right, Pastor Vriesen."

"By all means," he said, bowing in gratitude.

Slowly, Clara circled the fire, surrounded by a ring of glowing faces. Like a gifted mesmerist, she captured their attention. Her ebony eyes were particularly striking to Gustav. *What a beautiful young woman. What is Gerhardt waiting for?*

"Look into the fire," Clara said, "deep into the fire! We're traveling back in time to a place far away.

"Once upon a time, in the days of King Edward I, there was a small village in northern England by the name of Eden-on-Eden. It was a lovely village, tucked into western slopes of the Pennine Mountains. The cool, clear waters of the River Eden rushed past the east edge of the village and continued their way to the north, down through the valley, finally mixing with the waters of Solway Firth in the Irish Sea. A great bridge made of log and stone stretched over the river, joining the village to the land east of Eden.

"The villagers all said, 'Surely, there isn't a prettier, purer place on God's green earth, very much like the Garden of Eden in the beginning.' That's why it came to be called 'Eden-on-Eden.'

"The River Eden was the lifeblood of the village. Not only did it provide drinking water and fish for the villagers and power for the mill, but the river also gave the young people of the village endless hours of high adventure and fun. There were quiet side-pools for swimming in, roaring rapids to shoot on log rafts, boulders to climb, and to the south about an hour's journey there was a mysterious canyon to explore. There was, of course, the old village bridge from which to fish.

"In those days, there were three children growing up in Eden who were the best of friends: David, his sister Ann, and Jonathon, who was two years younger than David and the same age as Ann. Shortly after each child was born, the priest of the village church christened each one. As far back as they could remember David, Ann, and Jonathon knew each other, played together, did everything together.

"Any time the three of them weren't eating or sleeping or doing chores, they went down to the bridge, sat with their feet dangling over the edge, and made plans for what they might do together. Sometimes they just sat, mesmerized by the water rushing beneath their feet. It was the portrait of their childhood: three little friends sitting together, growing together, and absorbing the abundant life of Eden.

"One time, the three of them were sitting in a row on the bridge. Ann looked at Jonathon and said to herself, 'Someday Jonathon and I will be married and we'll live happily ever after.'

"On a warm day in late summer, when David was eleven years of age and Ann and Jonathon were nine, they packed a lunch of bread and cheese and made the hour's journey south to the mysterious canyon for the first time. When they reached the canyon, the three of them stood together at the top, staring down at the mammoth boulders and thundering water of the River Eden fifty feet below. From one new fascination to another they raced, filled with fear and excitement.

"At about midday, they realized they were hungry. Jonathon said, 'I have an idea. Let's eat on top of that!' He pointed and began running toward a massive stone column that rose out of the river and stood as high as the edge of the canyon and about six feet away. Without hesitating, he leaped out over the chasm, sprawling face-down on top of the column.

"Ann and David approached, and Ann said, 'I don't think that's such a good idea. I can't jump that far.'

"'I agree,' David said. 'You come back from there! That's far too dangerous.'

"Jonathon looked down at the swirling water surrounding the column and then at the edge of the canyon where his friends were standing and terror gripped his heart. His whole body began to tremble and he collapsed into a heap on the column.

"David said, 'Jonathon, I'll come over to you and help you across.' He ran toward a fallen tree nearby that appeared long and sturdy enough to serve as a bridge. With great effort he dragged it toward the canyon, and he and Ann stood it on end. 'Be on your guard!' he called, and let the top of the tree fall onto the column. He stepped carefully onto the tree and started balancing his way toward Jonathon.

"When David was nearly to the other side, the tree suddenly shifted and twisted. He lost his balance, and both he and the tree fell. Jonathon gaped in disbelief.

"Ann screamed. 'David! My David! No!'

"'Help! Help!' he cried. Then his voice went silent and he disappeared in the raging water below.

"That's enough story for tonight," Clara said. Instantly there was a howl of protest from the circle of faces. She smiled, held up her hands to calm the gathering, and assured them, "We'll continue tomorrow night, as I promised."

The campers dispersed and headed for their tents, and Gustav said to Clara, "That's a powerful story. Can you give me a synopsis of the rest of it?" She summarized the story and he said, "I think we'll be changing our plans for our daytime discussions. The whole group is obviously intrigued by your tale, though I don't know how useful it will be in helping us fall asleep. You're a skilled storyteller. This is a side of you I've never seen before. It's fascinating to me. Did you notice how, when you stopped, the two who moaned loudest were Simon and myself?"

"I did, yes," she said with a smile. "I'm glad you're enjoying it."

"Tomorrow," Gustav said, "we will imagine ourselves in the places of Jonathon, Ann, and her parents, and try to understand how they would react to this tragedy, and what a faithful response might be. We'll also help the students to think of Bible stories that raise similar issues. Thank you."

On Wednesday night after a great day together, the campers were primed for another campfire. They gathered wood during spare moments throughout the day to be sure they'd have plenty for a big fire and a long story. Again, just before bedtime, Clara rose and began circling the fire. The group focused on Clara. They were eager for the story to resume.

"Look into the fire," she said, "deep into the fire! We've traveled back six hundred years in time to Eden-On-Eden, to Jonathan and Ann. Can you see them? There, on the stone column. Jonathon's on his knees. His face is buried in his hands. And there's Ann on the firm land. She is kneeling and sobbing hysterically. David has just fallen.

"'You killed him, you evil boy!' Ann cried. 'If you hadn't been so foolish as to jump out there, David would still be alive!' She cried inconsolably and wandered away from the canyon and into the woods, leaving Jonathon imprisoned on the column, curled up and shaking more from fear than cold.

"The sun went down and nighttime fell upon the canyon. Jonathon shivered in the darkness on top of the cold, stone column. All he could hear was the menacing sound of the raging torrent below.

"The next morning, Jonathon was awakened by his father's voice: 'There you are, you worthless fool! 'Twould serve you right if I left you there!' He jumped over to the column, picked Jonathon up by the shoulders, threw him across to the edge of the canyon, and jumped across again. 'Such an awful thing you did! Unforgivable!' In silence the man stormed off toward the village, Jonathon following at a distance.

"Jonathon became an outcast. He became known as 'Eden's serpent.' Ann's parents were grief-stricken and overcome with hatred; they both died within the following year. Orphaned at the age of ten, Ann went to live with her aunt and uncle.

"It seemed to the people of Eden that, on the day when David died, a dark shroud of bitterness formed over the village, and they wondered if they would see the grace, mercy, and love of God again.

"Life became hard for young Jonathon, and he spoke to no one after that day; the most he did was let out an occasional grunt. Humiliated, his family moved from the village to an abandoned farm east of Eden. They showed Jonathon no mercy. He was banned from the family table; the only food he received was the porridge his mother set outside the door twice a day. He bedded with the horses, cattle, and goats in the shed; even they seemed to keep their distance. Because no one else forgave him for what happened to his friend, he was unable to forgive himself. After that, he shied away from all contact with the villagers; the east end of the bridge was the closest he ventured.

"By the time Jonathon reached the age of twenty, his appearance was that of an old beggar—thin and haggard in his shabby clothes, bent low from years of bearing a burden of guilt. By the time Ann was twenty and should have been in her prime, she looked like a wicked, old witch from a fairy tale. The ill will she harbored toward Jonathon caused her to change in ugly way, but being unable to get at him, she turned her hatred on others. She became adept at cruel gossip and said the most hurtful things to make her victims cry out in pain. Her face became creased with vicious lines, her back hunched from her oppressive bitterness.

"Twelve years to the day after Ann saw her brother for the last time, she remembered the anniversary with particular venom. Her body was so deformed by that time that she had to use a walking stick. As Ann passed a looking glass, she saw her reflection and let out such a savage string of insults that even she was repulsed. Something changed. She wept bitterly. 'I used to be so pretty,' she sobbed. 'How did I become so cruel and ugly?'

"The next day, Ann went to speak with the village priest, the one who christened her twenty-one years before, whom she had avoided since David's death. Over the years, the old priest's eyesight grew dim. But when she entered the church even he was startled by what he saw.

"'Be gone, evil witch!' he shrieked. 'Be gone from this holy place!'

"Leaning on her walking stick, she bowed her head and said, "I beg of you, sir! Hear what I have to say, for I am one of your lost sheep whom you christened as a child. My name is Ann.'"

Clara straightened her back and said, "We'll stop there for tonight."

Again there was a howl of protest. "Can't we finish the story tonight? I'm not tired." They all said the same.

Gustav stood and said, "We'll finish the story tomorrow, but isn't it wonderful?" The circle erupted in grateful applause, and the yawning campers filed toward their tents. He said to Clara, "Tomorrow we'll think about the changes that occurred in Jonathon and Ann, the effect a lack of forgiveness had on the village, and the Bible stories these things remind us of. This is a marvelous story."

"Thank you," she replied. "My mother told it to us when we were young."

That evening, after all the tents were closed up and the last lantern was turned out, Clara and the girls in her tent said good night to one another and settled down to sleep. Clara heard footsteps outside, as though someone were walking behind the circle of tents. Liesl heard the footsteps, too.

"It's probably Pastor Vriesen," Clara whispered, "making sure everybody's tucked in for the night."

The sound of the footsteps drew nearer. Clara noticed it was an uneven gait. There was a strong first step followed by a quicker sliding step. Now the sound was right behind their tent.

"Good night, Pastor Vriesen," Liesl said.

The footsteps stopped abruptly. "Hello?" Clara said. *Whoever it is—it sounds like a man—why did he stop? Why won't he answer?* She held her breath.

Liesl seemed unconcerned and soon she dozed off. For several minutes, however, Clara barely breathed. She waited and listened for what seemed an hour. The silence was oppressive. She wondered if she'd imagined it all. *Maybe it was simply an animal out for a midnight stroll. Maybe my ears were playing tricks on me.* Finally, Clara relaxed once more and settled down to sleep.

The footsteps started again from only a few feet behind Clara's tent, gradually trailing off in the distance. "That was odd," she murmured. Finally, she drifted off to sleep.

By Thursday, the campers knew the routine: cooperation during the activities of the day meant more fun around the fire that night. When it was time for another campfire, the children took their places around the circle. Catherine Klemme sniffed her arm and said, "I smell like bratwurst!"

Many of the others conducted the same test, announcing, "So do I! So do I! So do I!"

Gustav laughed and said to Clara, "It's often difficult to get an original thought out of a group of children."

"Yes, it is," she said. "Say, did you hear anybody walking around last night after everyone was supposed to be in bed? Somebody with a limp?"

"No, I didn't. I fell asleep pretty quickly." He paused for a moment. "Fritzie told me this morning that he had too much water to drink last night and got up to pay a little visit to the bushes. While he was up, he tripped and was limping around for a little while but he said he was over near the river. That's all I know. Is there a problem?"

"No," she said, "just wondering. It was probably some animal I heard."

Once more, after the singing and another Bible story, Clara rose and began circling the fire.

"Look into the fire," she said, "deep into the fire! Can you see them? There is Ann, leaning on her walking stick, looking very much like an old witch. And there is the priest, staring at her in wonder and fear.

"Even through the veil of years gone by, all at once the old priest recognized her and, overcome with pity, fell to his knees. He invited Ann to sit and tell her story. After listening carefully he said to her, 'You were so beautiful as a child, but over the years the hateful grudge you harbor against Jonathon has bent you low with a heavy burden. Your cruelty toward your neighbors has marked your face with lines of ugliness. Your true beauty remains locked inside, a prisoner of your hardness of heart.'

"'Then tell me what I must do to receive mercy!'

"'First, you must fill a sack with the down of thistles. Next, go throughout the village and place the thistledown on the doorstep of each person you have hurt and wronged. Finally, you must collect all of the thistledown again and return it to me.'"

"As quickly as she could, Ann followed his instructions. Of course, by the time she had distributed the last bit of thistledown, the wind had scattered the rest, so she returned holding only a small amount.

"The old priest said to her, 'You can never recall the cruel words that cross your lips. They are carried away like the down of a thistle in the wind, taking on lives of their own, still doing their harm. Their damage cannot be undone.'

"Ann collapsed on the floor of the church, sobbing, 'What can I do? What can I do?'

"He said, "'Confess your sin and sadness to God, and pray for forgiveness.' He stood silently by for several minutes as she prayed.

"When she finished, he said, "Rise, my child, your sins are forgiven. Go in peace, restored by the love of your Savior.'

"Ann returned home, unaware that anything had changed until she peered into the looking glass and saw the face of a beautiful young woman gazing back at her. She was, however, still as hunchbacked as ever. Hopeful, yet still troubled, she returned to the priest and said in perplexed amazement, 'My face is beautiful, yet I am still bent low.'

"He nodded and said, "Yes, the ugly lines of cruelty are gone from your face, but you still carry a heavy burden of bitterness against Jonathon. People often bear grudges against those whom we should love the most. Remember. "Even as Christ hath forgiven you, so do ye also." The second thing you must do is find Jonathon and be reconciled with him.'

"Ann knew where to find Jonathon. Every evening for the last twelve years, just after sunset when the streets of the village were quiet, he would come from the land east of Eden and stand at the end of the bridge, the bridge he hadn't crossed since his banishment. For several minutes he would gaze across at the village, as if studying ghostly images from the past. Then, he would kneel with his forehead touching the ground, crying out loud, 'Forgive me! Forgive me!' After several minutes, he would rise again and disappear into the gathering darkness.

"Ann knew this because every night for the last twelve years she had hid near the west end of the bridge, kindling her hatred against him, watching from one hundred feet away, the focus of her abhorrence just beyond reach.

"That evening, shortly before sundown, Ann walked to the bridge over the River Eden. She hid herself once more and waited for Jonathon. Again, he came and stood as usual, hunched over and leaning on his walking stick. She came out of hiding and stood at the other end of the bridge. He was startled and turned to flee. Although he hadn't seen her for so many years, he seemed to recognize her.

"'Wait!' she said, stepping onto the bridge. 'I have something to say. I forgive you, dear Jonathon. I know you loved David as a brother and that you didn't mean him any harm. I am sorry for holding his death against you all this time. I really do love you.'

"Jonathon turned his hollow face toward her, tears shining in his eyes. The years of lonely torment eased their grip, and he spoke to another person for the first time in two decades. 'When David died, I lost my two best friends at the same time. Now, perhaps, we have found one another again. Dear Ann, how I have longed for this day! Only because you forgive my foolishness can I forgive myself. You have set me free from my prison.'

"Slowly, from opposite ends of the bridge, they walked toward each other. The burdens of grudge and guilt were lifted from their shoulders. Another of God's miracles happened that night. What once was broken was healed. What once was bent was made straight. What was once lost was redeemed. In the middle of the village bridge over the River Eden they embraced, and the shroud of bitterness was lifted from Eden."

For perhaps a minute after Clara finished, the only sound coming from within the circle was the crackling of the fire. It seemed to Gustav that no one wanted to leave Eden. Gradually, however, one person shifted position and another coughed; they were all together again around the fire, next to the river in the church woods.

Gustav stood and said, "Let us pray. Everlasting God, Lord of heaven and earth, we give you our grateful thanks for the stories of our faith that help your power and love to live within our hearts. We praise you for families and friends and faith, for the ways we are renewed by each of these. We thank you for Clara and the gift of story she has shared with us. We are grateful for this time to be together. We pray, dear God, teach us how to forgive as you do. Bless us now with renewal and rest in your care, that we may be renewed in body, mind, and spirit and rise to new hope and new life in the new day. Let your whole creation live in your peace. Amen."

# Chapter Twenty ✑

On the Friday morning before Thanksgiving in 1908, there was a knock at the parsonage front door. Gustav Vriesen opened the door and found a boy of grade-school age bundled up like a woolen mummy, holding up a folded piece of paper for Gustav to take. "Thank you, young man! It's quite nippy out today. Would you like to—" But the boy was already racing away toward the road. Gustav opened the note and read it:

> *Dear Pastor and Mrs. Vriesen,*
>
> *Please excuse Emil and me, as we will be unable to accept your kind invitation for Thanksgiving dinner next week. The health of my uncle Walter in Milwaukee is failing and we will probably have his funeral that day.*
>
> *Kindest regards,*
> *Edna Dinkmeier*

Minnie came into the room, wiping her hands on a towel. "Was there someone at the door, Gustav?"

"Well," he said, scratching his head, "I'd say it was one of the Dinkmeiers' grandsons, but I'm not sure, really. It's the strangest note from them. They can't join us for dinner on Thanksgiving because they're planning to have a funeral that day. I wonder if Uncle Walter will have anything to say about that."

"A funeral on Thanksgiving? That sounds like a funny excuse," Minnie said. "One of the worst I've heard."

"Well, if folks have their minds set against doing something, one excuse is as good as another."

The two of them walked back to the kitchen. Minnie said, "Then I guess it will be Otto, Clara and Liesl, Gerhardt and Hilda, Willy and Marianna Grosscurth, the six D'Angelos, and us. And we'll have a nice time together."

"Eh, not the Grosscurths, either. I saw Willy yesterday. He said they both have to work all day at the printing shop."

"What? No time to give thanks to God, to enjoy a nice dinner? Even on Thanksgiving? Is there an unusual illness going around?"


On Saturday morning at the church, Gustav had the confirmation class thinking hard. Of the nine students in the class, all were present except for Johann Johannes. Gustav wasn't sure if Johann was ever completely there.

Gustav said, "The parable of the great banquet is a metaphor, an image that Jesus used to represent the kingdom of heaven, the realm of God. At first, only a few were invited, and they all made excuses as to why they couldn't attend the banquet, why the kingdom of heaven wasn't important to them. For the first one, material possessions took priority. For the second, work was more important. And for the third, family interests came before devotion to God. So, Jesus said, the invitation was extended to any who would come to enjoy the banquet with God, and the ones invited at first would be turned away.

"Now tell me. Who is the host at this banquet?" A hand went up. "Yes?"

"Christ Jesus?"

"Correct. And what does it mean when we accept our invitations to the great banquet?" Several hands went up. "Yes?" Gustav said, encouraging their answers.

"That we respond to Jesus' love with our love."

"Yes."

"That we're glad to receive God's blessings."

"Yes!"

"That it's a sign of our thanksgiving to God."

"Yes! Exactly so!" Gustav said. "And if we deny God's invitation to the great banquet?" Another hand went up. "Yes?"

"Then we must not love God very much."

"Ah," he nodded, "that's where we find heaven's sadness in this story. Can you imagine turning down an invitation to a banquet hosted by Jesus? Yet it happens all of the time. We say we're too busy. We have more important things to do. And we find ourselves missing a golden opportunity."

Johann Johannes entered the room and, without looking up, handed a note to Gustav. It said:

*Dear Pastor Vriesen,*

*Please excuse Johann's tardiness for confirmation today. I thought he had already left the house until I started to put his trundle bed away. He spoke up just in time.*

*Mrs. Julius Johannes*

Gustav smiled sadly at Johann. "Take a seat," he said. *Ah, dear God. That's how it is for Johann, isn't it? Never quite here, never quite found.*

At sunrise on Sunday, Gustav was out for his customary walk along the road; that's how he prepared himself to lead worship.

Lamps burned in the printing shop, and through the front window he could see Willy and Marianna Grosscurth hunched over one of the presses, hard at work. He crossed the bridge and headed east of Bierville. Just ahead, he saw Carl Mueller, who was walking toward a nearby woodlot with a hunting rifle tucked under his arm. "Good morning, Carl," Gustav said. "Trying to get a deer before worship this morning?"

Carl gave him a sheepish grin and said, "I'm willin' to gur-ricken stick it out all day if I need to. I weren't able to've gone to church anyhow. Gertrude's sick."

Each man continued on his way. Gustav shook his head and muttered, "Gertrude is sick, so he can't come to church! Excuses, excuses! All the excuses! Do they really think I'm that stupid? Gott im Himmel, hilf' mir!"

In a few minutes, Carl joined the rest of his hunting party; the other hunters were Reiny Hartung, Lester Mohr, Siegfried Burgener, Johann Johannes, and Fritzie. Fritzie, Johann, and Carl teamed up, as did Reiny, Siegfried, and Lester. Carl said, "Let's meet back here at noon, hey, and have a little lunch." The two groups of hunters headed out.

At about noon Reiny, Siegfried, and Lester reached the corner and were ready to eat. All at once they heard crashing and grunting in the woods nearby. They lifted their rifles, expecting to see a deer. But it was Fritzie and Johann, out of breath and drenched with sweat, dragging an enormous sixteen-point buck.

"Fritzie! Johann!" they shouted, running over to help. The three of them were bubbling over with excitement. "Palpitatin' polecats! He's a beauty! Looks like a moose! Congratulations! Did Carl see him? Where is Carl, anyway?"

Johann and Fritzie bent over to catch their breath. "Oh," Johann said, "he's about three-quarters of a mile back that-a-way.

This is Carl's deer."

"Carl's?" Reiny replied. "And he made you two drag it out?"

"Carl's been shot." Fritzie said.

"Shot?" Reiny said, "And you left him there?"

"Here's the thing," Fritzie said. "This big, ol' buck came into a clearing, Carl took aim, and got 'im. But he was so excited that then he shot himself in the foot. We set him up on a big, ol' log, looked at the wound, and saw he wasn't bleeding too bad. So we started to help him up and he said, 'No, gurricken take the deer! It'll take the two a-you to drag it.' We looked at him funny, but he said, 'I ain't goin' no place till you get back. But if we take and go off, leave this ol' boy here, and another guy comes along, hey, it's for sure this big, ol' buck would sprout wheels and disappear in a hurry.' That's what he said. So here we are and there it is."

"That's really smart," Reiny said.

"Smart?" Lester said. "That's really stupid—even for Carl— bless that poor addled brain of his! Let's go get him."

The first thing on Monday morning over at the mill, Lester opened the front door and saw Reiny coming across from the blacksmith shop. "Mornin', Reiny. Say, how 'bout that buck of Carl's? What a monster! I still can't get over it."

"Yeah, she was a beauty, that buck. Say, I just saw Siegfried there, and he told me to tell you he's sick and won't be in today."

"Sick?" Lester asked. "That's his sixth, maybe seventh miss this year. But just sick? No typhoid fever or malaria? What about 'My mother made me eat pumpkin seeds, and now vines are growing out of my ears'? That was one of my favorites. Oh! And then there was, 'I was just sitting there, minding my own business, when my pancreas heated up to seven hundred degrees!' That was good! But I bet he's just worn out after hunting yesterday."

"That'd be my guess. He did look pretty dragged out."

"Well, if you see him later, tell him the next time he misses work he should make up another one of his outrageous excuses. They're usually so entertaining."

At about ten o'clock at the general store, Otto was stacking tins of beans. Clara Schnuelle and Gustav were checking their mailboxes, and Herman Rickmeier came bounding in the door, as happy as a clam. He said, "Any day now our Emilie and Adam are going to have a baby, and I'll know then whether I'm a grandpa or a grandma."

Otto smiled and said, "You're not used to this yet, are you, Herman?"

Clara patted his hand and said, "Herman, dear, either way I hope you'll be very happy. However, Frieda's going to be upset if you turn out to be a grandma."

Herman chuckled. "Oh, you know. I guess I'm not used to this."

Gustav slapped Herman on the back, and said, "Well, Grandpa, we'll have a christening pretty soon. And if this grandchild of yours turns out to have the same character as the rest of your family, there'll be another saint among us."

On Tuesday at the general store, Otto was sorting the mail. In walked Helmut Holzkopf, the general store owner and new postmaster in Steinmauer, a little town about fifteen miles to the northwest. "Herr Holzkopf! Good morning! Do you have time for some coffee?"

"Well, maybe I do," Helmut replied, and the two shook hands.

"Hey, Fritzie," Otto called out, "finish sorting the mail, will you? So how's business, Helmut?" They settled down with their coffee at one of the checkers tables.

"Ah, it's been pretty slow. I think it must be that H. C. Prange store in town. Have you been in there?"

"No, but I hear it's somethin' different in there."

"Me neither, but I hear it's amazing. Three stories, an elevator, a basement, electric lights. How's a general store like yours or mine supposed to compete with a place like that?"

"Well, they say that's progress."

"I think they just might progress us right out of business."

They both sipped their coffee for a moment. Otto asked, "Say, how're things as the new postmaster? I haven't seen any mail from your neck of the woods in well over a month."

"I never realized," Helmut said, "how big those mail bags are. But as soon as the next one fills up, I'll send it right over."

"Helmut, Helmut, Helmut!" Otto said, chuckling. "Every day the mail is supposed to go out! Not when it starts to mold! Nobody explained that to you?"

"No. Well, yes. But it seems so wasteful. I'm just trying to be efficient."

"That's one way to look at it, I suppose. Maybe it'll catch on as the philosophy for postal service operations. Oh! And this would be our slogan!

*Efficient is better,*
*Trust us with your letter.*
*United States Mail,*
*We're slow as a snail!*

Hmm. No, I don't think that's the image they're trying for. Maybe you'd better just send out what you've got every day."

The oil lamp burned late at Clara's shop on Tuesday night. She had spent the first part of the evening with Gerhardt and Liesl. Now she was finishing work on Edna Dinkmeier's new Thanksgiving dress. Liesl was fast asleep in the other room. Edna had said to Clara, "Let's have this dress be festive and a touch flamboyant, but suitable for a funeral."

At nearly midnight, Clara was trimming the last threads and giving the dress its final inspection. "Beautiful," she said with a smile. "That's enough for tonight." She locked and barred the door, put out the lamp, and began feeling her way through the darkness toward their private quarters in the back of the shop.

She heard footsteps on the boardwalk down the way. *Who would be out and about at this hour?* She listened more closely. *The steps are getting louder. They're uneven, like the ones behind the tents last summer.* The silhouetted figure of a man passed her window. *Is that Reiny? He has a hat like that.*

The man reached the door and tried to open it. There was a dull thud. The whole building shook. The handle rattled and the door creaked as if under considerable pressure, but it held firm. Huddling in the far corner, Clara stifled a cry. *He's trying to force it open with his shoulder.*

"Reiny? Reiny Hartung?" she said, her voice quivering. "Is that you?"

There was no answer. She held her breath. Everything grew still. The footsteps resumed. The figure passed the window again and continued back up the boardwalk, and the sound of footsteps faded away. *Reiny? It looked a little like him, but it's really too dark to tell. That wouldn't make any sense anyway. He's never been anything less than a gentleman to me. But then, who was that? I wish Gerhardt were with me! I shouldn't have to be afraid in my own house. Some adult companionship would really help. Well, thank God for sturdy doors.*

On Wednesday, Gustav stopped at the Grosscurths' printing shop to pick up an order. "Hello? Marianna? I've come to pick up the booklets for the church. Are they ready yet?"

From the back room came Marianna's voice: "Oh, certainly, Herr Vriesen! I'll get them for you."

Willy was busy operating one of the presses and stopped only briefly to acknowledge Gustav, so he walked back to talk to Willy. "Can you take time to come to the service tonight? We haven't seen much of you lately, and I'm sure Marianna and you could use an evening off, even if you can't join us tomorrow."

Without stopping, Willy said, "This business is my life. I have every intention of succeeding and being well-to-do by the time I'm fifty. We have no time for giving thanks and other such foolishness. There's work to be done and money to be made."

Marianna entered from the back room carrying a large box. Her face was streaked with ink and tears, and her eyes revealed her despair. Gustav glanced at her, walked over to Willy, and rested a hand on his shoulder. Willy kept working.

"Willy," Gustav asked, "how old are Marianna and you? Twenty-eight? Thirty?"

"We're both twenty-eight."

"No one doubts that the two of you are hard-working and very capable. But if you continue at this pace, you won't be able to stand each other in twenty years. If you're both still living. You certainly won't know each other, and you won't know your God. If you hope to have a long life, there's always time for gratitude."

Later, Gustav was preparing for the Thanksgiving Eve service. *O Lord God, all of the excuses, all of the blessings of life and love that we take for granted. How is it that you still put up with us, your wayward children? Nevertheless, we who gather for worship tonight will rejoice in your presence and give thanks for your goodness.*

The church was full of warmth and love that night and many came in thanksgiving to God. Gustav greeted his people at the door, and the spirit of gladness and gratitude grew. They were going to celebrate Holy Communion, so he thought it felt like a family reunion—a banquet. Just before the service started, Willy Grosscurth came in.

Willy bowed in greeting and said, "Herr Vriesen. After you left the shop earlier, Marianna and I talked. We argued. You were right. There are so many blessings in life to savor, but I had lost sight of that. I decided that I needed to come tonight, but by then, Marianna said she was too upset. I've been pushing her too hard—myself as well. But I'd like both of us to live another twenty or thirty years, and what's the point if we're miserable? Or no longer together?"

"Ah, Willy," Gustav said. "It is so easy to get caught up in the busyness of life and forget its real value. I find myself doing the same thing sometimes, and I have to remind myself. Come in. Worship with us. I'll go talk with Marianna later."

Marianna slipped through the door, looking sad and uncertain. Willy went over to her and held her. "I'm sorry," he said, and kissed her on the forehead.

She said, "I didn't want to be alone. And I needed to be here, too."

Gustav walked up to them and said, "Come." With his arms over their shoulders, he led them to two chairs in the back of the church. "You can sit together back here. God has saved two places at the banquet table just for you."

# Chapter Twenty-one ∼

It was late April in the year of our Lord 1909, and Simon Klemme was surveying the landscape with satisfaction. Spring had arrived in full force. The spring routines of farming were progressing well. Most of the fields were being worked up. Hundreds of fieldstones that popped up during the winter were being laboriously removed, and a few of the farmers with higher, better-drained land were planting some of their fields. As usual—and partly out of necessity—it was a matter of neighbor helping neighbor, sometimes even managing to get along.

On Monday morning after chores, Simon went out just beyond his poultry yard to inspect the west fencerow bordering on Carl Mueller's property. Simon worked his way along, and he stopped to admire a meadowlark singing on one of the fence posts. He glanced over at the field on the other side and felt a little envious that Carl was already done planting his beans there. Simon was surprised by the sound of somebody digging just ahead on the other side of the fence. "Carl!" he said. "Fancy meeting you here! Say, that's a nice-size hole there. Gonna plant a tree there or what?"

"No, I'm plantin' some of my beans again."

"Well, that hole's a fair bit too deep for beans, don't you think?"

"Nope. Jus' right. They're inside one of your blim blam ducks I just caught. See? He weren't gonna give 'em up, an' I weren't gonna take no for an answer."

"Well, I'm terribly sorry," Simon said, looking down at the life-less duck. "Yeah, that one's name was 'Schlimmschnabel.' Never did mind his manners, always peckin' away at the little ones. You could have him for dinner, you know."

Carl straightened and said half-smiling, "I'm too agitated at 'im. Prob'ly gurricken get in'igestion."

"What?" Simon scoffed. "Angry at a duck? He's well fed, ya know. Make a tasty dinner. As I always say, 'When life hands you a dead duck, make soup.'"

"I never heard that," Carl said, smiling broadly. "But all right, hey. An' you an' Anna an' the children come join us."

Simon was relieved. The bean-eating-duck controversy was solved without a shot being fired. And Carl and he were still friends.

Tuesday was another beautiful day. By late morning, the temperature was already well up into the 60s. Over at the Rickmeier farm, they were gathering fieldstones. Calvin took the day off from high school to help his father. They also had a new helper: Herman and Frieda's five-year-old niece, Minna. She had been staying with them for the past month, pitching in with the chores like a little trooper. Calvin thought of her as his younger sister, and he took every opportunity to show her what life with a big brother might be like.

Minna, in her light-blue sunbonnet, took great care to place each stone on the wagon, the big ones specially positioned as testimonies to her strength and endurance. When the wagon was full of stones, Herman suggested they unload it and get some water for themselves and the horse. Calvin noticed two particularly smooth stones, each about the size of a cantaloupe. "Look, Minna! Those are elephant eggs!"

"Oh, elephant eggs!" she exclaimed excitedly, and she bent over to examine them closely.

Herman took off his hat, wiped his forehead. "Minna," he said, "those are, uh..." He winked at Calvin. "They're beauties! Real beauties!" Calvin doubled over with laughter.

They led the horse and wagon back toward the house, and Minna took charge of the "elephant eggs." Her spindly arms couldn't manage both at once, so she picked up one, struggled with it for about ten yards, carefully set it down, and ran back for the other one. All the while, she chattered excitedly about how she could make a nest for the eggs in the barn and keep them warm until they hatched, and she'd have two big elephants to love.

Calvin and Herman were having the best time, grinning from ear to ear—until they saw Frieda step out of the back door of the farmhouse, her arms crossed: "Herman, what do you have that girl doing? Elephant eggs? Calvin, you're as bad as your father! Now, which of you is going to explain it to her without breaking her heart?"


On Wednesday, Gustav Vriesen was over at the church changing the candles in the candelabra. Eduardo D'Angelo entered carrying two wooden boxes overflowing with sheet music. "Eduardo! Welcome home! Here, let me help you with those."

"Ah, Herr Vriesen, thank you." Eduardo said.

"How was South America? Your concert tour went well?"

They set the boxes of music down on the front pew and shook hands. Eduardo tried to stretch the stiffness out of his back and said, "Two months of travel and concerts is too much. But it was wonderful. The people of South America were very nice, though there were many strange things to me. And sometimes I was afraid for my life. In all the cities, the most popular pastime was not my organ concert. It was bull fights."

"Eh, isn't that barbarism?"

"Ah, perhaps so. Many seemed to prefer barbarism even to bull fighting."

Gustav chuckled. "So it's true, then, that there's so much social chaos down there?"

"I'm sad to say, that was my impression. It reminded me of home. No nation seems to be free from violence for long. What must our Lord think?"

"Is there nothing better than violence and retribution? The rebels attack because they want freedom. The government condemns the rebels as violent insurrectionists and executes its prisoners to show them that violence is not the way to solve disagreements. The rebels retaliate, the government strikes back. How can the heart of God stand such misery?"

Eduardo nodded and said, "If we all lived by that 'eye for an eye' kind of justice, before long we'd all be blind. Then who would lead?"

"The blind, I guess," Gustav said. "That's how it seems to be now. And where will it end? How can the nations of the world, built upon such a foundation of violence and retribution, continue to stand? And what becomes of the people? The children?"

On Thursday at the general store, things were quiet and Otto was restocking the shelves. Gustav entered the door. "Herr Vriesen!" Otto said, stepping from behind the counter. "Guten Morgen!"

"How's my friend Otto today?"

"Just fine! And isn't it good to have Eduardo home? He stopped in earlier."

"It certainly is. I don't mind being the substitute organist, but I'm sure the congregation is tired of singing the same twelve hymns over and over for the past two months. That's about all I can play."

"You did well. But it is good to have Eduardo home."

"Hasn't he made a remarkable adjustment to this community? He's lived here, what, six years, maybe? He and his family are now fixtures in the Bierville community. What would we do without them?"

"Ah, but remember it wasn't always that way," Otto said.

"People used to say, 'It doesn't so much matter how we treat him. He's not one of us. He's Italian.' And you said, 'It does matter! Has the Golden Rule become so tarnished? He is a brother in Christ and a child of God! Even if he were a Mohammedan or an atheist we should treat him with equal kindness. What good is the love of Christ in your hearts unless it first changes your life?'"

"I said all that?" Gustav asked, somewhat embarrassed.

"You certainly did," Otto replied. "I think that's what really opened people's hearts to the D'Angelos—and that they found out he's a world-class concert organist." Otto thought for a moment and asked, "Would we be so shallow as to embrace him only because he's well-to-do and famous?"

The two men glanced at each other. "No," Gustav said, smiling and shaking his head, "that would be incredibly shallow."


On Friday, Martha Schnuelle arrived in town on the ten-sixteen train after having lived with Conrad and Charlotte in Chicago for the last three years. Charlotte had fully recovered from consumption, so Martha was able to return home. Clara, Liesl, and Gerhardt greeted her at the station. Clara threw her arms around Martha and said, "Welcome home, Mother! The whole village, even Bruno, is excited to see you again."

"Oh, how is Bruno?" Martha asked. "He must be getting pretty old."

Gerhardt said, "He's fine, although Otto has noticed he doesn't keep up with the children as well as he used to."

"Oh, Mother," Clara said, "I want to show you the hats I've been working on. I've already sold ten dozen at Woolworth's!"

"Clara, that's splendid! I had no idea you were doing so well on that."

"I help with some of the hat bands," Liesl said proudly. "Mama put me on the payroll for ten cents a week."

"Liesl," Martha said, "I hope you save some of that money. The pennies make the dollars, you know."

"Sure thing, Gramma! I keep 'em in a Mason jar. That's my bank."

"And Gerhardt," Martha said, "how are you? How are things at the store? Your mother? We've been gabbing away. You can't get a word in edgewise."

"Oh, everything's fine—my mother, the store," he replied. "I was enjoying listening to the three of you catch up."

That evening, Clara invited Martha for dinner. Martha brought pickled beets to add to the meal. Clara was delighted to have her home.

At one point, Martha said, "Oh, Clara, I meant to ask. Did that man ever find you? Do you know the one I mean? His name was—oh, I can't remember!"

"No," Clara said. "Was it someone you met in Chicago?"

"Yes, he stopped by one day when I was alone, asking if Conrad had a sister named Clara. I said yes. He said you used to work for him years ago, and I asked if he wanted to leave a message for you. But he just asked for your address and said he wanted to surprise you sometime."

"Did he have a beard?"

"No, he was clean-shaven. Maybe a mustache."

"Did he walk with a limp?"

"I'm not sure. I don't think so, but I guess he might have. I really wasn't paying close enough attention."

"Did this happen just recently?"

"Oh, no. I'd say a few years ago—shortly after I went to live with Conrad. Did I do something wrong?"

"No, I don't think so," Clara said hesitantly. "Anyway, it doesn't matter."

"It does matter, Clara. I didn't mean to do anything against your wishes."

All of this caused Clara to wonder. Her mind was preoccupied, and she didn't talk much the rest of the evening.

On Saturday morning over at the church, confirmation school was meeting. Gustav led the class in a discussion on Christ-like mercy, grace, forgiveness, and love. He noticed Johann Johannes staring blankly out into space and wanted to see if his point was getting across. "Johann," Gustav asked, "what would Jesus have you do if some boy came up and slapped you on the cheek?"

"Well, uh," Johann said, "do you think I could whang 'n whomp 'im?"

"No, no, Johann. What would Jesus do?"

"Well, why would some boy slap Jesus?"

Gustav strolled over to the window with his hands clasped behind his back, searching for answers in the sky. He mumbled, "'... and upon this rock I will build my Church.' Hmm, hmm, hmm! I'd look for another quarry."

On Saturday evening over at the Rickmeiers, Frieda was just finishing a bedtime reading to Minna, who was contentedly curled up on her lap. "The Owl And The Pussy-Cat" by Edward Lear was one of Minna's favorite poems:

> *... And hand in hand, on the edge of the sand,*
> *They danced by the light of the moon,*
> *The moon,*
> *The moon,*
> *They danced by the light of the moon.*[iii]

Minna was nearly asleep, a blissful smile on her face. Calvin walked quietly into the room with his hands behind his back.

"Minna," he said, "I rode into town down by Woolworth's today, and guess what? You know those elephant eggs? They hatched!" From behind his back, he brought out two stuffed calico elephants—one green and one yellow.

Minna beamed. Reaching out and taking one elephant in each hand, she tucked them under her chin. "Thank you, Calvin!" she said. "They're just what I thought they'd look like."

Frieda smiled up at her son and said, "You are as kind and wonderful as your father."

"Aw," Calvin said, "it really doesn't matter, Mama. They're only little stuffed animals."

"It does matter," she replied. "Kindness makes all the difference in the world. And it warms the heart of God."

# Chapter Twenty-two 〜

Once again, the rhythms of life were evident in the changing of the seasons. Otto pondered the calendar on his desk; it was the second week of September in 1909—still summer. The fields and forests suggested the same thing. But the flocking blackbirds reminded him that summer was passing; so did the shortening days and the unmistakable aroma of declining vegetation.

After school on Tuesday, Anna Klemme and Simon Jr. were at the general store. He seemed to want everything in sight and was driving her crazy.

"How 'bout this clown bank, Mama?" he asked. "Can I have it?"

"Do you need it?" Anna replied.

"I want it. Oh, Mama. Look at his outfit. Red polka dots, a white suit, a pointy hat to match. It's fine, Mama. All you do is put a penny in the clown's hand and press the top of his hat. The clown raises his arm, opens his mouth, and swallows the penny. It's really nuts."

"Nuts?"

"Sure, Mama. That's what Calvin says. 'It's nuts,' he says."

"Do you have enough money to buy the bank?"

"Ya mean I have to pay for it?"

"Well, of course you have to pay for it. For anything worthwhile, there's always a cost. So, if you really want it to be yours, you have to pay the price."

"Herr Steitz," Simon said, turning toward Otto, "how much does this clown bank cost?"

"Let's see," Otto said, walking over and picking up the bank. "I wrote the price on the bottom here. Two dollars, Master Simon."

"Two dollars? That's really expensive."

"Yes, it is," Otto said. "Two dollars is what I paid for it. But, for the right person, it'll be worth every penny. This was an extraordinary find. It's a mechanical bank from France and it's made of bronze. And don't you like the detailed hand painting?"

"That's really expensive," Simon repeated, as if in a trance.

Anna said, "It's a nice bank, Simon. But a bank's real purpose is to hold treasure. So if you never put much into it, it won't be worth much in the end."

"Shall I wrap it up for you, Master Simon?" Otto asked.

Before Simon could answer, Anna said, "He'll need to save his pennies for quite some time before he'll be able to afford anything like that. Thank you." She guided her son toward the door.

On Wednesday morning, Lester Mohr was finishing a transaction with Gustav Vriesen. He'd come in to buy some oats for his horse. Lester recorded the sale in his ledger. Julius Johannes came through the door.

Gustav hoisted the fifty-pound sack to his shoulder and headed for the door. He said, "Mind the mill, Lester! Guten Tag, Julius," and went outside.

"Who was that?" Julius asked Lester.

"You know. Herr Vriesen."

"From the church? Right. I'm surprised that he's strong enough to carry a sack of oats like that."

"I forgot," Lester said, "you wouldn't know him."

"Don't get me wrong," Julius said. "I believe in some sort of God and all that. I send my children to Sunday school. I don't know how much they get out of it, but it's probably good for them. Still, I have better things to do on Sunday mornings than dress up in a monkey suit and sit with a bunch of hypocrites in church."

"We are people," Lester said, "who at least recognize our need for God and try to live better lives. And remember, your children are always learning from your example."

"But it's pointless," Julius replied, "wasting all that time when you could be doing something productive."

Lester set his ledger and pen on the desk, leaned back, and said, "Honoring the Sabbath has many benefits that cannot be recorded in a ledger."

"They're not things I'm interested in," Julius replied. "I care about the productivity of my fields and how much I harvest at the end of the season. Being successful in farming doesn't happen without a lot of hard work. And I'm more than willing to pay that price."

"There's always more work to do than can be finished, and you can work yourself to death trying. I almost did." He paused for a moment, stroking his beard, then continued: "That's why my wife left me fifteen years ago. You've heard the expression, 'All work and no play makes Jack a dull boy'? Well, I became even worse."

"I've often thought that," Julius said, smirking.

Lester smiled and continued: "I had no time for anyone, just work. When she left, my relatives said, 'Good for her!' I had no friends. I didn't have any shoulders to cry on, not even God's. It's true, there's a cost to keeping the Sabbath. You have to give some things up. But so much more is gained. It's even more costly to ignore the Sabbath."

Julius replied, "I have never noticed God punishing me for working on Sundays. The fruits of my labor on the Sabbath are equal to anything I do the rest of the week. In fact, let's make a wager that my harvest this year will be greater than that of any of my neighbors. Let those who are stupid and lazy take time off, and I will acquire the wealth that could have been theirs."

"Ah, Julius," Lester said, shaking his head. "The consequences of ignoring the Sabbath are not necessarily seen at the harvest of one season, but after the harvest of many years, the harvest of a lifetime. Some day, I'm afraid you'll find that your overflowing storage bins don't contain anything you really value. Those who are wise learn from the mistakes of others. Those who are not insist on making their own mistakes. But it's your choice, Julius. Your choice."

On Friday morning, Otto was sweeping off the boardwalk in front of the store. He straightened his back and noticed somebody walking up the road from the west. Porkpie hat, outlandish plaid suit, salesman's satchel. "Well, I'll be a skinny-dippin' ol' mule!" Otto said. "J. T. Whitley." Shouting this time, Otto said, "Hey! J. T. Whitley! Is that you?"

"Say there, Old Timer! Is that all you do—sweep off your boardwalk? That's what you were doing the last time I was through here. I figured you'd be runnin' out of Doctor Whitley's Miracle Elixir by now. How 'bout a fresh supply?"

"Nein, da—" Otto caught himself. "Eh, no, thank you," he said. "We're still pretty well set. But I have to say, the neighborhood cats love it—they sing real well."

"Well then, Pappy, you'll be interested in our newest product. May I introduce you to Doctor Whitley's Fountain Of Youth, guaranteed and scientifically proven to take years off of anyone's appearance."

"What about babies?" Otto asked.

"Of course not! It's not recommended for anyone under the age of thirty-five. That's when people start to get desper—I mean, that's when it's most effective. Here, try a spoonful."

"Whew!" Otto said, staggering backward. "The mooooon is shinin' brightly!"

"'Tisn't moonshine, but a distillation of Nirvana. Let me ask you, Pappy. How old are you? Ninety? A hundred?"

Otto frowned. "Sixty something," he said.

"Good grief, man! I hope it's not too late."

"Mister Whitley," Otto said, "I won't be buying anything from you today. But why don't you come in for a cup of coffee? I'll treat. And, uh, please leave your satchel outside so nobody inside is tempted."

"Mightn't it be stolen?"

"You city folks worry about that too much. If your supply of Fountain Of Youth elixir is missing, we'll know the culprit is a youthful-looking drunk. Come on in."

Otto poured some coffee for each of them and they sat at one of the checkers tables.

Whitley sipped his coffee and surveyed the room. "Say, Old Timer, did I mention I do some business consulting on the side? I tell ya, we could turn this sleepy, little store of yours into a gold mine."

"Why would I want that?" Otto asked.

"Why, to make more money, of course. Let me ask you, how much do you charge your regular customers for coffee?"

"I don't. It's free."

"Hey! I thought you said you were treating me?"

"That's right. I always treat."

"How much do you charge for a game of checkers?"

"Charge? It's free."

"Free? Do you see the problem here, Pappy? How much do those shirts over there go for?"

"One dollar."

"One dollar? My stars, man! The same shirts are going for twice that much in the cities. You'd more than double your profits. What

221

about your bakery goods there? How much for a dozen rolls?"

"Ten cents—and I give 'em a baker's dozen."

"Highway robbery!" Whitley said. "Pappy, Pappy, you're givin' away the store. No more free coffee! Or checkers! Double your prices! Fire that lazy Fritzie fellow over there. And no free samples of anything. Then you'll be making some REAL money."

Otto leaned back in his chair, folding his hands behind his head. "Mister Whitley," he said, "I make a fair living from this store. If I take more than I need, isn't that stealing? My friends shop here. They depend upon the things I sell, and many of them aren't very well off."

Whitley said, "The freedom to make as much money as you can is a store owner's prerogative. That's what's gonna make some of us a lot wealthier than others. And that's what makes America great."

"I disagree. It's individual freedom tempered by love—personal responsibility to the community. I love these people. I would rather make a little less, help them as I can, and go to bed at night knowing that these good people are also looking out for my welfare. I try to live not by the rule of gold but the Golden Rule, as Jesus would have us do. That gives me a great deal of satisfaction. And," Otto said, smiling and waving a finger in Whitley's direction, "people don't hide their wallets when they see me coming."

On Saturday afternoon, two women were chatting on the boardwalk in front of the general store: Sophia Boeger, who had recently moved to the area, and Giesela Johannes, Julius' wife. It was a lopsided conversation, one that Sophia had walked into by mistake.

Giesela was doing most of the talking. She said, "Being you're a newcomer to these parts, I'll help you get acquainted with some of the neighbors. See that heavy-set man across the road in the blue shirt and overalls?"

Sophia looked and nodded.

"That's Jacob Schmalfuss, one of the dumbest people you'll ever meet. If you ever talk to him, remember to speak s-l-o-w-l-y. That way, he'll have a chance to understand some of what you say. And that woman, standing in the doorway of the seamstress shop?" She pointed across the street.

Again Sophia simply nodded.

"That," Giesela continued, "is Clara Schnuelle. She wants people to think she's become a model citizen, with her operating the shop and being a Sunday school teacher and all. But I know better. She's not married, yet she has a child. Everybody around here knows that, in her younger years, she was quite the little harlot. And now she keeps pretty close company with an ex-convict. Not the kind of person I want teaching my children."

Sophia glanced at the door of the store and was about to escape inside when—

"Now that woman," Giesela said, motioning with her head, "is Martha Schnuelle, Clara's mother. Is that a package she's giving to Clara? Martha was the worst of mothers. She obviously couldn't control her children. Her son Conrad was as bad as his sister, only somehow he managed to become a doctor—goodness knows how many bribes he must have paid. I know I wouldn't take a dog to get treated by him."

Sophia felt her face flush. She glanced at the door again, then looked back to see that Martha was heading toward them.

"Shhh," Giesela said. "Try to be kind to the elderly." Smiling, she said more loudly, "Hello, Mrs. Schnuelle. We were just talking about you. All good, of course."

"Of course," Martha said, smiling. She winked at Sophia and said, "And who is this? Our new neighbor?"

"Yes," Giesela replied. "Martha Schnuelle, allow me to introduce you to Sophia Boeger. They recently moved here from the ghastly state of Ohio—the poor dears. Now where was I? That man walking toward the blacksmith shop—is someone I don't know. But, just from the looks of him, he's a real hayseed. I don't think I'd care to know him."

"Well," Martha said, "I met him earlier, and he seems to be a fine gentleman. Sophia, isn't that your husband, John?"

Sophia forced a smile and said to Martha, "Excuse me."

Giesela cleared her throat and said, "I'm sure the two of them deserve each other. They're obviously not a high quality of people."

Martha looked squarely at her and said, "It is most often the case that those who go around spreading poison end up giving themselves a double dose."

"Nonsense," Giesela replied. "It's just a little harmless gossip. Don't you enjoy spreading all these tasty tidbits around, adding some of your own spice?"

"Actually, no," Martha said.

"But think of all the juicy gossip you're missing."

"By controlling my tongue, my thoughts? Just some poisonous drivel that doesn't do anyone any good. And look at what I gain— the trust and respect of my friends and neighbors. Can you say the same?" Martha turned and walked away.

Giesela was quiet.

On Sunday, Lester noticed a new face at church. About ten minutes before the service started, Julius slid into the pew next to him.

Julius leaned toward Lester and said quietly, "I was missing much more than I knew. I have been feeling poorly lately, and I feel alone and afraid. My children are all almost grown up, and I was too busy to notice. My wife—I hardly know her, and the woman I see is someone I don't like. She's terribly vain—only cares about herself. I realize that I don't even have any friends, no one that I trust. And I really have no knowledge of God. My whole family has paid a terrible price."

Lester glanced at Julius and patted him on the knee. "Welcome," he said.

"Thank you."

# Chapter Twenty-three ∼

In June of 1910, some of the farmers in Sheboygan County, including Simon Klemme, were having quite a time of it. There hadn't been any major catastrophes, just far too much rain for Simon's liking. It was hot and humid on Monday and it rained, on and off, most of the day. At mid-morning, Simon found himself sitting on the front porch again, gazing gloomily toward the road, through a curtain of rain.

*Rain, rain, go away, water someone else's hay! Say, that's pretty good. We farmers spend a lot of time complaining. Too little, too much, too soon, too late. But it's tough. My fields are all so low. They're always among the last to dry out. That's what's so frustrating. Sure, the ones who have their crops in already are enjoying this. Everything's growing. But for me, it's just weeds. I've hardly had a chance to plant anything yet. It's getting kind of late, and it's hard not to get fidgety.*

His thoughts went to a bath-time game he used to play with his three children when they were little. He'd set the large washtub in the middle of the kitchen floor and pour a few buckets of warm water in it. Catherine, Caroline, and Simon Jr. would climb in and get all soapy and clean. When it was time to rinse off, Simon would fill the bucket with more warm water. Then, using a Mason jar as a ladle, he'd dip it into the bucket, hold it high above the children's heads and say, "And then, it began to rain!" pouring it over the heads of the squealing children. After a few times, all he needed to say was, "And then..." and the children would shout in chorus, "it began to rain!" The four of them loved this game.

Anna didn't. It was always the same. "Simon, you're making such a mess! You'll ruin the linoleum."

"Don't worry, dear. It's just a little water. I'll clean it up."

Simon's attention came back to a large puddle that was forming in the yard, but he realized he was smiling. *Nothing to do about it. Might as well just float with it. Hey, that's pretty good, too.*

On Tuesday afternoon, Gustav walked to the general store to pick up his mail and buy some lamp oil. The bell on the store door tinkled as he entered. Gerhardt and Otto looked up.

Gerhardt said, "Good morning, Herr Vriesen. I mean, good afternoon. Why do I do that? Say good morning to you, no matter what time of day it is?"

Gustav laughed. "Lots of people do that. I think it's a reflex. Mornings are when most folks are accustomed to seeing me. And maybe it's my merry morning sunshine disposition."

"That's the reason," Otto said. "If you were a fire and brimstone preacher, they'd say, "'Hello, Herr Hades.' without even thinking."

"Hmm," Gustav replied, "Herr Hades. That's a commanding appellation. But not very pastoral." He looked around the store. "Say, no Fritzie today?"

"No," Otto said, "Fritzie and Johann left on the train for the U.P. this morning. The way they figure it, they'll be rich young men in a week."

"Oh, right. It's that wolverine scheme," Gustav said.

"Yep, that stranger passing through a few weeks ago put the idea in Fritzie's head. The fellow said the going price for skins is high, and there's still a good number of wolverines to be found along the southern shore of Lake Superior. With Johann being his cousin and all, Fritzie told him they'd go halvers on the deal. Though, being the senior partner, Fritzie will get the bigger half."

"The bigger half?" Gustav smiled. "Sounds like something Johann would agree to. When will they be back?"

"On Friday, if things go as they plan. We'll see. If they come back in one piece, it'll be a success. In the meantime, Gerhardt and I will hold down the fort."

On Wednesday morning, Clara Schnuelle unlocked her shop door and walked across the road to check her mail. "Good morning, Herr Steitz. Has the mail been sorted already?"

"Yes," Otto said, "Gerhardt just finished with it and I sent him to Sheboygan for something. He'll be sorry he missed you. Is there something for you?"

"I'm sure I'll see him later. And, yes, I did receive something. Hmm, I don't recognize the writing." She opened it and found this printed on a piece of paper:

When does 11 + 12 + 20 = 0?

"Oh, it's a riddle," she said. "I like riddles—especially since things have been so dreary lately."

"May I see it?" Otto asked, reaching for the paper. "That's interesting. When does 11 + 12 + 20 = 0? I'll have to think about that. Let's see. It's postmarked in Sheboygan, but you don't have any idea who sent this to you?"

"No. But it does look interesting. I think I'll pin it up in my shop and let my customers have some fun with it."

Wednesday was Gottfried Mohr's eighty-fifth birthday. He and Lester invited all of Bierville to stop by during the afternoon or evening for some chocolate cake and frozen custard that Gottfried had made himself.

Otto closed the store at five o'clock and went to see Gottfried. After getting some of the birthday treat, he sat next to the guest of honor and said, "So, Uncle, what's it like to be eighty-five?"

In the husky voice of an octogenarian, Gottfried said, "Well, it's better than having to stop counting at eighty-four, if you know what I mean. Otherwise, pretty good. You know, 'Too soon old, too late smart.'"

"How's that body of yours holding together?"

"Oh, all right, I guess. But I think I've been getting rather forgetful lately. I remember things from my childhood as clearly as if they were yesterday, but things from even five minutes ago—why, they go in one ear and out the other."

They each took a bite of cake and frozen custard, and Otto said, "Well, for someone who's eighty-five, I think you're doing quite well."

"Ja, but I think I've been getting rather forgetful lately. I remember things from my childhood as clearly as if they were yesterday, but, uh. What was I saying? I think I've been getting rather forgetful lately."

Otto took his uncle's hand and said, "Just do the best you can and don't worry. Keep that sense of humor of yours and things will go well."

"Ja, ja," he said, chuckling. "'Of all the things I've lost, I miss my mind the most.'"


On Thursday morning, it was already hot, hazy, and humid by the time Simon finished his chores in the barn. After Anna and he finished breakfast, he gave her a kiss and said, "It appears the lower ten has finally dried out enough to plant, so I'll be down there till dinner. If you have some time later, I'd appreciate it if you could bring out some more seed and some water to drink."

Simon headed out to the shed, got the planter ready, and hooked up Ol' Billy. With the reigns in hand, he set out for a promising day of planting. When they reached the field, Simon got off the planter seat, set the lever so the seed would fall, and said, "Well, Ol' Billy, it appears we're in luck. I think we've got a good day of planting ahead of us."

He hopped back up in the seat and—"Thunder? Well, the sky is still a hazy blue. It can't rain now." He looked up and a big drop hit him in the eye. And then, more thunder and a lot more rain. "Aw, Billy. Not again." He felt like crying, or maybe smashing something.

Simon disengaged the lever on the planter. They headed for home and he said, "Well, Ol' Billy, I guess we're done." At that point, they weren't in a hurry. By the time they'd gone a hundred yards, Simon was soaked to the bone. So was Ol' Billy, but Ol' Billy seemed to be enjoying it more.

Anna was in the kitchen when Simon walked through the back door. She glanced at him and burst into hysterical laughter. "Simon, you look like a—" She wanted to say "a drowned puppy wearing a soggy, straw basket," but she couldn't get the words out.

He glared at her and said, "This is serious, Anna!" For a moment, she suppressed her laughter. However, she made the mistake of looking at him again and she giggled uncontrollably.

Still laughing and gasping for air, she staggered over to Simon, removed the hat from his head, and showed it to him. This time they both erupted with laughter. They hooted and howled till the tears streamed down their cheeks and held on to each other to keep from falling over.

After about five minutes, they regained enough composure to sit at the kitchen table. "Whew!" Simon said, and gazed out the window at the falling rain. The smile faded from his face. "Ya know," he said, "if rain is a blessing from heaven, then I wish heaven would bless somebody else for awhile."

"I know," Anna replied, "it's just too much of a good thing, like a big Thanksgiving dinner where everybody stays at the table gorging themselves until all the food is gone. But all we can do is do what we can. Things have a way of working out. Nothing is impossible for God."

On Friday morning, Herman Rickmeier had just finished in the barn and was heading toward the house when he noticed little Minna standing near the back door. She was crying. "Minna," he said, "what's wrong?"

"Look," she said. Taking him by the hand, she led him toward the road. She pointed at a dead raccoon lying at the side of the road.

"Aw, Minna," he said. "It appears the poor thing was run over." He saw this as an educational opportunity for his niece.

Gently, he lifted her up and set her on a fence post so they could talk face-to-face. "Minna," he said, "death is part of life, and life is awfully fragile. Many times, there isn't very much difference between the living and the dead. That's why life is so precious."

"Was that raccoon a baby once?" she asked.

"Oh, sure, and some mama is going to be sad to find out her young one was killed. But ya know, Minna, nothing is too difficult for God, and I think maybe there's a raccoon heaven where that little one lives with God now."

"Really?"

"Sure, why not? But, with all the horses and wagons and now automobiles going by, you'd better be careful by the road there or you could end up like that raccoon. And we'd all be sad."

On Friday afternoon shortly after lunch, Catherine, Caroline, and Simon Jr. were out at the edge of the woods picking bouquets of wildflowers for their mother. Caroline began shrieking, "It's a bee! It's a bee!" One was buzzing persistently around the flowers in her hand.

"Let it perch on your hand!" Simon said, dancing with excitement. "Let it perch on your hand! It'll die. When bees sting people, they die."

"Nooooo!" Caroline wailed.

"Why don't you put the flowers down and walk away?" Catherine said.

"Let it perch on your hand!"

"Put your flowers down!"

"Nooooo!" Caroline zigzagged toward the house, leaving a trail of flowers.

Back at the Rickmeiers' on Friday, Frieda spent the afternoon preparing a celebration for the thirty-third "monthiversary" of Adam and Emilie's wedding. Theirs was a torrid love affair. What they lacked in sophistication they more than made up for in sincerity. The tone for their marriage was set at their first breakfast as newlyweds. Adam raised his coffee cup to toast his beloved, saying with great affection, "Here's mud in your eye!"

And she, all dreamy-eyed, answered, "And lots of it!" What did it matter? They were in love. Frieda treasured that story.

In the evening, everyone gathered for the festivities and the preparations were nearly complete. Herman glanced into the parlor. "Look," he said. "Emilie and Adam are sitting together in the rocking chair. I didn't know that chair was sturdy enough to hold two people like that."

Frieda smiled and said, "Remember how we used to sit together like that when we were newlyweds?"

"Yes, but we'd both never fit in there now." She elbowed him in the ribs. He said, "Well, it's mostly me," giving her a kiss on the cheek. "How long do you think they're going to act like newlyweds?"

"As long as they love each other, I hope."

"Their son Thomas is eighteen months old!"

"Why should that discourage them?"

"Remember Calvin at that age? He would have discouraged anybody."

She put her arms around his waist and said, "We did just fine. After they go home later, why don't we try out that rocking chair?"

That night, Frieda tucked Minna into bed and asked, "Liebchen, did you learn something from what your uncle told you about that poor, little animal?"

"Yes," Minna replied, "I learned to be careful near the road, or I could turn into a raccoon and be dead."

"Oh, dear," Frieda said. "I don't think that would happen, but you do need to be careful. When you're near the road, make sure you stop, look, and listen."

On Saturday morning, Otto was ringing up a sale on the cash register when he heard the front door open. He looked up. "Fritzie!" he said. "Welcome back! So how was the big hunt?"

"Herr Steitz," he said, smiling, "you're not gonna believe it."

"Ah, just as I expected. You didn't see any wolverines, did you?"

"See any? We were lucky to get out alive! Those critters are ferocious!"

By this time, a crowd had gathered near Fritzie and Otto. "All right," Otto said, smiling and shaking his head. "I can tell there's a good story here. Why don't you tell us all about it?"

"Ladies and gentlemen," Fritzie said, his eyes lighting up, "it was the adventure of a lifetime! Here's what happened. Last Wednesday, we were about a mile south of Lake Superior. We had just finished lunch, after not seeing a trace of a wolverine all morning. Johann and I decided to go on a little hike, just to let our food settle.

"'No need to bring our rifles,' Johann says. 'We won't be gone long.' And wouldn't ya know? I believed him! So there we were, followin' this little trout stream along, tracin' it through rapids and pools, meanderin' its way toward Lake Superior.

"Well, by an' by, that stream went an' grew into a full-size river. In the shallows, we could see dozens of nice brook trout. And, at one point, the water went tumblin' down twenty-five feet into the shadows and rocks at the other side of this bowl-shaped gorge. The whole river disappeared underground.

"Well, we figured we'd climb into the gorge for a better look. When we were partway down, there was this powerful smell. Wolverine! I pointed and froze. 'Johann!' I whispers. 'Look! There's a wolverine eatin' a big trout!'

"'Yessir,' he says, 'that's a wolverine, all right! How old d'ya reckon he is?'

"'Looks like a yearling,' I says. 'Look it! We can get it. Let's put on our gloves. We both got our knives along, and there's two of us!'

"So down into the shadows we climb. When we reach the bottom, we draw our knives, ready to strike. 'Jumpin' jackrabbits!' Johann says. 'What a smell! Pert near as bad as a skunk!'

"'Don't worry,' I says, 'the stink's worth it. If what that fella says is true, we'll get three, maybe six dollars for this one.'"

"'In that case,' Johann says, 'I got really good news! There's at least fifteen more over here, and some of 'em are really big! We're rich!'

"I turn to look, an' my heart jus' stops. I says to myself, 'Fritzie, I hope you're happy! Sixteen wolverines cornered in the bottom of a twenty-five foot gorge. This is good news!'

"Well, somebody starts makin' this nasty snarlin' sound, an' somebody else joins in—and I'm pretty sure it's not Johann an' me. So I whispers, 'Nice an' easy, now. Back away nice an' slow. On a count of three, we'll make a beeline outta here. One. Two—' Well, wouldn't ya know, Johann trips an' falls on his behind. Hell's bells!

In a flash, it's pandemonium, I tell ya! Snarlin' an' clawin' an' bitin'! We were lucky to escape with our lives! All that for nothin'! But, boy, talk about excitement!"

The crowd exploded in laughter and applause.

Fritzie bowed. "Thank you. Thank you," he said.

The crowd dispersed.

Otto patted him on the back. "Quite a story, young man," he said. "Any of it true?"

"The whole thing. Gospel truth. Jus' look at my boot here! This big one had me right there. Woulda eaten me for dinner if he'd had the chance."

"Let's see that," Otto said, kneeling for a closer look. "Well, you could have scraped that boot up on some rocks. Or maybe you tore it in some of the heavy underbrush. But, uh, what's this? There's something stuck in the heel." Otto found a pair of pliers and pulled the object out. "It's a tooth that was broken off in there!"

"Really?" Fritzie said. "I feel a bit queasy."

Otto examined it in his open hand. "Looks like a canine tooth, Fritzie. Well, what do you know?"

On Saturday, Frieda was tucking Minna into bed and Minna asked, "Will there be cheese in church tomorrow?"

Frieda chuckled and replied, "Well, I don't think so, dear. We don't normally have food at church."

'That's not fair," Minna said. "They never give us any, so why do we sing 'Bringing In The Cheese' there?"

Frieda tried not to laugh. She thought about trying to explain why they sang about sheaves, but it was late. She kissed Minna on the forehead, and said, "I think we have some cheese we could take along tomorrow and share."

It was a lovely day on Sunday, and Gustav was enjoying welcoming a great flock of his people for worship. On his way into church, August Schmidt said to Gustav, "My barn is nearly as clean as when it was built, my machinery has been repaired and oiled and polished—three times! And I've taught three of my cows to play pinochle with me. But I want to plant something!"

Gustav commiserated with him. "I'm sure you're frustrated. But you know this weather pattern can't last. In the meantime, remember Proverbs 17:22: 'A merry heart is a good medicine: But a broken spirit drieth up the bones.'"

"That's true," August replied. "It doesn't help to moan and groan about things we can't change, and it feels much better to laugh."

"Soon, I'm sure," Gustav said, "you'll have more work than you'll be able to manage. By September, I imagine things will seem about normal once again. What was it that God said after the flood? 'While the earth remaineth, seedtime and harvest… shall not cease.' Now, August, let us worship together and enjoy the presence and love of our gracious God."

# Chapter Twenty-four 〜

*'Twas the twelfth of December*
*And all through the village*
*Neither burglar nor robber*
*Would venture to pillage.*
*Yet one damsel's spirit*
*Was sore in distress,*
*"The danger—I fear it,*
*I humbly confess."*

For everyone in Bierville, the middle third of December, 1910 was marked not by the joyful anticipation that would normally be expected in the days prior to Christmas but a growing sense of apprehension. They were aware that Clara Schnuelle might be in danger, yet neither she nor anyone else was certain why.

On Monday over at Clara's shop, Martha and her daughter were discussing the atmosphere of uncertainty. Martha said, "Whoever sent those letters might be a madman, but I don't think he's a danger to you."

"Madmen aren't dangerous?" Clara asked. "How can you be sure? It seems to me the main advantage a madman has is surprise. Nobody knows what he's going to do because he doesn't act rationally. What does he want from me?"

"You have a point, dear. But we don't know who's behind this riddle or that anyone means you harm. It could be nothing more than a series of coincidences. After all, nothing really bad ever happens in Bierville. Some day we'll look back at this and laugh." Martha went over to the wall and read the riddle again:

When does 11 + 12 + 20 = 0?

Beneath it were posted three clues to the riddle Clara had received during the past three months. They were written in the same hand-printed characters as the riddle. Because each of the other riddle pieces had arrived about one month apart, Clara expected another one to come soon. That's why she'd become so apprehensive. The clues said, in the order they were received:

11 years
the 12th month
the 20th day.

"What does it mean?" Clara asked. "This isn't fun anymore. Eleven years, the twelfth month, the twentieth day—that could mean something just short of twelve years, I suppose."

"Or," Martha said, "the twelfth month, the twentieth day— that would be December twentieth, but eleven years from now or eleven years ago? I'm not sure."

"Liesl turns eleven soon," Clara replied, "but that's on Christmas Day. And why would all of that equal zero?"

"It's puzzling, dear. And a little ominous, I admit." Martha said. "But it's not necessarily a reason to be worried. At any rate, you have all of Bierville standing with you."

"I know," Clara replied, "and that helps."

"Now," Martha said cheerfully, "can I help you with those table linens for the Rickmeiers? Frieda wants them by Saturday."

"Thank you, Mother. What would I do without you?"

The next several days were a blur for Clara. On Friday morning, she and Liesl walked over to Rickmeiers and delivered the table linen—a day early. Frieda was delighted. "They'll be perfect for our Christmas dinner," she said. "We'll have a full house with you two, your mother, Gerhardt and his mother, Emilie's three, and the four of us here. It'll be wonderful!"

"I'm glad you like them, Frieda," Clara said. "The work helps to keep my mind occupied."

"How are you?"

"Nervous. But the strangest thing is, I'm not even sure why."

Frieda hugged her and said, "Try not to worry. It might not be anything."

After morning chores on Saturday, Simon Klemme Jr. said to Anna, "Mama, may I go find Calvin now? I want to see if he'll play football with me."

"He's quite a bit older than you. Do you think that's a good idea?"

"Sure, Mama! We're just going to play catch. That's all."

"All right, as long as you wear your hat and coat. It's a warm day for December, but it's still chilly."

"Thanks, Mama," he said, and headed out the door.

Simon Jr. went to find Calvin and his football, but the business about playing catch was mostly a ruse; he needed Calvin's help on a project. When the two of them reached Simon's planned destination behind the general store, he said, "Calvin, wait'll ya see this—behind the outhouse. It's the berries!"

"Great slimy slugs!" Calvin said. "This looks interesting! Tell me about it."

"Well," Simon replied, "since the general store's privy is a twin seater, it can hold more people than most private ones. That gives us more chances. This piece of stovepipe, here, I found at the village dump. It runs down to that hole in the back of the privy and goes inside. We hide back here in this thicket."

"So how's it work?" Calvin asked. "Do ya pour somethin' down there? Down the pipe?"

"No," Simon replied, "it only runs into the empty box between the seats.

First we need a customer—a lady would be best. Then we count to twenty and say…" Simon whispered something into Calvin's ear and they both burst out laughing. Simon continued: "You should be the one to say it. Your voice sounds more official-like."

The plan was set, and they hid in the thicket. Being a busy Saturday morning, they didn't have to wait long for their first visitor. It was Edna Dinkmeier. When she closed the privy door, Calvin counted to twenty and said into the pipe, "Lady, we're cleaning down here. Could ya use the other side?"

Shrieking and wailing, Edna bolted out of the privy. She disappeared across the lawn, doing her best to tuck and run at the same time.

Calvin and Simon Jr. made a beeline toward the millpond. "Oh, that was great!" Calvin said, laughing. "Where'd ya come up with that idea?"

"From my Papa. Ha ha! He was right! It worked really well!"

"How old are you? Seven or eight?"

"Almost eight."

"My boy, you have a promising future! You'd be a prime candidate for The Easy Boys Club."

"'The Easy Boys'? What's that?"

"I'll tell ya all about it!" Calvin took Simon Jr. under his personal tutelage.

Early on Tuesday the twentieth, Otto and Fritzie sorted the morning mail. It was another mild December day, but the warmth couldn't mask the cold foreboding they felt. Otto noticed another letter for Clara, postmarked in Sheboygan, similar in appearance to the riddle letters. Rather than wait for her to come after her mail, he walked across the road to get her.

Clara read the letter, gasped, and buried her face in Otto's shoulder.

"No," she cried, "it's happening!"

Still holding Clara, Otto took the letter from her and read it out loud:

When does $11 + 12 + 20 = 0$?
(11 years, the 12th month, the 20th day)
When it's the last day of your life. 10:00

"Fritzie," Otto said, "I want you to ride into town and alert the sheriff. Explain the situation. We're trying to prevent something bad from happening. He might be able to give us some help—maybe send his deputy. Hurry back!"

Bruno sat up, looked at Otto, and gave a muffled bark.

"Yes, Bruno," Otto said, "we might need your help, too. Clara, let's call a village meeting here for eight-thirty. That gives us about an hour and a half to notify people. Gerhardt will be back any minute. He can escort Liesl and you to your mother's place. Then he and I can finish spreading the word. Sound good?"

"Yes, I think so," Clara said.

"Fine. See you at eight-thirty. And try to stay calm."

By eight-thirty, the general store was packed with more than forty people from the area. Gustav Vriesen stood on a chair and convened the meeting with a prayer: "Good Shepherd, as your people and the sheep of your pasture, we entrust ourselves to the wisdom of your care. We seek your guidance and strength to do what you would have us do, to live as the people of your kingdom in this hour of trial. Hold us all—particularly Clara and Liesl—in your tender care. And bless our enemy with a sense of your redeeming presence and eternal peace, in Jesus' name. Amen."

Otto stood on a stepladder next to Gustav and said, "Here's the situation. Clara received what appears to be the last part of the riddle today. We're not sure who sent all of these riddle pieces, but altogether it reads:

> When does 11 + 12 + 20 = 0?
> (11 years, the 12th month, the 20th day)
> When it's the last day of your life. 10:00

"With this being the twentieth day of the twelfth month," Gustav said, "it appears likely that something is being planned for ten o'clock today, but we don't know what. Whoever has been sending these seems to be three shades of a madman and focused only on Clara. It might help to keep these things in mind."

Otto said, "Fritzie should be back any time with word from the sheriff. In the meantime, we need a plan to keep Clara safe. Any ideas?"

Hugo Putz said, "Why don't we just look for a stranger and plug 'im between the eyes? That'll make a quick end of it." Several others voiced their approval.

Otto held up his hand to quiet the gathering. "We get strangers through here all the time. Are you planning to kill them all?"

"Beyond that," Gustav said, "as followers of Jesus we are called to do what he would do. He was holy and pure, and we must strive to be so. Our Lord does not give us license to commit immoral acts, even for moral purposes. 'See that none render unto any one evil for evil; but always follow after that which is good, one toward another, and toward all.'"

"What if we hide her?" Gertrude asked.

"What's to say he won't gurricken find her?" Carl said.

"What if we send her away?" August asked.

"Where?" Martha replied. "She might be running for the rest of her life."

Fritzie entered the front door. He was frowning and glanced at Clara.

"Well?" Otto asked.

Fritzie said, "I'm sorry, Clara. There's a strike at one of the furniture factories. The sheriff and his deputy are busy there, trying to keep the peace. The sheriff said one of them might be able to come out this afternoon."

There was a collective groan from the crowd.

"Any other ideas?" Otto asked.

"I have a suggestion," Adam Schroeder said, rising to his feet. "What if we act like a flock of sheep?"

There was an explosion of derision and contemptuous laughter from many in the gathering.

Otto held up his hand again to quiet the crowd. "Wait! Wait! Hear him out! Let's see what Adam has to say."

Adam stood next to Otto. "When many species of animals seek protection from a predator, instead of fleeing or hiding, they flock together. It's a kind of camouflage. They all look so much alike and the movement is so confusing that the predator is unable to pick out one to attack, gets confused, and gives up."

There was another explosion of voices, this time of delighted enthusiasm and laughter. A plan was devised.

"Well?" Otto asked. "What do you think?"

"A plan sent from heaven," Gustav said, "delivered to us by an angel."

"I say we do it!" Herman Rickmeier said. "It's crazy enough to work against a crazy man. Well done, Adam!"

Gustav said, "Before everyone scurries off, I want us to remember something from the Gospel of John, 15:12-24: 'This is my Commandment, that ye love one another, as I have loved you. Greater love hath no man than this, that a man lay down his life for his friends. Ye are my friends, if ye do whatsoever I command you.' God be with you, my friends!"

Clara walked over and hugged Otto and Gustav. "Thank you! I have a feeling this will turn out all right."

"Let us hope so," Otto replied.

"Amen," Gustav said, nodding.

At nine-fifteen, Otto stepped outside of the store. People were starting to gather on the road through Bierville and the plan took shape. A distant spectator would have thought the whole village was filling up with women of all different shapes and sizes; black and shades of gray and blue were the colors of the day; bonnets were the preferred headwear.

Many of the women weren't really women. Reiny made an imposing, broad-shouldered *Frau*. Lester's full beard was arresting in its shock value, cascading down the front of his blouse; he held onto Gottfried, who was wearing a blue calico dress and black shawl. The two of them made a handsome pair.

Anna winked at Simon and said, "You know, you're a more attractive woman than I am."

Simon tapped her hand and said in falsetto, "Don't make advances on me, dearie! I'm spoken for."

"Reiny," Jacob said, "would you like to go—"

"Don't even ask," Reiny snapped in feigned irritation. "I have a headache."

"Calvin," Dominique said, "those old clothes of Emilie's fit you pretty well. If you run out of things to wear, you can borrow some of my dresses any time."

"Thanks," he said. "I think this'll be enough."

Otto mustered his sweetest smile and said to Gustav, "Would

Jesus have dressed up like a woman?"

"To save the life of a friend," Gustav replied, "I think he would have. He went to greater lengths than this."

Otto was delighted to see the more than seventy "Claras" milling about in the road between the general store and the printing shop. He even tied a blue bonnet on Bruno, who seemed to enjoy it. For a half hour, there was a carnival-like atmosphere among the flock. Adam stood off to the side and said to Otto, "This is exactly what I had in mind—the movement, the confusion. It's disorienting to see sideburns, mustaches, and beards poking out from under so many bonnets. Perfect!"

"Fritzie?" Otto called out. "Anybody see Fritzie?" He turned to Minnie and said, "I wonder where he is. He should have had time to change by now."

"Maybe he snagged his stockings and had to get a new pair," Minnie said, smiling. "That's a joke, Otto. I'm sure he's fine. He hasn't missed anything yet."

"Gerhardt!" Otto shouted, getting his attention. "Come here, will you?" He put him arm over Gerhardt's shoulder. "Son," he said, "just some fatherly advice. When all this is behind us, you need to marry that woman," pointing at Clara. "It's obvious you belong together. That's what you want, and you'll both be happier. Liesl, too. She needs a father and she loves you. Beside that, you have the blessing of all of Bierville."

Gerhardt smiled. "I know. You're right. I'm thinking of a June wedding."

The "women" continued milling about. Clara—the real one—mixed into the middle of the flock and held Liesl by the hand. Clara appeared to be choking back tears of gratitude and said, "Thank you all for helping me! Thank you!" Smiling, she turned to Otto and, taking the locket from around her neck, said in a playful tone, "Here, why don't you wear this? It'll look nice with that dress you're wearing."

"Why, thank you, Clara," he said. "I've often admired this locket of yours. As I said before, my wife had a similar one. May I open it? I'm curious about something."

"Be my guest," she replied.

"Let's see. On the left side here," he said, "is where you said the picture of your husband and you was? And behind it was that foreboding poem. Correct?"

"That's right," she said.

"Now on the right side here, behind this picture of you, my wife's locket had a kind of secret compartment. The picture comes out and with your fingernail you can—pry it open. There we are." Otto gazed into the secret compartment and froze in disbelief.

"Otto?" Martha asked. "What is it?"

Martha looked inside the locket and gasped. "Otto," she said, "this photograph. This is Elsa. When you were married. It's been thirty years."

"How can it be?" Otto said. "Elsa?" He removed the photograph of his wife from the locket. A small piece of newspaper was tucked inside the compartment. He unfolded it, read it, and staggered a few steps.

"Otto!" Gustav said, steadying him. "What does it say?"

Martha took the paper from Otto and said, "Oh, dear. It's a headline. 'WOMAN, TWO CHILDREN MURDERED—Killer At Large.'"

Becoming frantic, Clara cried, "What does this mean? What does this mean? Why are these things in my locket?"

"Oh, Clara," Gustav said softly, holding her in his arms. "It appears you were married to the man who murdered Otto's family. When he murdered them, he must have taken the locket from Elsa. I'm so sorry. I'm so sorry."

After digesting the information for a moment, Clara said numbly, "I've been wearing a death notice around my neck for thirteen years, and now he's coming for me." Her face was expressionless, as if she'd given up all hope.

"Oh, this is too much for any of us to absorb all at once," Gustav said. "Your former husband, Edward Mackey, is the same as Evan McKay, the one who boarded with Otto and killed his family? If he's the riddle writer, that's all the worse. That means he's both crazy and deadly. Beloved," he said so the whole flock could hear, "let us join in the prayer of our Savior."

They joined hands and prayed. Fear was replaced by courage. Doubt gave way to conviction. Weakness was transformed by power. The enemy approached and they were ready.

Fritzie came stumbling up from behind the general store. "Did I miss anything?" he asked, all out of breath. "I was in the outhouse changing when I got stuck inside this corset with my arms above my head. Then the corset got caught on a nail. I'm never puttin' one of these on again!"

The flock laughed and Otto patted him on the back.

It was ten o'clock.

"Someone's coming!" Adam said, pointing east toward the bridge. "Is that Mackey? Or McKay?"

Martha looked up. "Clara," she said, "I think that's the man who came looking for you in Chicago. Is he your Edward?"

"Not mine anymore," Clara replied, "but the man I was married to. Yes, I'm sure that's Edward."

Walking across the bridge with a pronounced limp was Edward Mackey. His broad-brimmed hat covered his eyes from view. Two milk cans hung from a yoke that was slung across his shoulders. He approached and the flock continued milling about, slowly drifting away from him and settling in front of Reiny's blacksmith shop.

"Clara?" Mackey shouted. "Clara, I've come for you!"

"Stand firm, beloved!" Gustav said, glaring at Mackey.

Mackey now stood between the flock and the blacksmith shop. He set the milk cans on the ground and lifted the yoke from his shoulders. He appeared mesmerized and confused by the constantly changing pattern of "women-folk" before him.

"Clara," Mackey said, "come forward! I could have taken you years ago in your tent, or late one night in your shop. However, it is most fitting that our lives should end on the anniversary of the end of our marriage."

"So he was the one those other times," Clara whispered to Otto. "And of course. This is the twentieth. Our divorce became final eleven years ago today. Oh, I've tried so hard to forget!"

"Edward Mackey, listen to me!" Gustav said. "Her life is not yours to take."

"Clara? I know you're there. Come, we shall die together. One can is for you and one is for me." Mackey pulled the lid from one of the milk cans, picked up the container, and started dousing the flock with its contents. It was gasoline.

"No!" Gustav shouted, stepping forward. "You may not have her!"

"No!" Gerhardt shouted, standing next to Gustav.

"No!" Martha shouted, coming up next to Gerhardt.

"No!" Otto shouted, forming a barrier with the others. Bruno growled and stood at Otto's side. The entire crowd moved forward.

Mackey stopped for a moment and squinted at Otto. "You are Otto Steitz. We meet again, after all these years." His eyes became wild. "I loved Elsa. I wanted to be with her. But she wouldn't have anything to do with me!"

Otto was filled with rage, but he stood firm.

"No! No! No! No!" The flock began shouting as one. Mackey continued splashing them with gasoline. It tingled on their skin and burned in their eyes. "No! No! No! No!"

"No!" Liesl said sternly. She broke free of her mother's grip and stood before Mackey. "Don't hurt my mother!"

Silence fell over the village. Mackey leaned forward and studied her face. "Whose trick are you?" he asked.

"Don't hurt my mother!"

"It can't be!" Mackey said, becoming increasingly agitated. "In your face, child, I see myself. No! I was wrong! This isn't how it was supposed to end."

Mackey hoisted the other milk can and dumped the gasoline on himself. "Ahhh!" He wailed in anguish and ran toward the blacksmith shop.

"Mackey, no!" Gustav shouted.

"Ahhh!" Mackey disappeared through the open doors.

"Get back!" Reiny said, waving his arms at the flock. "Get down!"

A hellish ball of orange flame and black smoke exploded from the heart of the shop. The flock fell to the ground. Angry tongues of fire lashed out, but stopped well short of the flock. Some of the contents of the blacksmith shop caught on fire. Those who weren't soaked with gasoline ran to extinguish the flames. A few minutes after the explosion, the fire was out.

Reiny, Simon, Carl, and Adam carried Mackey to the middle of the road. He was badly burned, beyond recognition. Sitting on the ground, Gustav cradled Mackey's blackened head in his lap.

Mackey gazed blankly at the sky. He convulsed and coughed and said with his last breath, "This isn't how it was supposed to end."

Kneeling beside them, Otto wept.

# Chapter Twenty-five ∽

With the changing of the calendar from May to June in the year of our Lord 1911, there was no doubt in Otto's mind that summer had arrived—finally. It was Thursday, the first of June. He was out for a walk with Bruno. They stopped on the bridge, and Bruno sat to rest. Leaning against the side rail, Otto followed his gaze up the village road to the west, past the mill and the general store, the shops and the dance hall, out of Bierville and into the countryside.

*What a beautiful sight. All of our farmers seem pretty happy. Their crops are all in and growing well, thanks to a warm and cooperative spring. The sun is staying up a little longer each day, allowing more time in the evening for folks to sit on their front porches and greet passersby. It's a glorious time of year. And the times are changing. Everything looks different today.*

It was the first day of Otto's retirement from work at the general store and post office; he was officially "a free man," as he said. This wasn't a spur-of-the-moment decision; Otto had been mulling it over for years. Then, last January, he asked Fritzie and Gerhardt to sit with him at one of the checker barrels.

"Gentlemen," he said, "I'm retiring at the end of May. And I have a plan for making this work for all of us. Having no children of my own, I started thinking several years ago about who might take over at the general store. The business has grown steadily. The post office is also much busier than it used to be, to the extent that it needs its own postmaster and building. Are you with me so far?"

Fritzie and Gerhardt nodded, but remained silent.

"Good," Otto said. "Fritzie, I'd like you to apply for the postmaster position. I've already spoken with the regional supervisor and he sees no problem with your being placed here. Gerhardt, I'd like you to become the general manager of the store. You will each own half of the business."

Fritzie and Gerhardt remained silent but Otto noticed that their mouths hung open.

He continued: "I've saved more than enough money over the years to meet my needs, so it will be best for all of us if I simply step out of the way and let you two run things. I continue to be impressed with how well you two work together and have every confidence that this will continue. Any questions?"

What could they say? The three of them stood together in a huddle, arms draped over each other's shoulders, laughing and crying all at once. For his part, Otto was closing a chapter of his life, opening another, and changing his identity. His decision affected Fritzie and Gerhardt just as dramatically. He knew they'd all miss working together, but new horizons were opening before them.

"One thing, though," Otto said. "I get to keep Bruno. We can keep each other company in our old age."

"I have a question for Fritzie," Gerhardt said. "Now that we're going to be partners, I was wondering if you could tell me your last name?"

Glancing at the floor, Fritzie said, "Well, it's 'Schnauze.'"

"Schnauze? You're joking."

"Schnauze. Keep it a secret, will you?"

"Keep what a secret?"

Otto smiled and said, "You boys will be just fine."

On Friday, Clara, Liesl, and Gerhardt waited excitedly at the Chicago and Northwestern station in town as the morning train pulled ceremoniously in. Conrad and Charlotte Schnuelle stepped off of the train, luggage in hand; their three little ones followed behind, bounding onto the platform. Clara threw her arms around her brother and kissed him on the cheek. "Welcome home, Conrad!" she said. "Welcome, Charlotte, children! We're glad you could all come to our wedding."

"Congratulations, Gerhardt!" Conrad said, extending his hand. "Welcome to the family."

"Thank you," Gerhardt replied, bowing in appreciation.

"Dear sister," Conrad said to Clara, "when you wrote to us about Doctor Hess' death in April, we were saddened, of course. I realized the village would need another physician. So, here I am. We're moving to Bierville."

"Wonderful! But where will you live?" Clara asked.

"I recently exchanged letters with Lester Mohr. He and his father agreed to sell us Gottfried's old place. I understand he lives with Lester now. Charlotte and I made arrangements for our automobile and belongings to be shipped from Chicago next week. We're here to stay."

With that, there were more hugs and the children joined hands in a circle and danced with delight.


On Saturday at four-thirty in the afternoon, Gustav Vriesen welcomed an intimate group of people to the parsonage for Clara and Gerhardt's wedding ceremony. The bride and groom had invited their immediate families to be with them; in addition, they asked Adam and Emilie Schroeder to stand with them as witnesses. During the ceremony, Liesl stood between Clara and Emilie. Minnie Vriesen provided music on the pump organ. Despite it being a small gathering, Gustav thought it felt warm and festive—just right.

"Clara," Gustav asked, "Do you take this man as your lawfully-wedded husband?"

"I do," Clara replied.

"I do, too," Liesl said.

"Sorry, Liesl," Gustav said, patting her on the head, "one per customer."

The wedding reception was held a short time later at the dance hall. Calvin Rickmeier took it upon himself to stand at the door and greet the celebrants; even he wasn't sure why. He simply felt like doing it and no one seemed to mind. After twenty minutes of welcoming people, Calvin thought that nearly all of Bierville had already entered the hall; they were primed for a celebration, ready to um-pah-pah the night away. When he saw Dominique D'Angelo coming through the door with her family, he forgot about welcoming anyone else. Her eyes met his, and she beamed.

"Hey, Dominique, come here!" he said, pulling her aside. "Wait till the band starts playing later. It's going to be great!"

"Calvin Rickmeier," she said, smiling and waving her finger at him in a motherly way, "what have you done this time?"

"About a half hour ago, after the band had tuned up and went outside for a smoke, I went over there and stuffed a peeled hard-boiled egg into the bell of the trumpet. Oh, this'll be great!"

"Oh!" she said, wincing and covering her ears. "I don't want to know this."

After the wedding guests ate and the tables were cleared from in front of the stage, the eight-piece waltz and polka band assembled with their instruments. The guests paired up on the dance floor, waiting for the music to begin. Calvin and Dominique stood to one side, barely able to contain themselves.

Finally, the moment came. The other instruments played the um-pah-pah introduction, and the trumpeter awaited his entrance.

The dancers began waltzing with the music, the trumpet was raised, and—nothing for a second—then BLAAH!

The egg soared elegantly through the air, plopping on Herman Rickmeier's head.

Calvin and Dominique clung to each other, laughing hysterically. The rest of the guests chortled with surprised amusement. Above the commotion, Calvin heard his father fuming, "Hey, what's the big idea? Frieda, where's that son of yours?"

On Sunday morning at worship, August Schmidt and Jacob Schmalfus sat together on the men's side. Several times during the service, August noticed that Gustav seemed unusually distracted. In the sermon, Gustav talked about the compassion of Jesus for his people at a time when they were like sheep without a shepherd. His voice broke and he was unable to speak for a moment. During the pause, Jacob commented to August, "I never knew he was so fond of sheep."

This made more sense to August at seven o'clock on Monday morning. While at the post office picking up his mail, August opened a letter from Gustav Vriesen addressed to the congregation and posted right before closing on Saturday. Copies of the letter had apparently also been sent to the other members of the church. It said:

> Minnie and I have had the privilege of serving this congregation for the past eighteen years. Now, after spending much time with God in prayer over this decision, I am confident it is time to step aside as your shepherd. I have accepted a call to a church in Des Moines, Iowa. My last day as pastor of this congregation will be Sunday, June 11, 1911.
>
> May God continue to bless this community with faith, hope, and love.

August began to cry. It felt to him like the death notice of a dear friend. He refolded the letter, wiped his tears with the back of his hand, and left the post office. Riding home in his wagon, he had time to think. *Ah, what news. Gustav. Minnie. My dear friends. Leaving. How will the church continue? Many will cry and think it's the saddest news they've heard in a long time. A few will greet this letter with a cheer, thinking they will soon be rid of the thorn that has tormented them for too long. And some will simply say, "Ah, Vriesen has resigned. Ja, ja."*

August returned home and opened the kitchen door. "Lena?" he said. "I have the saddest news. Gustav has resigned." He listened for her voice. "Lena?" He walked into the living room and saw her body face down on the floor. "Oh, Lena. You poor, little thing. Lena."

At about nine o'clock on Monday morning, Gustav heard the news about Lena's death and walked over to August's house to console his friend. When August came to the door, Gustav said, "I'm sorry, August. Peace be with you!"

"Ah, Gustav—dear friend! Thank you for coming." The two of them embraced in the spirit of comfort and understanding. August sighed and said, "Ja, ja. She's been in such frail health for so many years that, on the one hand, I was prepared for this. On the other hand, she's been this way for so long it seemed she just might go on forever. But it's funny. The thing that makes me the saddest at the moment is the news of you leaving us."

"So you read my letter of resignation. I've never resigned from a church before. I've always been asked to leave. I didn't know what to do, whether to talk to you personally before making my decision public."

August nodded. "That's all right, Gustav. There's really no good way to receive such news. But the more pressing matter at hand is making funeral arrangements for Lena. The poor, little thing. I know my son Julius would like to say good-bye to his mother, but I don't even know where he lives or how to get word to him. It's my own fault that I'm all alone now."

"No, August. God is here. And things have a way of working out."

The obituary for Lena Schmidt was in Tuesday's newspaper; the funeral service was set for eleven o'clock on Wednesday morning at the church. About an hour before the service, August stood near the coffin greeting the mourners who were beginning to arrive. At one point, he looked toward the door and saw Julius entering the church with his wife, Rebecca and three children. August had never met his grandchildren. He hurried toward Julius and burst into tears of relief.

"My son, my son. I didn't know if I'd ever see you again." The two sank into one of the pews, crying and holding on to one another. August asked, "How did you know?"

"I saw the notice of Mama's death in yesterday's paper," Julius said. "I knew we had to come to you. We moved back to the area three years ago and are living in an apartment in town. But I wasn't sure if you would ever want to see me again."

"Oh, Julius, my son. I never should have let Rebecca and you leave. You needed us then more than ever."

Rising to his feet, August embraced Rebecca and said, "Thank you for coming, my dear!"

Julius introduced August to his grandchildren. "This is Julia. She's almost nine. This is Elroy. He's seven. And this is Clarence. He's five."

Kissing each one on the forehead and gently touching their heads, August said, "My little ones, I'm so glad to see you! I want to learn all about you."

Julius said, "Pa, I've told them a great deal about you already—what a fine man you are. Now they can get to know you themselves."

After the committal service, August walked through the cemetery with Julia hanging onto one hand and Elroy holding the other. Julius, Rebecca, and Clarence followed behind. They read the different names and dates on the markers, and Elroy asked, "Grandpa, why did all those people say 'Happy symphonies' to you?"

"Happy symphonies," August said, trying to think what Elroy meant, "happy symphonies. Ah, ha, ha! I think what the people said was, 'You have my sympathies.' That means they were sorry your grandmother died."

They continued walking and Julia asked, "Grandpa, did you know all of these people?"

"No," August said, "but a great many of them. Some of them died before I was born or was too young to remember. But most I can still picture. As for your Grandma Schmidt, your father and I will tell you about her and show you some photographs so you can picture her, too. Even though she never met you, she loved you."

On Thursday the eighth, Lester Mohr helped his father celebrate his eighty-sixth birthday. In the months after Gottfried turned eighty-five, it had became clear to Lester that his father was unable to stay by himself anymore, so he prepared a place for Gottfried in his house. Lester answered a knock at the door. It was Otto.

"Shhh," Lester said. "Father is just beginning a story."

Gottfried stood in the middle of a room full of people and, with twinkling eyes, sweeping gestures, and a huge smile, continued his story: "So, there we were, ah—and the four! Ah—ah—and there we go! Lickety-split—bouncin' and hollerin', ah—and the chickens and the horses—BAWK! and WOA! DOWN, DOWN—heh, heh—and OVER! OVER! HooHOO! Oh, and the MELONS! The MELONS! And, uh. And THERE WE WERE!"

"Oh, my," Lester said, applauding with everyone else. "That was quite a story."

"Hja!" Gottfried chortled, smiling from ear to ear. "Hja!"

Lester and Otto walked back to the kitchen, and Otto asked, "What was that about? I'm afraid I couldn't tell."

Lester replied, "He was telling a story about a time when he was a young lad. His wagon flipped over in the ditch."

"Oh, right. I remember that. He sure has slipped a bit."

"A bit? I can't make heads or tails of what he's saying half the time."

"Yes," Otto said, "it's very difficult to see his mind fading away like that and not be able to do a thing about it."

Lester thought for a moment and said, "Well, sometimes you just laugh or cry. Might as well laugh."

"He seems happy enough."

"Well, he's still alive and all, and I still love him dearly. But he can't carry on a conversation anymore. His memory's disappearing fast. Then what's left? That's who we are. In most ways, I've already had to say good-bye to my father."

"Ja, ja," Otto said. "We're all beginning to miss him."

Early in the evening on Friday, Gustav and Minnie were out for a walk around the village. They approached the river near the mill and saw Calvin sitting in the middle of the south edge of the bridge. Rex was lying next to him. Calvin's feet dangled over the water, his arms rested on the crosspiece, and his head rested on his hands. Gustav studied him for a moment. *My little friend is becoming a man.*

"Mind if we join you?" Minnie asked.

"Sure, be my guest," Calvin replied.

Gustav sat next to Calvin on the left and Minnie sat on the right, next to Rex.

"Hello, Rexy," she said, giving him a scratch on the top of his head. There they were: four friends, sitting in a row, gazing into the flowing water below.

"'There is a river,'" Gustav said, "the streams whereof make glad the city of God, the holy place of the tabernacles of the Most High.'"

"Psalm 46, verse four," Minnie said. "This is such a lovely river. Oh, and look at the family of mallards!"

Gustav smiled. "The ducklings are like little balls of fuzz, aren't they? Bobbing on the water." After a pause, he said, "Calvin, you seem to be thinking hard about something. Can we help?"

Calvin threw a stone into the water near the ducks, causing them to scurry downstream. He said, "All of these changes, they're happening so fast. Everything seems to be falling apart. I don't think I can take it."

"I sometimes feel that way myself," Gustav replied. "I don't like saying good-bye, whether it's to loved ones at the time of death, or to beloved friends when we have to move. I hate it. You don't know how my heart is breaking."

"Then why do you have to leave?" Calvin asked. "Stay here!"

"Ah. I'm afraid it's time. This church needs new leadership, someone with more energy to help you on the journey of faith. I seem unable to challenge and inspire you as a church anymore. I love you as my own family, but I'm afraid we've grown too comfortable with one another. And that simply doesn't work. This is perhaps the most painful part of being a pastor. No place can ever truly be our home. We can only be visitors. Now I believe God has other hopes for you here and for us in Des Moines."

"But I don't want you to leave," Calvin said. "Nobody does. You're the only pastor I've ever known. The church is going to die."

"Calvin, we are proud of you. You were one of the first babies I christened here, and I believe God has great plans for you. I love you, and I hope to remain in contact with you for the rest of my life. But did you know I'm the fourth pastor to serve this congregation? And after me there will be many more who will lead the church into the future and help it to grow."

"But I don't want things to change—you moving, Herr Steitz retiring, Doctor Hess and Frau Schmidt dying, Herr Mohr losing his mind. It's too much."

"Yes, I know the feeling. Sometimes there is too much sadness and loss. Yet good things are also happening," Gustav said. "Doctor Schnuelle and Charlotte moving to town, Gerhardt and Clara's wedding. And I noticed Dominique and you enjoying each other's company at the reception. She's a wonderful young lady. Still, people have struggled to deal with changes in their lives for as long as there have been people. But, if something stops changing in any way, there's a good chance it's no longer alive."

"God doesn't change."

"The nature of God doesn't change, that's true. But God is love and the love of God grows. There was a Greek philosopher named Heraclitus from about 500 B.C. who said, 'There is nothing permanent except change.' I would say, 'The only permanence in the midst of change is God.' That's because GOD IS."

"Calvin," Minnie said, "look into the river as the water swirls past. If you were to step into the river now, and then a minute later, it would have changed in that time. Yet it would be the same river. Do you understand?"

"I think so," Calvin said.

"So it is," she said, "with this community, with this church family. Things are always changing, and yet the community endures. The church is not sustained by one person or group of people, but by the indwelling Spirit of God."

As the four of them continued sitting together, other folks from the neighborhood seemed drawn to the bridge and began congregating around them. Herman, Frieda, and Minna came up and sat next to Minnie.

Otto walked up behind Gustav, patted him on the shoulder and leaned over his friend, resting his arms and chin on the top rail.

Bruno nuzzled in between Rex and Minnie. All six D'Angelos walked onto the bridge; Dominique went over and stood behind Calvin. August Schmidt and Reiny Hartung, Adam and Emilie Schroeder and little Thomas, Simon and Anna Klemme and their three children, Gertrude and Carl Mueller, Gottfried and Lester Mohr, Clara, Gerhardt, and Liesl, Martha Schnuelle and little Norbert, Ida Klietz and Hilda Schultz, Fritzie and Johann—they all gathered on the bridge, watching the shining river meander its way south and west, across the meadow, near to the church, and into the woods.

Gustav gazed into the flowing water and listened with affection to the quiet voices and laughter of these good and faithful people whom he loved. "Ah, beloved," he whispered. "This is the river of life."

---

[i] Henry Alford, "Come, Ye Thankful People, Come," 1844.

[ii] Joseph Mohr, "*Stille Nacht,*" 1818, Tr. John F. Young, ca. 1863.

[iii] Edward Lear, "The Owl And The Pussy-Cat," 1871.

# A Glossary of Foreign-Language Words and Phrases

*(in alphabetical order—German, except as noted)*

| | |
|---|---|
| Ach! | alas! |
| Ausländer | foreigner |
| Blitzkrieg | sudden attack (lit. lightning war) |
| Danke! | Thank you! |
| Das ist eine gute Idee. | That is a good idea. |
| Dickkopf | stubborn person (lit. thick head) |
| Donnerwetter! | My word! (lit. thunder weather, thunderstorm) |
| Fraülein | young woman; Miss _____ |
| Frau | woman; wife; Mrs _____ |
| Gottesdienst | worship service (lit. service of God) |
| Gott im Himmel, hilf' mir! | God in heaven, help me! |
| Gurricken | an interjection of unknown origin or meaning |
| Guten Tag! | Good day! |
| Hallo | Hello |
| Herr | man; Mr. ____ |

| | |
|---|---|
| Holzkopf | blockhead (lit. wooden head) |
| Ja | yes |
| Liebchen | sweetheart (lit. little loved one) |
| Morgen | Good morning; morning. |
| Nicht | not |
| Natürlich | naturally |
| Oh, la, la! | Oh, my! (French) |
| Richtig | right, correct |
| Ruhe sanft | rest peacefully; quiet rest |
| Schlaf gut | Sleep well; have a good sleep. |
| Schlaf im himmlischer Ruhe. | Sleep in heavenly peace; tranquility. |
| Schlimmschnabel | nasty beak |
| Schnauze | nose; snout |
| Schönes Wetter, nicht wahr? | Beautiful weather, isn't it? |
| Schweinkopf | pig head, stubborn person |
| Sí | yes (Italian) |
| Sicherlich! | Certainly! |
| Trés bien! | Very good! (French) |
| Verzeihung | Pardon me; excuse me |
| Wie geht's Ihnen? | How's it going? How are you? |
| Wunderbar | Wonderful |